CHALLENGE THE HEAVENS!

Odan stared up, as the cloud grew, black and massed, while the lightning struck and the thunder rolled. Staring, Odan saw the long radiant arms of fire reaching out across the heavens. He knew this vision was his alone; this was not visible from proud Eresh over the horizon.

"Come, you great god!" he bellowed. "Let me see you and your chariot of fire!"

He was mad. He was quite mad by this time. He must be insane, thus to stand, head jutting, glaring up as a god descended in fire and glory from the heavens.

In a great burst of maniacal frenzy he had conjured a god. And a god had answered his call and his challenge.

"I am Odan and I am of Eresh! Show me your attributes, show me your face, if you dare! For I am Odan the Khuzuk and my father is a god—*is* a god!"

About The Author

Because of prior commitments and contractual options by the author, the publishers are not at liberty to reveal the true identity of Manning Norvil. We can say that, as his realistic account of the first days of human civilization under the tutelage and power of those ancient astronauts known as "gods" shows, Manning Norvil is a learned student of the dawn of culture in the Mediterranean and Mesopotamian basins. He has written extensively of subjects celestial and terrestrial. His books have sold in millions of copies throughout the world and have been translated into many languages. The legend of Odan, offspring of a human mother and a "divine" father, is based upon the extraordinary prevalence of such demigod lore in all the most ancient records and primitive theologies of all races and on all continents.

WHETTED BRONZE

Manning Norvil

DAW BOOKS, INC.
DONALD A. WOLLHEIM, PUBLISHER

1301 Avenue of the Americas
New York, N. Y.   10019

FIRST PRINTING, MARCH 1978

1 2 3 4 5 6 7 8 9

PRINTED IN U.S.A.

Prologue

This is a story of the days when a mighty River flowed southward between two seas that rolled their blue waters where today lies the Mediterranean Sea. A lofty procession of kingdoms and empires followed one another in pride and power along the broad curves of The River in the land of Ea and upon the sunlit shores of the two seas. Many a king looked upon his rich lands and was wantonly not content and coveted the land and city of his neighbor king. Many a poor laborer looked up from the toil of the fields and saw in the ranks of the king's army a brighter horizon. Many a sorcerer wove a dark spell to bring the heart's desire closer, many a beauteous maid languished for her lost lover, many a hero sought heroic death in relentless combat against the malefic forces of evil.

The gods lived in the land of Khepru in those days and walked among their people, and each shining city of The River and the two seas cherished its own god who took sacrifice from the city and returned sacrifice with power and wealth and protection.

Then all this bright tapestry of high living and joyous adventuring and dark sorcery was swept away in the green rushing waters as the Atlantic swept in and the two seas joined to drown a world.

Not gold or silver, not shield or sword could hold back the cold dark onrush of the waters. Not the proud curvetting beauty of the chariot horses or the most potent gramarye of the sorcerers could stem the deluge. A world vanished and the lights of civilization flickered and went out for thousands of years. Only a few survivors were left to return to scraping an existence with the flint tools of their ancestors.

Lost and forgotten lay all that high culture of The River and the two seas, and today there is no record of all that beauty and brilliance and terror of the world of Khepru—save in the accounts that follow.

Chapter One

Kufu the Ox

Fire cut through the waterfront of the proud city of Eresh. Black smoke rose chokingly. Zamaz the sun cast a mocking brilliance of light upon the black smoke and the curling tongues of flame. The warehouses and jetties burned. Lurid reflections danced upon the waters of The River.

Through the chaos of fire and destruction the devils of Endal moved with a sure quick purpose. These were the second wave of barge-borne infantry and they intended to smash utterly and forever the power of Eresh along The River. Their bronze helmets and spear points caught the twin lights of fire and sun. They glittered bravely below the roiling clouds of smoke, glittering darts of fire breaking along the waterfront. The noise and the stinks and the bright spilt blood accompanied their progress.

Kufu the Ox, shield bearer of the Fifth Kisraen of the Leopard Archers of Eresh, felt the jarring blows all along his arm and shoulder as the murderous arrows battered down against his upraised shield. He licked his lips and his eyes glared above the curved rim of the massive gerrhon behind which Fadu the archer stood to loose his shafts upon the devils of Endal. The gerrhon bristled with arrows. Chunks of the wicker had been ripped from the right hand side of the shield. An arrow pierced clean through the foolishly exposed throat of Bagu, the second-class shield bearer.

Bagu tired to screech as the blood stained around the arrow.

Fadu, letting fly, bellowed his annoyance, reaching for the quiver which Bagu dropped.

The two shield bearers protected their archer's head with their shields, as the wide gerrhon protected the bodies of all three. Kufu the Ox contorted his body in the attempt to keep his shield aloft and to reach the fallen quiver. Bagu had not been too useful, but a first class archer needed two assistants, and Fadu was a haughty archer who demanded an impossible degree of service.

"Hurry, Kufu, you fool! The devils run on us—their spearmen attack!"

Kufu reached the quiver. The fingers of his left hand gripped around the embroidered strap.

And then Wadu the archer was dead, staggering back with a last surprised look on his heavy face, the blood pouring down from his eye, staining his brown cheek and dribbling into his massy black beard.

The arrow from Endal stood up in that eye, as though triumphant.

Excited yells burst above the hubbub. Crouching behind the curved hood of the gerrhon Kufu shot a quick look out at the advancing enemy. They were coming on at a run, screaming, bellowing, shaking their spears in anger, their oval shields up. Above them arched the arrow storm, covering them, tearing into the thin line of Eresh's Leopard Archers.

Kufu the Ox saw that all was lost here.

At his left side the waters of The River rolled endlessly on toward The Sweet Sea far to the south, at his right the mud-brick wall of a warehouse without windows offered no protection. They would have to fall back to the wider area before the foot of the Bridge.

As he realized that, Kufu saw and heard Jaipur, captain of the Fifth Kisraen, gesturing and shouting.

"Back! Fall back!"

About a score of the Kisraen were left on their feet. They turned and ran. The gerrhons were abandoned, tall wicker shields, curved and equipped with grips for transportation, they must be abandoned, for there were too few shield bearers left to carry them.

Kufu the Ox ran with his comrades of the Fifth.

He had snatched up Wadu's great bow and he retained the quiver slung over a shoulder. With his own small oval shield held at his back he ran.

The hard of mud brick, faced against the water with costly stone, widened as the Bridge was approached. Eresh was built upon the west bank of The River, and the Bridge provided access to the east bank. The warehouses drew back here, as though in respect for a great feat of building, unique upon The River.

Wondering just what Jaipur, captain of the Fifth, intended, Kufu saw that intolerant man abruptly stagger. He drew himself upright, reaching imploringly for the sky. The arrow protruded from his neck under his left ear, for he had been turning his head to bellow back when the shaft struck. Blood dropped upon the brave leopard skin slung over his left shoulder. Blood stained all that finery, symbol of the Leopard Archers of Eresh. Jaipur staggered, and fell, and sprawled lifeless upon the dust of the hard.

At Kufu's back an oil store burst into violent flame. Blue and violet tendrils of fire licked up as the oil from shattered amphorae ran across the waterfront. For a space, as that richness was consumed in fire the infantry of Endal were halted. For a space, the men of Eresh might regroup and draw breath and set their hearts more firmly in the bronzen resolve never to give up to Endal.

For Endal, the city southward along The River, was a jealous city, and sought only to destroy proud Eresh. Kufu had heard a quick and garbled report that the chariotry of Endal had been routed and destroyed to the south of the city. He had rejoiced as they slew the barge-borne infantry. But then the second wave had come in. Clouds of arrows had darkened the sun, Zamaz, and under the protection of their shields with the blasphemous designs and symbols of Nirghal inscribed upon them, the spearmen had carved their way ashore and driven ahead under the arrow storm.

No officers were left to the Fifth and the Third Kisraens. The Fourth had been destroyed in the first onslaught. Kufu looked among the jostling throng to see if any officer remained of the Sixth Company. He could not see the nodding yellow and white plumes that denoted a captain. The noise continued in a long screaming bellow of sound. The thunderous smashing as roofs collapsed, their withy and mud burned and dried away, continued as a tumbling counterpoint to the clamor of battle.

"We're done for, friend," gasped an archer as Kufu stood, glaring back at the burning oil store.

Kufu did not know him, but his insignia proclaimed him as from the Sixth Kisraen.

"Maybe we are. But we shall send many of the devils to the seven hells before they send us there, by Zadan!"

"Ay," said the archer, setting arrow to bow and nocking the shaft with a finicky care. "Aye."

The men of the Leopard Archers milled uncertainly. They had been charged with holding the central section of the wharves and they had failed. Now the infantry of Endal were almost upon the foot of the Bridge. Once they had swept away the last defense here they could turn upon the Gate. The men holding that, weakened by detachments, would not hold long. Then Eresh would fall.

The city would burn. Blood would flow. The great statue of Zadan, the Sword God, would be taken from his sanctuary in the Ziggurat of Zadan, taken in triumph to be paraded through the streets of Endal, to be contumed and defiled, and then to be burned and destroyed utterly.

When that happened the god of Endal, Nirghal, would have gained a mighty victory over the god of Eresh, Zadan.

Kufu's clipped black beard glistened with sweat. His conical bronze helmet with the scrap of leopard skin wrapped about its base weighed upon his head, pressing down into his thick black hair. His woolen tunic was soaked in sweat. Dust clung to his naked legs and feet. But his bronze sword was sharp within its scabbard, and he would never surrender.

He saw the uncertainty of the archers. He did not wear the proud leopard skin, he did not flaunt the brave feathers of an officer in his helmet; but he was a man of Eresh, a shield bearer, one of the Leopard Archers of Eresh.

He drew in a breath and he expanded his chest, and he shouted.

"Leopards! Archers of Eresh! Men! Are we to let the devils of Endal wreak their will? Never! Never! Let us form and fight and break them into pieces for the crocodile pool!"

One or two of the archers who had continued their retreat more enthusiastically than the others halted at this. They turned to stare at this shield bearer, a mere shield bearer, who reminded them they were Archers of Eresh.

"We are finished!" shouted a burly rascal with blood staining over his left shoulder where he had ripped out an arrow. "Let us save ourselves."

"Aye!" bellowed another. "Where are the chariots the king promised us? We shall be slaughtered if we stay here."

Just why he said what he did say, Kufu the Ox could not explain. Boldly, he lifted his bow and shouted the cries down.

"The chariots will come. The king, whose name be praised, will never forget the Leopard Archers. Stand and fight like men!"

An archer with the scars of long service on his face hitched up his corselet of bronze scales. He spat.

"We will fight if—"

"No ifs!" screamed Kufu the Ox. "If we run, the Bridge and the Gate are gone. The city is doomed."

Cut off, marooned by the foot of the Bridge, the group of archers could see no way to save themselves except by running.

The smoke from the oil store wafted by the breeze blew in billowing black masses across the wharves and over The River. Occasionally snatches of forms running could be glimpsed through the smoke. The inglorious rout of the archers had surprised the infantry of Endal. But in only moments now they would burst through the smoke. Like wolves they would hound down the men of Eresh, and break them and burst past to take the Bridge and the Gate.

The upstream gates were out of this. Once a Kisraen of infantry of Endal gained an entrance then the city would fall. There would be fighting in the streets and across the flat roofs; but the outcome would be inevitable.

"Where are our spearmen?" shrieked an archer. He waved a bloodied hand about. The Leopards stood alone. "We have no shields. If we stand, we will all die."

In a single movement of great venom Kufu the Ox reached the man. He grasped him by the ear and tugged. He dropped his shield and the bow and he drew his bronze sword. The keen blade kissed the man's throat.

Surprised, he gagged in horror as he felt the kiss of death upon him.

"You will die if you do not stand!" bellowed Kufu the Ox.

He glared about, madly, and saw the multi-colored feathers and the glitter of bronze bursting through the smoke curtain.

"Here they come! Bend your bows with a will, brothers! The Leopard Archers of Eresh will never surrender or flee!"

Sight of those vulpine shapes, the brisk and bracing words from Kufu the Ox, all worked upon the archers. Swiftly they shook out into line. What few shield bearers were left lifted their oval shields. The archers bent their bows.

And then—and then they looked as one man to Kufu for the order to loose.

No sense of incongruity in the situation affected them. Accustomed to obeying orders without thought, they responded to the bronze note of command in Kufu's voice. The arrowheads lifted, all in line, the bows bent. And Kufu raised his voice and, judging the oncoming spearmen to a nicety, shouted in a clear bell-like voice: "Loose!"

The man whose throat Kufu had offered to slit stood with his comrades and shot shaft for shaft with them.

That sleeting deluge plunged into the oncoming ranks of spearmen. Many an arrow lodged in the devilishly painted shields of Nirghal; but very few missed. The Leopards were renowned archers in the army of Eresh. The spearmen staggered; but trumpets blew brazen notes of urgency, and the infantry gathered and came on.

Then the return shafts rained down. Men of the Leopards shrieked and spun out of line as the cruel bronze birds skewered them. But Kufu the Ox kept up his impassioned flow of orders, recollecting the tactical maneuvers through which the regiment had labored so many times, sending men to extend the line, rallying the shield bearers, intemperately berating those who were slow in proffering arrows to the archers.

"Loosen your swords in your scabbards!" he screamed.

In only moments now the oncoming spearmen would reach the thin line of archers. Then it would be spear and shield against sword and shield if the archer could snatch up a shield in time. Here the shield bearers would fight, also. Here was where each man earned his salt.

Smoke and flame smothered down across The River as

the spearmen of Endal advanced under cover of their archers.

In the normal way of the standing army of Eresh each
Kisraen of archers would contain about fifty archers with
their shield bearers and assistants. The Fourth had been
destroyed. Of the three companies left charged with this
duty there remained fewer than sixty archers and about a
hundred shield bearers. Not a single captain—a Greatest
of Fifty—had survived. With these men Kufu the Ox
prepared to receive the wild skirling charge of the spearmen of Endal, shot in by Kisraens of Archers of Endal.

He stepped out, his shield high and held contemptuously
against the arrow storm. He glowered along the line of
men—along the line of his men. No one could explain
how a man, a certain man, would rise to an emergency
and take over and by his personality and dominance control and dictate to others.

Kufu licked his lips. He saw the way his men shot, the
way the shield bearers slanted their wicker shields so as to
deflect the shafts. More stuck than were deflected, for
these were not the shields of the spearmen which were
covered with sheet bronze over their wicker.

"On my command!" he shouted. "And not before."

They understood. They knew.

He saw their glittering eyes, their drawn-back lips, the
bared teeth. He saw the bulge of arm muscle and the
supple dropping away of the string hand. Yes, with men
like this properly led Kufu would go up against the devils
of Endal. But, all the same, they were done for, doomed,
ripe meat for slaughter. If only the captains of the Elev-
enth and Twelfth, just upriver, would bring their Kisraens
down into action!

As for the spearmen—they must be fighting elsewhere.
The chariots promised by the king, Neb-ayin-Ke, would
never arrive now, and, with a quick stab of betrayal, Kufu
the Ox felt that the earlier report of a great victory south
of the irrigations was a lie. The chariotry of Eresh had
been beaten and scattered by the chariotry of Endal. That,
he felt sure, must be the truth.

"Hold fast!" he bellowed. These men—*his* men now—
would stand and fight until all were slain.

The Standard Bearer of the Fifth lifted high the pole—
it was a true sweet piece of wood brought down from the
upper reaches of The River—and the bronze leopard glit-

tered in the sunlight. The yellow and brown streamers
waved defiantly. No other standards from the other Kisraens had survived to reach here; all these survivors would
fight and die under the standard of the Fifth. Kufu the Ox
felt that to be apposite.

Beneath the yellow and brown streamers of Eresh
twirled the black streamers of the Leopard Archers. Above
the bronze leopard lifted the sun emblem, and twinned
with it the emblem of the sword, sacred to Zadan. Below
the leopard the hand symbol of the Fifth Kisraen, the five
fingers widely stretched, would summon on men of the
Third and Sixth also.

The arrow storm diminished. The spearmen came on at
a trot and their own shafts would drop perilously close to
them had their archers continued shooting.

Now was the time for each Leopard Archer to stow his
bow away in its gorytus and hand the decorated case to
his shield bearer. Now was the time for swords to be
drawn. What shields were available were brought forward,
and dropped into line, and so, with set faces and fists firm
on sword hilts, the archers of Eresh awaited the onslaught.

Kufu the Ox swore. He glared over his shield rim at the
oncoming infantry. He could see no javelinmen among
them. This was no way for a close-fighting force to oper-
ate. He sensed that. Memories of the brawls and fights of
his childhood in Mankalu, the little village on the western
edge of the irrigations, sprang into his mind. His father
had been a skilled workman in wicker, and the small Kufu
had tussled for many happy hours with the shock-headed
children of the ditch workers. Attack! That had always
been the way his gang of cronies had routed their op-
ponents.

Kufu the Ox sprang forward, sword lifted. The blade
caught the sunlight and flashed like beaten gold.

"Forward!" he bellowed. "Follow me! Attack!"

Well-trained though the archers of the Leopards were,
they were a missile force. For an instant they hung. Kufu
half-turned, being careful with the skill of a shield bearer
to keep his wicker covering face on to the foe.

"Follow me!" he screamed. He thrust the sword stiffly at
the oncoming foe. "Charge!"

The moment hung surcharged with energy, as the moment passes in the instant before the Floods surge down
The River.

A single trumpet pealed, high and chiming, ringing silver against the light.

Kufu switched his impassioned gaze to the Gate. A silver trumpet meant chariots . . .

The gates opened. Everything happened with blurring speed.

A single chariot dashed forth. Its two horses were wounded, streaming blood, they frothed at the mouth and licks and gobs of froth blew back like thistledown. A man dressed in a driver's harness hung head downward from the rear of the chariot. He was dead, and his head battered the dust of the hard as the chariot bounded on. With wheels spinning discs of light, with the maddened horses leaping on as though uplifted by divine wings, with light striking from bronze spearpoints and harness bosses, the chariot hurtled on.

Every eye fastened upon the man driving the chariot like an insane man, like a maniac, like a messenger of the gods.

Tall, this man, but hunched, stooped over from constantly bringing his head down to a level with his fellows'. Massive in arm and thigh, with corded muscles roping, he lashed on the crazed horses, bursting at full stretch toward the line of spearmen from Endal. He wore no helmet. Wounds covered his body so that he glistened like a crimson statue. He grasped the reins slackly in his left hand and plied the whip with his right. A fillet of unbleached linen bound his brown hair, so unlike the dark polls of the folk of The River, and his hair falling forward over his face was blown savagely back by the wind of his passage.

Straight as an arrow the chariot flew at the spearmen.

Alone, unsupported, insanely, the single chariot charged.

And the Leopard Archers set up a great shout, a mighty voice of thunder, rolling outward to overpower the devils of Endal.

"It is Odan! Prince Odan! Odan the Half-god—Odan the Khuzuk!"

Chapter Two

Chariot Dust

Odan flung the reins in a quick loop around the driver's post in the left front of the chariot. He slammed the whip into its socket. The lash streamed and rippled behind. He glared with enormous venom upon these devils of Endal, these men of the city whose god had entrapped and betrayed him, and his lips ricked back in the feral fighting snarl of the Hekeu, the dagger-tooth lion of the far Hills of Zumer.

His left hand clenched around the forward rail and his right hand lifted the first javelin from the tall upright quiver fixed to the front right of the car. The javelin was merely a javelin, it was not the massive hunting spear of Zumer; but with such a weapon Odan the Khuzuk could cast clear through a man's neck . . .

The chariot whirled on over the hard and dust plumed. The noise and flames, the smoke and the crash of battle, bellowed all about. On flew the chariot past the thin line of Leopard Archers, and Odan saw them waving their swords and caught fragmentary snatches of their shouts.

"Odan! Prince Odan! Odan of Eresh!"

"Charge!" The stridency of Odan's voice snapped them up, brought them forward at an eager run after the chariot.

One man ran at their head, a stout, shock-headed fellow whose bronze helmet showed the dints of battle, who carried himself like the powerful oxen of the fields between the ditches.

Odan judged his maneuver well, because the desperate situation demanded nothing less. His friend Ankidu who

16

had taught Odan, the wild primeval savage, much of the art of chariotry would have smiled in satisfaction. But Ankidu was not here. He was to the south, bringing up what he could scrape together in the way of Eresh's chariotry. Odan had fought that battle in the desert and Eresh had won. Now he had brought the reserve to this spot of danger—and where, in the name of Ke the Creator, were those chariots supposed to follow him?

Had the devil sorcerers of Endal cast a spell to break down the defenses of the thaumaturges of Eresh? Had disaster overtaken the remnants of Eresh's chariotry hurried here by Odan the Half-god? All Odan could do was fight the battle here and now, and put his trust in Zadan the All Powerful, the Sword God of Eresh, a god for whom Odan entertained a lively suspicion and a god, moreover, he had attempted to avoid in the past.

With the reins looped and gripped once again in his left hand, Odan hauled back. The horses, panic-stricken, streaming blood, their eyes rolling, slewed. The chariot raced along the front of the spearmen of Endal.

And, as that careering chariot span down the line so Odan's right arm lifted and snapped forward, his hand reached for a new javelin and lifted, and so once again that mighty right arm of Odan the Khuzuk snapped forward in the lethal throw. Man after man pitched screaming from the ranks. Like some impossibly speeded-up spirit of The River, that arm rose and fell .

The edge of the road whirled nearer. The River, itself, welcomed him if he did not turn.

He swung the chariot with a savage burst of power.

The horses screamed. Odan felt no pity for the beasts. They had their place in the scheme of things, as had every man and woman, every beast and bird and fish. Everyone, except Odan the Half-god who would be a true god.

Once more before the lines closed the chariot raced between them. Halfway along, Odan exhausted the javelins. Without hesitation he swung the chariot left once again and sent it crashing into the line of spearmen.

In the instant before the terrified horses smashed into the upraised shields, Odan leaped off the back. His sword was gripped in his right fist, and the chariot's oval shield snugged up on his left arm.

As the two lines met in a frothing smother of bronze weapons and bright spilled blood, Odan the Half-god smote onward at the head of the Leopard Archers of Eresh.

They would have been beaten and crushed and totally destroyed. They would have been—but with the shrilling of silver trumpets rending the hot air, a fresh wave of chariots burst out from the Gate, spun with whirring wheels into action. A rain of arrows descended upon the spearmen. Javelins scored as the chariots flashed past.

"Now we have them!" bellowed Odan above the hub-bub. "Oh! On for Eresh and the king!"

In the melee he slanted the shield to deflect spear thrusts, drove his sword in with that sweet economy of effort so painstakingly drummed into him by Nadjul the Quick, forged deeper into the enemy mass.

A man at his side hacked and slashed with the zealous indiscriminate way of a strong man wielding an unfamiliar weapon.

Odan took a spearpoint on his shield that would have degutted this fellow.

"Steady, steady," shouted Odan in the din. His bronze blade licked, and the spearman screamed and dropped.

"At them, my prince!" screamed Kufu the Ox. He swung his sword wildly, hacking and cutting, driving on, always on. Odan smashed his way ahead, not to be out-done. At the head of a wedge, Odan and Kufu bored into the spearmen of Endal.

They could never have done it, of course, had not the chariotry arrived and shot them in, had not the spearmen of the Seventh and Tenth Kisraens of the Bullock Spear-men of Eresh run up to add their weight. Now it was a matter of push. More spearmen from Eresh arrived, the Gate filled with the brown and yellow. Brazen trumpets blew.

Along the waterfront past the sullenly smoking roofs the men of Endal were thrust back.

Many men fell into the water, and as their blood stained that ages-old flood so the long sinuous backs moved pur-posefully in, and mighty jaws opened and closed.

Back and back the men of Endal retreated. Their own archers, losing heart, turned and ran. After that it was a matter of mopping up.

Or—so thought Odan.

He stood with his legs braced, his massive body hunched, his magnificent head jutting arrogantly, glaring at the running men of Endal. Chariots whirled past in pursuit. Spearmen wearing the yellow and brown trotted past to rout out the last survivors of the attackers who might attempt to hide in some crevice of the proud city of Eresh.

Odan breathed deeply. He had been wounded here and there—but he had been trained as a savage primeval in the mountains and valleys of Zumer far, far to the north of the land of Ea between the two seas. He was the son of Odan En-Ke, a god, and his mother was Queen Momi of Eresh, brought to the king, Neb-ayin-Ke by Odan-En-Ke. But, was Odan in truth the son of Odan En-Ke? Or was the very existence of all the old gods, of whom Odan En-Ke was one, a myth, a construction of the first men out of fear and superstition?

All Odan could say was that he was half a god, that was certain, for it had been vouched for by the priests and the sorcerers. He was going to make himself a whole god, a true god, and nothing—nothing—would stand in his way.

So, breathing easily and smothered in blood, Odan the Khuzuk watched as the last of the men of vile Endal were routed and dispatched.

The pursuit passed away to the south along The River. The barges in which the Endalers had pulled upstream were mostly caught or set on fire; some few escaped. The noise and hubbub receded. A chariot drove up, with enormous sedateness after the hurly-burly of the battle, and Ankidu jumped down.

His bronze corselet was splashed with blood, and his helmet bore two savage dints; but he was unharmed.

"I rejoice to greet you still alive, my prince! But your wounds—"

"I shall have them attended to by and by—and I, too, Ankidu, rejoice to see you." Odan looked at his sword. The bronze edge was nicked so that it looked like a badly made saw. "We fought them, though, did we not?"

"Aye!"

Young Ankidu, the son of the lord Andan, was one of the very few nobles of Eresh to show friendship for Odan. This was understandable, this hostility from nobility and priesthood, for had not this wild Zumerian from the savage lands returned from the dead to claim his inheritance as the son of Queen Momi and, on the wishes of the god Odan En-Ke, the adoptive son of the king, Neb-ayin-Ke?

They stood separated by a space of bloodied dust from

the wounded and the exhausted Leopard Archers. A few
spearmen bound their wounds nearby. A number of over-
turned and smashed chariots lay strewn about, a half
dozen dead horses. Already the flies were at work, great
glistening black and green bodies.

"Is the king safe, my Ankidu?"

"Aye, praise to Zadan the All-glorious. The king, your
father, may his name be praised, lives."

"You saw no sorcerer in action? I saw none."

"No, prince. Although I saw none, be very sure that
Master Kidu was most earnesly at work, thwarting the vile
spells of the devil sorcerers of Endal."

"I will believe that. By Odan, yes!"

Both men spoke in a short and almost breathless way
that was indicative of their differing reactions to the battle.
For Ankidu, a bright and breezy young blood of Eresh,
for all that he harbored a secret sickness of the heart, the
fight had been a wonderful example of right triumphing
over wrong, of men fighting, of blood flowing, of great
deeds and the high silver notes of the war trumpets beckoning on to glory.

For Odan the fight had been a technical exercise once
his initial savage feelings had been overcome. Accustomed
to hunting barefooted in the hills, hunting the incredibly
powerful hekeu, the dagger-tooth lion, and, later, to han-
dling a sword in guard combat with Nadjul the Quick,
Odan knew this battle had presented him with many new
impressions he needed time to consider and from which to
learn fresh lessons.

The blood and the stink of death meant nothing to him.

To Ankidu they were an offense under the heavens.

Blood ran in the dusty crevices between the baked
bricks of the hard. Men lay sprawled in the obscene pos-
tures of death. Flies buzzed, black and green. The smell of
death, raw and choking and fresh, hung in the bright air.

Odan wiped his sword methodically on a scrap of a
dead man's tunic, as Nadjul had drummed into him.

"I will go up to my father the king. There will be much
to do. Now that we are secure here the captains must
restore order."

"With your permission, my prince, I will go with you.
My father fought at the king's side this day."

A noise as of running naked feet, and of men and
women screaming, drifted across the shining surface of

The River. Both young men turned to stare at the Bridge. A confused mass of people ran along the Bridge, shouting and waving their arms.

"What new deviltry is this?" exclaimed Ankidu, sharply.

Methodically, Odan went on cleaning his sword, wiping every last smear of blood away from the hilt, where a firm grip would mean life or death. Still wiping, he walked slowly to the foot of the Bridge.

Set on stone footings, brought down The River at great expense, and supported on arches of oven-baked brick, the Bridge's spans held a roadway wide enough for two wains to pass each other. This marvel of architecture gave access to the east bank and to the tidy collection of houses and shops there clustered around the eastern end of the Bridge. This offshoot of the city was known as Eresh Minor, or Eresh the Lesser. It possessed little of fame, apart from a sumptuous temple to the goddess Tia, patron deity of the city of Karkaniz, the goddess of love. The main claim to fame of Eresh Minor was the great Golden Gate of Eresh, the Eastern Gate, the portal that led out onto the Golden Road to Shanadul.

"There!" said Ankidu, sharply. He swung about to the scattered body of wounded and exhausted soldiers. "Men of Eresh! To me! The Bridge is attacked!"

Odan saw past the confused mob of screaming fugitives. Back there and pouring over the Bridge roared on a chariot force of nomads of the desert, fierce dark men in swirling white robes, their eyes glittering in envy and malice, their spears darting, their every intention plain.

"The devils stab us in the back when we grapple with Endal," said Odan. He had no love for the nomads, for many reasons. "But they are too late. Had they struck a glass earlier . . ."

"They may be too late to cooperate with the Endalers," said Ankidu. "But yet can they deal us a mortal blow and break through into the city. They must be stopped, here and now."

"Oh, aye, my Ankidu. They must be stopped. Yet it seems to me that there are precious few of us to do the stopping."

Ankidu swung a startled glance at Odan. Odan did not smile or nod reassurance. He calmly went about picking up discarded spears and javelins. He knew just how much time he had. After that first surprised look, Ankidu started in yelling at the bowmen, arranging them in formation, set shield bearers and assistants to collecting arrows and quivers. The spearmen formed up. They were, in truth, a pitiful force to check the overwhelming rush of the desert chariotry.

"Let the people through, Ankidu," shouted Odan as the noise battered nearer. "The chariots must be stopped on the Bridge. Once they debouch and flank us—"

He had no need to be explicit. A child could see the play here.

He saw the burly shock-headed man at whose side he had fought in the melee strutting about bellowing orders. The man looked to be a shield bearer by his dress and the thin strip of leopard skin about his helmet. Yet he gave orders and the Leopard Archers obeyed. There was no time to unravel the riddle now.

"Me?" said the fellow, looking at Odan with a suddenly uneasy face. "I am Kufu the Ox, if it please you, my prince."

"Then, Kufu the Ox, tell your archers to loose when those damned chariots pass the last span. Not before—and not later. Understood?"

Kufu braced his shoulders back. "Understood, my prince!"

Two more companies of the Bullock Spearmen trotted up, together with a Kisraen of the Tiger Archers. They had seen action; but were in better case than the Leopards. As the frightened and screaming mass of fugitives poured over the Bridge and fled in all directions as they debouched, Odan bellowed forcefully for the captains to place their men in line, to brace up, and to loose on his orders.

"We must enfilade them," he bellowed, his strident voice lifting over the hubbub. "Do not let a single dog set foot upon the west bank."

There had been fighting in many parts around the city and he could hope for reinforcements only in tiny driblets as the danger was realized and the generals sent their captains and men to the spot of danger. Trumpets pealed to warn Eresh. But Odan the Half-god knew that this battle was down to him and the men he had with him now.

The nomads had picked their time well, if a little late, and before the sun had passed a hand's breadth across the sky the issue would be resolved.

The last of the fugitives ran and stumbled along. The leading chariots were up with them, and the nomads shot their arrows and hurled their javelins with great glee into the fleeing backs. Odan half-turned.

"The last people are doomed, either way." His voice was as hard as the rocks of the Hills of Zumer. His archers must shoot when the chariots drew near, and if some poor wight of Eresh was caught in the storm from his own soldiers, then this was the price each citizen paid for the glory of his city, the demand made by Zadan the Sword God, the god of the proud city of Eresh.

Now the triumphant shouting of the nomads reached Odan. Over the mingled sounds of screaming and the trampling of the horses and the squeal of leather-bound tires, he heard the nomads screeching out the name of their damned desert god. "Belpeor! Belpeor! Slay the men of mud! Belpeor!"

"I'll give 'em men of mud," said Ankidu, with vast savagery. No man of the city who lived in a decent house built of mud-brick liked to be called a man of mud by the desert nomads who lived in skin tents, when they bothered to erect a dwelling-place at all.

With their white chariot scarves wrapped about their throats and mouths and noses, the nomads drove on. The scarves fluttered out to the rear, whirling with colored tassels. Above the scarves the brows of the nomads drew down in sharp notches of anger, and their dark eyes glittered with the baleful light of slaughter to come.

Odan lifted his sword high. He shot a penetrating, a commanding look along the line of archers, each man braced, bow lifted, arrow half-drawn, the curve of bow and arm and back like the lifted head of a dragon before striking.

"Loose!" bellowed Odan the Half-god.

The bows bent fully, the arrows notched under ears, the strings hummed sweetly. As one, the archers loosed. The bows snapped forward, the strings sang their martial songs, and the bronze birds flew. In mere heartbeats those bronze birds of death would feather down onto the leading chariots and the last few struggling wretches of Eresh seeking escape.

And so Odan looked under the flight of the arrow storm and saw the figure in the white gown staggering on, falling only to rise and lurch on. He saw. He saw the Princess

Zenara, his beloved, running from the chariots. He saw her stumble and fall, saw the chariots upon her, and he saw the sleeting hail of death pour destructively in, falling with indiscriminate malice upon nomad raider and upon desperate citizen of Eresh alike.

Chapter Three

The Fight for the Bridge

"Zenara!" screamed Odan.

He set foot on the Bridge. He could hear everything going on about him; yet the world consisted of a high keening whine shot through with the buzzes and rumblings of volcanoes. He could see everything going on about him; yet the world consisted of the white-gowned form of Zenara and the stumbling chariot horses and the flaming bronze of nomad weapons striking down toward her.

He struck through the last panic-stricken refugees. He reached Zenara. Arrows stuck in the wicker of the chariots and other shafts rebounded from the bricks of the Bridge. He clasped Zenara in his right arm. His left rammed the shield aloft so that arrows and weapons smashed against it. He breathed evenly, barely feeling the blows, feeling only the soft pliantly firm form of Zenara within the curve of his arm.

"Odan—my brother!"

"Aye, Zenara, my sister, it's me—and now we're both like to be killed!"

She laughed at him. An arrow skittered from the bricks and lanced past her head, tearing the russet fillet, and she laughed and snugged into him.

"If only we might truly die, here and now!"

"That is not the way of the Hekeu."

Keeping the shield cunningly slanted before her, Odan crouched. The first chariot went past to one side and he could do nothing against it and so let it go. The scent of the horses stank in the hot air. The noise burst about him as the noises of a beck tumbling from the high alps of Zumer burst about the lower crags.

"Grip the shield," he said, short and sharp, thrusting the wicker tightly over Zenara, releasing his right arm. He'd flung his spear—he had a chaotic memory of it arching high to fall into the mass of oncoming chariotry—and so now he must rely only on the sword. Noise and movement and the tumbling movement of bodies all about blended into an animal uproar. Shrieks knifed the air as men and women fell. The chariots rolled on.

Odan smashed away the foam-dripping mouth of the near-side horse, sent him staggering away and the chariot careered past, its driver swearing and hauling at the reins. For a space all was a weltering confusion and then another shield slanted in over Zenara and Kufu the Ox's hoarse voice rasped out.

"I am here, my prince."

"And right welcome, my Kufu."

A long spear flashed and Ankidu was there, half laughing, half in frenzy. The shields formed an immovable clump and the spear drew back dripping red. Somehow Odan wrenched a nomad spear away and reversed it and so plunged it deeply into the white-gowned breast of a desert warrior who flung forward from his chariot, shrieking. The wheels skittered past crazily, and the chariot lurched over onto its side. A following pair of horses smashed bodily into the toppling car, and in an instant the air filled with spinning chips of wood and whirling splinters, and the frenzied shrieking of wounded horses.

The clump of shields remained fast.

Ankidu and Kufu the Ox braced their bodies and with swelling muscles held the shields above the Princess Zenara.

And Odan the Khuzuk carved with all the primeval savagery of a man of the Hekeu, carved bloody chunks from the hides of those nomads foolish enough to allow him to approach.

More arrows skewered in. The confusion boiled now in an ebbing tide as the nomad chariots wheeled, breaking, collapsing as slender wheels refused to take the strain. All the bright pageantry of the desert could not stand against those murderous shafts as the Archers of Eresh shot and shot. Hard on the discharges the spearmen ran in. Odan saw that there were many more now than when he had run onto the Bridge, and so he understood—with a quick prayer of thankfulness to Odan and to Zadan and to Ke—that reinforcements had come up.

He had not thought that possible. But when the last chariot collapsed in a wild sundering of lashed beams and shredding bronze plates, and he stood up, carefully, over the last corpse, and so looked back, he saw the king brilliant in his regal chariot, and with him many of the nobility of Eresh.

"So the king, may his name be praised, is here at last!" said Ankidu. He was smothered in blood to rival Odan.

"And your father, the lord Andan, is with him and unharmed," said Odan. "Truly, out of great misfortune we have gained a victory."

He looked at Zenara. She smiled, uncertainly, and smoothed her long pale brown hair. Blood spots defiled her white gown; but they were not the blood of the Royal Princess of Eresh.

Odan could not touch her. He held himself stiff in the back, trying to force his head up against the habitual hunching forward of his massive shoulders. She was his sister—his half-sister, daughter to the king and Queen Momi. He could not touch her. He stood as attendants ran forward and she was conducted with all reverence back to the chariot of the king where she mounted up. Grasping the ivory and golden rail at her father's side, she looked at Odan.

He lifted the sword, bloody and gleaming.

"Hail the king!" bellowed Odan. He might be a wild man of the Hills; but he had learned much. He knew when the gesture of a moment would bring great profit for the future. "Hail the king, beloved of Zadan the All-Glorious!"

The soldiers took up the cry. The wharf and the Bridge resounded with the triumphant battle cries of the army of Eresh.

So Odan the Half-god marched back with the soldiers, back into Eresh. Many applauded him, and cried their congratulations and vowed to serve him past the point of death. But for Odan the Half-god, who would be a god in the fullest sense, the future lay opaque and unreadable.

The interview with the king would be painful, might be highly uncomfortable—and could all too easily be fatal.

Master Kidu, the court wizard, plucked thoughtfully at one down-drooping end of his long black moustaches. His habitually mournful face wore a look of indecision most unusual in him. Since his early days in King Neb-ayin-Ke's warren of a palace Master Kidu had grown ever more powerful both in overt and in darker and hidden ways. Now all men recognized him as a power in the city, a man to cherish, a man to beware of, a man above all never to cross.

"You are perplexed, Kidu," said old Master Asshurnax, in a chiding voice, hitching his second-best embroidered robes up to settle himself in Kidu's guest chair. The two wizards conversed within Kidu's eyrie atop the Tower of Relicts. The suite of apartments had been redecorated only three times since Kidu had come here to live as the king's wizard. He found the color schemes most restful to his eyes and art not worth continual change. Down in the palace the architects had the painters perennially searching for fresh color combinations and greater realism in frieze and wall-painting. Here time and dust and the secret cobweb ruled.

Kidu roused himself at Master Asshurnax's words. The old wizard was a friend, a good friend, and, if the truth be told, more than a little of a fool to himself. But he had befriended the young prince Odan when no one had known Odan was the son of Queen Momi and the god, Odan En-Ke, after he had returned from his experiences growing up among the primeval savages of Zumer. Nowadays Prince Odan was tender toward Asshurnax in ways he could never even begin to regard others—except, perhaps, and here Kidu pulled even harder at his moustache, except the young lord Ankidu. Those two were ripe hellions, always ready to arouse the night watch, to play merry hell with any and every poor wight who crossed their path.

"Aye, Asshurnax. I ponder what best to tell the king."

"My advice," said old Asshurnax, stoutly, "is to tell the king nothing of Odan's wishes. Only trouble can follow."

"But are we not bound by oaths?"

"By Kurd!" said Asshurnax, spitting in his excitement

all down his beard. "Since when have mortal men's oaths bound a sorcerer already sworn to other powers? I love the king and his family—and you, Master Kidu, know that to be true—but I love this wild Odan also. I weigh one against the other, and I—"

"And you prattle thoughts that could see you dangling by your ankles from the battlements."

"That might be so. But if the king learns that his true daughter, the Princess Zenara, is loved by and does love her half-brother—why, Kidu! The kingdom will be convulsed!"

"All this we have settled—or so I had thought. It is the matter of Odan's treachery that concerns me."

Asshurnax sighed, feeling the weight of his years pulling at his scrawny body. "Aye, Kidu. Treachery is not too foul a word for it. But you can see why? Surely, you can see that?"

"I have said—the cowlike sighings of children who imagine themselves enamored one of the other can never be allowed to interfere with the well-being of the king and the safety of the city. Mark me well, my Asshurnax. Odan the Half-god did promise to betray the city of Eresh to the devils of Endal, he did offer to open the gates to them, working under the cloak of invisibility, he sought to sell himself to the devil, Nirghal."

"But he did not!" Asshurnax wiped his shaking lips. "Odan remained true, at the end. And—see the way he fought for Eresh!"

"Oh, aye, he fought. I'll allow he fought. By Kurd, never has there been a fighter like Odan the Khuzuk. But that was after he discovered the trap Nirghal the Damned had set for him. Nirghal's own demigod son, Nirghi, did right to laugh at the deceit practiced in his name on our Odan."

"Our Odan. Yes, my Kidu! For are we not all of Eresh? And can we sleep at ease while one brick is left upon another in vile Endal?"

Kidu nodded and half smiled.

"Yes, that is a true reading. But had we not practiced our gramarye in this last battle, the sorcerers of Endal, and particularly Sebek-ghal, would have overwhelmed us."

"They recovered from the plague the blessed Zadan sent to vex them. Let us pray they do not recover so rapidly from their losses in the battle."

Using a little magic, a mere vanity of chiming a silver bell in an adjoining chamber, Kidu called for wine for his guest.

Despite all the bronzen resolve he tried to bring to his high calling as the king's wizard, Kidu felt an unreasonable affection for Master Asshurnax. The old wizard scraped a living preparing spells and griftings for the merchants of the city, and he did well enough, all in all. He had taken Odan as his famulus quite without understanding. Now that Odan had been recognized as the Prince of Eresh, kidnapped as a child and now returned as a savage Khuzuk, a wild man of the Zumer Hills, Asshurnax rebelled at the life of luxury Odan had offered him. He would continue to cast his spells and make a living and study the writings and the evil lore of the ancient Worm People as he had always done.

Littly walked gracefully into the eyrie. She carried a bronze tray of goblets and bottles, with a dish of sweetmeats.

As always—as always!—Kidu sighed as he watched her go gracefully about her tasks, setting out the goblets, pouring the wine, offering sweetmeats. For Littly still possessed a marvelously beautiful body, all creamy curves and delectation, lithe and seductive. But, perched atop that delectable body, poor Littly's head and face presented a macabre and grotesque monstrosity. A thing of wrinkled green skin and scarlet eyes, with sagging dewlaps and jagged uneven teeth caught by slobbering brown lips. Coarse strands of grey hair hung down beside that blasphemy of a face, a face spelled upon her out of frustrated lust by the last court wizard, Unsherbi, who had long since gone to feed the crocodiles.

The only difference in Littly's appearance now from what it had been when Kidu had taken up his appointment could be seen in her ears, which had been reasonably round and were now quite clearly donkey's ears. These ears were the result of an unfortunate and completely unsuccessful attempt made by Kidu to spell her own beautiful face back. He still searched for the correct formula; but he was increasingly losing confidence, year by year, that he would ever discover where Unsherbi had found the grifting that had so blasted all Littly's hopes in life.

For a space the two wizardly friends sipped their wine and nibbled their sweetmeats and talked. Their own thoughts remained veiled. At last, Kidu set down his goblet, and leaned back, and said: "I think, for the general good of the king and of Eresh, we should allow Odan to continue. No satisfaction is to be obtained from petty revenge. I feel he can see the folly of his conduct. Now he is for Eresh wholeheartedly."

"You are right, Master Kidu." Asshurnax felt the relief. "Odan the Half-god will fight for Eresh as a loyal son, never fear."

But, all the same, Asshurnax felt a vague breath of unease stirring his old heart, for he remembered with what enthusiasm Odan had received Asshurnax's suggestion that he might become a whole god, and not a mere Half-god.

And, Master Kidu, nibbling a honey-stuffed date, smooth and sweet, reflected that his surveillance of Odan the Khuzuk would not abate, for all his reassuring words.

The most northerly riverine gate of Eresh was called the Tik-bird Gate. Here Gabal-ayin, the king's uncle, had commanded his bearers to carry him as the devils of Endal attacked. He gripped onto the gilded wood of the chair's armrest now and his brown fingers ridged hard and mercilessly, as though he grasped the neck of the king his nephew, Neb-ayin-Ke. Long and long had Gabal-ayin waited and plotted and still his strength and still his purchase of sorcerous powers had failed to topple the king. As a cripple, Gabal could not ascend the Crocodile Throne. But his son, Galad-ayin, might do that—no! Not might. Gabal possessed the burning fanaticism that made him supremely confident that, one day, his son Galad *would* sit in the Crocodile Throne and rule all proud Eresh.

Now all those thoughts must temporarily be brushed aside. Now he must hurry immediately to the king and hail him, congratulate him on winning the battle and of retaining his life unharmed. From the Tik-bird gate a boat would have carried Gabal to safety had the city fallen, for he was a man who liked to keep open a line of retreat. But the city had not fallen and the devils of Endal had been thrashed and behooved Gabal to make his joy at the king's success known to Neb-ayin-Ke at once.

So he hurled vicious commands at his slaves as they hurried his litter along. He had a story ready, a farrago about bringing in reinforcements from the north. The king was booby enough to believe what his uncle told him.

There might be a raised eyebrow from Kephru-Ket, the chief priest of Zadan; but Gabal was working toward an understanding with Kephru-Ket. The major problem lay with Master Kidu, the court wizard, a man who had previously thwarted Gabal's attempts to slay the king and wrest from him the scepter and the power.

One such attempt including the kidnapping of the young prince Odan had gone awry, and Gabal had fallen from the high window to be transformed on the instant from a strong and ferocious fighting noble to a weak and crippled noble forever condemned to a chair or a litter.

Yes—the bastard Odan must be slain. There was nothing else for it. If Gabal's plan to marry his son, Galad, to the Princess Zenara was to succeed, then Odan the Khuzuk must be disposed of.

He would send for his son. As a matter of policy Gabal kept Galad always on the move up and down The River, making him learn the ways of different people, currying friends, sizing up potential enemies. Galad had turned into a rough tough fighting man of great physical prowess, of a lowering dark appearance, and of enormous capacity for deceit. Gabal knew, with a pang he felt as so strange as to be insupportable, that once his son was king then the father to the king must look cautiously to himself for his own head.

Chapter Four

Intrigue in Proud Eresh

Kephru-Ket, high priest of Zadan the All Glorious, Zadan of the Sword, moved in priestly dignity down the immense expanse of steps before the Ziggurat of Zadan in proud Eresh. Incense smoked bluely on the air and the de-

clining rays of the sun threw indigo shadows into crevices
and corners. Many lesser priests moved with Kephru-Ket,
chanting in sonorous chorus the rote phrases and the ful-
some praises of Zadan of the Sword.

Among the glitter of costumes, the bright flash of jewels, the liquid gleam of bronze and the multi-colored haze
of feather fans, the face of Kephru-Ket appeared as hard-
set and as merciless as the stone axes used to break open
the skulls of evildoers who had blasphemed against the
god.

The sacrifices had been made. Many bullocks had been
burned to the greater glory of Zadan. Thanks for the great
victory had been offered up. The city of Eresh might once
more sleep peacefully. The sun, Zamaz, might rise on the
next day after the mysterious passage through the nether-
world to regain the eastern horizon, and could shine down
upon the maze of waterways and the viridian fields of the
irrigations, upon the battlemented walls of the city, and all
Eresh would know the shadow had been lifted.

But Kephru-Ket was not satisfied.

He had spoken long and deeply with Gabal-ayin, the
king's uncle. He was well aware of that darkly ferocious
man's plans. Little could escape the many eyes and ears
available to a high priest of the chief god of a city of The
River.

So Kephru-Ket slowly descended the sacred steps. He
turned at the foot, crossing the marble pavements with
their religious symbols inlaid in precious stones. He cast a
single glance up at the massively towering bulk of the Ziggurat. The wisp of smoke rising from the topmost tier told
him all was well. Up there, in the airy realms of the gods,
all might very well be in order. But the chief priest knew
that down here, among the runnels of the city, all was a
dark miasma of intrigue and ambition and murder.

In his private chambers he dismissed the last of the servitors who withdrew with much bowing and scraping, gorgeous in their ceremonial robes. He was left with the vicar
of Zadan, an old man who was trusted by Kephru-Ket
only as far as he could keep him under observation. The
vicar's confidant, a young-seeming priest of ascetic features who would as lief slay anyone who did not bow the
head at the name of Zadan as attempt to convert him, remained half hidden in the shadows by the curtained window.

"You look tired, vicar," said Kephru-Ket. He removed his own simple garment left after he had been disrobed of the sacred vestments. "You would do well to retire early."

"I shall retire when all my duties to Zadan and you as high priest have been discharged."

The vicar's confidant stirred, and then was still.

Kephru-Ket did not look pleased.

"I have an audience of the king before the Royal Hearing in the Hall of Reception tomorrow. I would be alone, vicar."

The vicar inclined his head. "As you command, Kephru-Ket, so it shall be."

Watching the two men leave, the high priest caught the confidant's eye. The confidant, a slender man with the wolfish face of the religious fanatic, moved his head slightly within the blue cowl. Kephru-Ket smiled.

The apartments of the chief priest at the base of the ziggurat extended for a wide area of passage and court, of covered way and secluded chamber. He sought out a certain private room where, later, he would summon the dancing girls to please him and soothe his cares. On a gilded couch he lay back, feeling the strain in his neck muscles, until the soft voice of his personal slave, Shafti, aroused him.

"The confidant comes, master."

"Let him in. And let no other in, as you value your immortal soul."

"As you command, master."

The confidant bowed deeply.

"You honor me by your sympathy, your reverence."

The high priest motioned the confidant to a chair, a gilded monstrosity of eagle's feet and vulture wings and uncomfortable, overstuffed seat. The confidant sat with expectation.

Kephru-Ket leaned forward. His heavy face betrayed a deep suspicion. His lips showed a riper flush of red in the gleam of the lamps.

"I give you my confidence. I do not have to warn you of the consequences if you betray me."

The confidant had sense enough to make no reply.

"You went with the vicar and Queen Momi to Dilpur. With you went Prince Odan." Kephru-Ket put a plump beringed hand to his lips. "What of the Prince?"

The confidant did not hesitate.

"He carries a dark secret, my lord. The Queen is devoted to him. Her son has been returned to her after many years in the wilderness. Yet he bears a secret—"

"I know, you dolt! What is the secret?"

"That I do not know, your reverence."

Kephru-Ket's eyes showed in their abrupt murderous flash all the turmoil of his feelings. If what Gabal hinted at should come to pass, as it very well might, then Kephru-Ket intended to continue to be high priest of Zadan in Eresh when a new king sat on the Crocodile Throne.

"There is much gold, a casket of gold, for you if you bring me the secret."

"Yes, your reverence." The confidant hesitated. Then: "The vicar has been won over by the queen and by Odan. He does not speak well of the Prince Numutef."

"Nor does anyone with sense." Numutef, the son of Queen Fretti, the king's second wife, was all show and glitter and beneath that carapace of brilliant wit was a dark monster of passion and desire, willful, feckless, a betrayer of men and women, a destroyer. "Numutef will naturally wish Odan to die so that he will inherit. All men know this."

"Yet no man dare speak it for fear of the wrath of the king." The confidant licked his lips, hesitating and then plunging on boldly. "Yet the vicar will say so, out of love for the Queen Momi and her son. He will risk his head."

Slowly, Kephru-Ket nodded.

"This may be used. It seems to me that I may need a new vicar of Zadan. I may not have to look far."

"No, your reverence."

The confidant lowered his eyelids. Ambition burned in him; but caution held him back, also. The higher a man rose the farther he had to fall, the more horrible the way of his departure from the Land of Ea and his entry into the seven hells.

All the gorgeous trappings of high rank, the gold and jewels, the magnificence of clothing, the dancing girls, the sumptuous food—all those great and glorious things availed a man nothing when he was dragged naked and screaming to be impaled or to be hung head first over the battlements.

Intrigues within the palace flourished like weeds in the irrigations and must be cut down with the hoe. Secret plans fomenting in dark places, the glint of vengeful eyes, the scarf drawn across a distorted face, the quick lunging stab of knives plunging into backs—all these were daily hazards to those who served the king and his nobles, who placated the gods in the temples and in the great ziggurat.

And, always looming over all men, the threat of the sorcerers dampened down too reckless plots and attenuated the boldest schemes of hardy adventurers. The vicar's confidant looked to the time when he would be appointed vicar in his turn, and he was as fully prepared to play his part in the downfall of Prince Odan as, it seemed to him, the high priest Kephru-Ket was. Let Zadan smile on this enterprise! The confidant knew, also, in the fierce fanatical pride of the zealot, that he was fully fit to hold the position of high priest. One day—and he prayed to Zadan that the day be not too long postponed—he would seize and take and hold the position of high priest of Zadan of the Sword in proud Eresh.

The Royal Hearing in the Hall of Reception wound inexorably on to a preordained close.

At least—for all his savage and rebellious nature, Odan the Khuzuk felt a stab of anticipatory hope that the Hearing would resolve in a fashion favorable to himself.

Within the many-towered and turretted palace of Eresh had been built many halls and courts. Lavishly had the past kings spent on decoration, money and talent and sumptuous materials had been poured into the structure and its embellishment to make of the Royal Palace of Eresh a wonder even to the blasé cities of the central arm of The River. The Hall of Offerings was too large for this gathering and the king and his high priest had instructed the chamberlain, Narpul the Staff, to prepare the Hall of Reception. Here Neb-ayin-Ke sat upon the lapis-lazuli throne encased in his regal garments, and sweated and shifted uncomfortably and yet retained the stiff and unforgiving frown upon his face that protocol demanded until the outcome of the Royal Hearing was made manifest.

Looking at the man who was king in this city, Odan pondered. This man, Neb-ayin-Ke, he felt to be as good a king as an ordinary mortal might be. Odan had little experience of kings. But he felt he knew his mother. Momi exhibited all the love and affection and wifely duty to be expected in a woman wholly devoted to her husband. And, then, Momi was the first wife, the senior wife. Neb-ayin-Ke had taken only two wives—Momi and Fretti—where the laws allowed any man to take four wives, and women expected the pleasure of companion wives to share their burdens and lighten their days. So for Odan the Half-god delivered by his father, the god Odan En-Ke, into the hands of the king of Eresh for safe-keeping, this king deserved good at his hands.

He had been rewarded by treachery.

Odan was too well-versed in the treacherous ways of the bazaars, where in his young days he had been a bazaar pirate, the leader of the Terrors of the Souks, to shrink from naming his own conduct.

He would be a god. That simple fact had drawn him into the trap set by Nirghal, the devil god of vile Endal. He had promised to open Eresh to the chariotry of Endal. Only at the last minute had he seen the truth, and so turned and fought for Eresh to defeat the Endalers.

If old Asshurax, his sorcerous master, or Master Kidu, the king's wizard, spoke out against him, he was doomed.

So Odan, whom men called Odan Crookback, waited in the crowd of courtiers and nobles lining the steps leading to the lapis-lazuli throne, and he sweated along with everyone else.

The proceedings began with propitiatory offerings as was proper. The small altar to Zadan within the Hall of Reception stood within a decorated niche and here Kephru-Ket carried out his first and most essential part of the function. Unless the god smiled on the enterprise it must be abandoned.

Everything proceeded well and the smell of burnt flesh as well as wrinkling everyone's nostrils, also told of the beneficent interest the god took in the city dedicated to him.

Narpul the Staff banged his great staff of office thrice upon the marble flags. Then, with a curt gesture, he ordered forward one of his minions, a stout lesser-chamberlain with lungs of boiled leather, to bellow the necessary reasons, charges and demands for calling the Hearing.

Odan watched with the fascination of any country bumpkin gawking in a great city.

His youth had been spent here; but he did not remember. He recalled only vague snatches of a boat and The River, and had only recently heard how the old high priest, Mnenon-Ket, had died in his defense. Odan had

been trained in the fantastically hard life of the wandering
savages of Zumer, northward of the barbarians who peri-
odically raided down The River. Odan held a contempt
for the ferocious barbarians that came from a conscious
knowledge of his own prowess. A man of Zumer—and
particularly a Hekeu, a member of the dagger-tooth lion
totem, could thrash a whole village of barbarians with one
hand lashed behind his back.

Sunlight poured through the wide embellished opening
in the roof, glittering from jewels and spear-points and
sword-hilts. Evidence was given. Of how the army of
Eresh had been called to arms. Of how they had waited in
ambush. And here Ankidu, sworn comrade to Odan,
stepped forth and loudly proclaimed his joy and admira-
tion for the way in which Odan, Prince of Eresh, alone
and desperately wounded, lured on the chariotry of vile
Endal to their destruction. People nodded and murmured
their approval. Odan shot a quick dark look at Master
Kidu. No discernible expression could be read on the long
mournful face of the court wizard.

Evidence was given by the captain of the outlying patrols. He said, simply, that subsequent investigation had
discovered the smashed chariots and the bodies of his men,
far out in the southern desert. Endal had planned well.

Then it was the turn of men to speak of the fight along
the waterfront. Kufu the Ox, loud, brash and confident
even within the glories of the king's palace, outdid himself
in praise of Odan.

Odan stepped forward and a hush fell for the prince.

"I but fought for my city and my king and my god. I
would say that this man, this Kufu the Ox, fought as well.
He it was who held the Archers when all appeared lost.
To Kufu the Ox, my king, my father, should go the praise
and the reward."

The king inclined his head. His massive ornamental
crown swayed, glittering in the falling sunbeams.

"Kufu the Ox shall be richly rewarded. Be it known to
all men that the King of Eresh knows well how to reward
those who serve him faithfully."

The back-hander to that was not lost on Odan. Again
he looked across as Kidu remained silent. The king's
wizard held powers unknown to mortal men. But Odan
who shared many of those powers in a patchy, incomplete
way, was under no illusions. Kidu knew about his treach-

ery. Quite instinctively, as the dagger-tooth lion gazes
about for prey and for quick runnels, so Odan Crookback
looked about to see the way he would carve for himself as
he escaped—if Kidu spoke the words.

But Master Kidu remained silent.

There were no shufflings of feet or fidgetings in any hall
or court where the King of Eresh presided. Now a stir began at the entrance. Gigantic blocks of stone, cut and
shaped into the fearsome forms of winged bulls, with pa-
tient, bearded, human faces, guarded those portals. High
towered the bulls' heads and higher rose their feathered
wings. The man who ran in past the yellow and brown
ranks of the guards looked shrunken and shrivelled. He
held up a hand and he gasped with the effort of speaking
after running so hard and fast, for the palace demanded
legs of bronze.

"My king!" bellowed this man in a high gasping voice.

Instantly a captain snapped a harsh order. A rank of Tiger Archers bent their bows, all in unison, and their cruel
bronze arrowpoints centerd all together on the bedraggled
figure as the man struggled to cross the open marble space
toward the lapis-lazuli throne.

Kidu said. "Hold, captain! It is Master Asshurnax."

Like a hekeu, Odan spun about. His old master, a
wizard who was the comrade of Kidu, knew also that
Odan had sought to betray Eresh. He had said all was
washed clean. But—was he come here in such haste to reveal all, to denounce Odan the Half-god, to pitch him into
the hands of his destroyers?

"Dilpur!" Old Asshurnax's first mighty bellow had exhausted him after the long run through the palace. He
could not send a grifting here, for Kidu's seals prevented
thaumaturgy within the immediate presence of the king.
"Dilpur!" he croaked and would have fallen, tangling himself in his third-best robe, for there had been no time to
don his best robe to crave an audience of the king.

Odan leaped, put an arm under Asshurnax, helped him
stand.

Asshurnax's face was tinged with blue and his mouth
opened and closed like a landed fish.

"Thank you, my lad—my prince—but Dilpur! The city
is attacked. While the devils of Endal attacked us—"
gasp "—the army of Sennapur went up against Dilpur."
Asshurnax whooped in a draught of air, and wheezed, and

managed to finish: "King Norgash of Dilpur commanded his chief mage, Master Skeltu, to send a grifting for our aid. The alliance—"

The king lifted his golden flail. Complete silence.

The king spoke.

"The city of Eresh lives in unbreakable alliance with the city of Dilpur, for is not Fretti, the daughter of King Norgash, my second wife? Has she not borne me a son, Prince Numutef? Then we will rise in our wrath and ride forth in our might and drive the devils of Sennapur utterly into the waters of The River."

The golden flail gleamed a brilliant shaft of light. Nebayin-Ke lowered the flail and men might speak once more.

At once a great full-throated shout of anger and determination rose.

"Eresh and Zadan! Dilpur and Redul! Death to Sennapur and Farbutu!"

Sennapur as the arrow flies stood a hundred and ten miles from Eresh, a trifle north of west, upriver. Odan knew the journey could be accomplished by fast chariot in practically no time at all, compared with the time an army would take, compared especially with the time taken by an army travelling upriver in boats.

In the uproar Kidu and Asshurnax were talking quickly, their heads together. Odan, who knew a little of the ways of thaumaturges, knew they were planning some kind of deadly sorcerous intervention. But, also, Odan knew that the mages of Sennapur would be ready. They would know that the treacherous attack by Endal on Eresh had failed. In all probability the master mage of Endal, Sebek-ghal, assisted by the renegade Chaimbal from Eresh, would be called on for help. Whatever the soldiers did on the earth with bronze and fire, the sorcerers would battle more fearsomely still in the unseen and hideous realms of the occult.

Narpul the Staff banged down on the marble until the noise subsided. Odan stepped away from Asshurnax, knowing he was all right and already hard at work at diabolical plans with Kidu. At once, as though his father, the god Odan—if Odan En-Ke *was* his father—had thrust the thought full-grown into his heart, Odan saw what he must do.

He stepped out boldly and ran a half-dozen treads up the enormous marble stairway, pausing beside the left-hand golden chalice with its lambent oil flame burning straight and steadily. He lifted his hand, saluting the king.

"King Neb-ayin-Ke! My father! Command me to take our army to Sennapur and drive out and destroy utterly the devils of Sennapur to the greater glory of Eresh, and of her king, and of her god, Zadan the All-Glorious!"

"Aye!" burst out the tumultuous uproar. "Prince Odan! We follow Prince Odan to Sennapur! Slay the dogs of Sennapur and break down their idols of Farbutu, the false god!"

It was a magnificent spectacle as the bronze swordblades flashed aloft, catching the light, creating a dazzlement within the Hall of Reception. The noise continued. Eventually Narpul the Staff restored a little order and Odan, flushed as a young man with the dizziness of the moment, turned to stare triumphantly up at the king.

Hard on the heels of the commotion and before the king could speak, a commanding figure strutted forward and ascended the marble steps, halting a discreet one step lower than Prince Odan, as was proper. The disturbance, Odan saw with a quick stab of understanding, had been artificially prolonged just so that the king would not speak before this man stepped out. The last of the noise subsided. Odan saw those who perpetrated the applause and thus afforded a space for fresh speech, a small group of nobles clustered to one side among whom stood no one who bore him any good will.

He detested the whole pack of them, with their pampered ways and oils and unguents and lovelocks and gilded armor and scent bottles. But among them were a number who possessed stout sword arms, for all their affectations.

Ankidu did not stand among them. He remained a little isolated, separated from the mass of courtiers, the space where Odan had stood vacant at his side.

Now the man who had strutted forward lifted an arm in the ritual request for speech; and the king lifted his flail— for only a moment, only a moment—and lowered it. In absolute silence this man, this Hillul from Dilpur, spoke.

"Your wisdom is renowned throughout the whole land of Ea between the Two Seas, O king! I beseech you, as I speak for my master, King Norgash whose name be praised, your friend and ally, your father-in-law. This is a task laid upon the sons of Dilpur. This is a task that

should be undertaken by a son of both Dilpur and Eresh.
This is my plea, O great king, live for ever."

Odan stared down evilly at this Hillul. The fellow was a
Ras, a high-ranking officer commanding a regiment; but
he had been attached by King Norgash to the person of
Norgash's grandson, Prince Numutef, son of Fretti and
Neb-ayin-Ke. He was a stocky, thickly built man, with the
round head and jetty hair of the peoples of The River. He
wore magnificent clothes, bronze armlets, a profusion of
jewels, the sash of power about his hips, supported by a
wide belt of white linen, over which the sword and dagger
belts glittered with plates of gold and silver, each finely
chased and engraved with scenes of war and carnage. His
dark-featured face with the curling nostrils and thick lips
showed in every line his knowledge of his own power and
prestige under the kings.

As for his beard, massy, square, threaded with gold and
silver wire, that was as false as his heart, a formality
prescribed by ritual. His own beard was shorn short, as
would any warrior's beard be shorn who did not wish his
foeman to grasp it in the heat of conflict and so drag his
neck down to the decapitating slash.

Ankidu had warned Odan about this Ras Hillul. A dangerous man, serving Norgash utterly, devoted to the
worthless piece of turpitude, Numutef, he would stop at
nothing to perform his duty.

Odan, staring down with his own head jutting from his
hunched shoulders, saw well enough what Ras Hillul was
about.

The king saw, also.

"You speak with sense and reason, Ras Hillul. And I
wish Prince Odan to keep my side for a space. It is right
that my son, Prince Numutef, who is also the grandson of
King Norgash of Dilpur, should lead the army of Eresh
against the devils of Sennapur." The king lifted his solid
gold mace of power. The weight caused him to lift and
then let drop the holy object. "It is my command. Let it
be done to the greater glory of Zadan."

A burning stain spread painfully over Odan's cheeks.
His forehead furrowed and grew red. His brows drew
down and he glared with the fury of a baulked hekeu
upon this Ras Hillul.

Above him, the blaze of the throne and the figure of the
king, leaning, looking down. At his side and a step lower,

Ras Hillul, smirking, stroking his beard, very pleased. Below, the mass of courtiers arranged in neat hierarchical patterns within the Hall of Reception, with the knot of nobles looking up with expressions as close to jeering contempt as they dared in the presence of the king; with Ankidu, isolated, looking up with despair. At the side, half hidden in shadows from the high mantle of the altar, the blocky form of Kephru-Ket.

Odan was still a young man—more, he was a wild, untamed, primeval savage. He had been so thoroughly enjoying the homage paid him his sensations had been quite beyond his understanding or his control. His heart seemed to want to burst with emotion. He was the king's son, the son of a god, Prince, and he was in full stride, riding high on honor and glory and the superiority of his own conduct. Whatever he wanted within this Hall it seemed to him might be vouchsafed to him. And, right in the full flow of his young untamed pride, he had been checked.

Someone had dared to stand against his wishes! The king had been thoughtless. Surely he could see that he would shame Odan if he refused this request?

Odan turned abruptly. He opened his mouth. His face was congested with dark blood. He was about to bellow out to the king, to demand that he, and not Numutef, be entrusted with the expedition to Sennapur. He caught a quick glimpse of Master Kidu and Master Asshurnax, very close together, looking up at him.

His own powers as a demigod would prevent their interference.

He opened his mouth to shout and with a sudden dizziness, a feeling of cold, the high priest of Zadan, Kephru-Ket, stood between Odan and the king.

The high priest took Odan's arm in a grip that felt firm and yet melted as though a rock had been smothered in butter. Odan tried to pull away and the high priest said: "Come down the steps a way, prince."

For a space, a wheel of violet and indigo color swirled about Odan. He did, indeed, take three steps down. Kephru-Ket walked with him, hand on arm.

Master Kidu looked up from very close at the bottom of the steps.

"Odan!" The words punched through an echoing vault to Odan's ears. "Odan! Do not speak your mind to the king, else you are destroyed!"

So Odan turned and tried to shake free of the high priest, and lo!, Kephru-Ket was no longer with him upon the stairs but stood in his shadowed alcove by the altar.

Odan understood.

Kidu and Asshurnax might not play directly with their sorcery upon him. So they had performed a most potent grifting. They had projected an image of the high priest, because he might stand upon the steps higher than the young prince, and so had checked Odan in a career of headlong destruction.

Young, Odan might be. Savage, he most certainly was. But the Hekeu taught him survival. In any situation: survival, self-reliance. He understood. In the court proprieties to speak against the king was death.

He looked up and he said: "My king, my father. Let Prince Numutef lead the army against Sennapur. For the greater glory of Eresh and of Zadan the All Glorious." Then, remembering, he added: "And I await the commands of my king in the place he reserves for me at his side."

At Odan's side, Asshurnax whispered in his shaky old voice:

"By Kurd, my lad! You nearly had your head rolling down those stairs, mark my words!"

The passion and fury and resentment washed away from Odan's face. Son of the king he might be; the laws of Eresh demanded inflexible obedience. As he had as a wild youngster in the wilderness of the Zumer hills, Odan learned and stored up wisdom from his experiences.

He must survive. He had to survive.

Far sweeter than any cup of water to the thirsting man in the desert, the thought of Zenara drove him remorselessly on. Once he was a god, a whole god, recognized as a god by all the pantheon of heaven—why, then what might not he do!

Chapter Five

The Witch Amenti

Galad-ayin, the king's cousin, drove his chariot along the Processional Way from the North Gate of Eresh with all the panache and glitter of glory rightfully due to a blood-kinsman of the king and a noble prince high in favor. Zamaz the sun shone benignly upon the prince, light splintered from his golden armbands, from the chariot bosses, from the bronze plates embellishing his chariot. The white plumes of the chariotry of Eresh nodded from the heads of his horses. His erect stance in the car, his head held high, his left arm jutting tautly wrapped with reins, his right hand casually throwing silver pieces to the running crowds at his wheels, the sparkle and glitter of his gilt bronzen coat of scales, all these munificences bespoke the true prince, the man of glory—perhaps, the man of destiny?

Following in their own rigs his cronies felt the surge of reflected glory. Truly, Galad-ayin was the man of the future!

Summoned by his father, Gabal-ayin, the prince drove swaggeringly through the shouting multitudes. Always, he and his father had lavished largesse on the mob, on the scum, the ditch workers, on all those poor who yet were not slaves. From their ranks came the bulk of the army, save for the chariotry. From them could be expected loyalty when the time to slay the king came, a loyalty bought and paid for, a loyalty as yet undeclared but deep running as watercourses of The River in flood.

After due obeisances and sacrifices had been made at the middle altar of the ziggurat, as custom decreed, prince

Galad could turn his impatient horses towards the palace of his father. Gabal had built a fine strong house, and year after year he had extended it at the expense of further demolitions among the huddled houses of the people. But all wrath was turned aside as Gabal cunningly arranged for those he dispossessed to move into areas freshly rebuilt after mysterious fires, or subsidences, or plagues. Devious and subtle in the ways of the city was Gabal. To be called a man of mud was to him an accolade—as, indeed, it was to any who felt contempt for the nomads and their skin tents and the barbarians and their wooden villages.

Father and son greeted each other with the cautious aloofness that had grown between them over recent years. Galad was only a few years younger than the king, and Gabal remained a crippled force forever chained to his chair.

"My son!"

Gabal stared down from the high seat shadowed with cloth-of-gold hangings in his ornate Room of Reception. Attendants and guards and quick, obedient slaves gave to this place a little of the atmosphere of the great Hall of Reception within the royal palace. Gabal, as the king's uncle, liked to keep up his pretences and appearances, to make sure no one forgot his power and position.

Standing with one foot on the topmost step, Prince Galad lifted his head to look at his father's face. Old, he looked, old with the years, wasted with the grievous hurt done his body in the long ago. As always, Galad shuddered at the thought of remaining chained to a chair for the rest of his life.

"My father!"

The lord Gabal motioned impatiently, his scrawny hands loaded with rings that caught the light, flashing grotesquely.

"Thonga," he said, speaking pettishly, the spittle flying from his lips. "Clear this rabble away. Attend me in my private chambers. Son, do you walk at my side."

The man addressed as Thonga stepped forward and crashed his cumbersome staff upon the marble floor. Staff and marble, here in the land of Ea between the two seas, spoke eloquently of power and wealth. This man Thonga, middle-aged but still enormously powerful, rough and tough, looked in the harsh coarseness of his features to be a strange choice for a palace chamberlain. His big body moved with the deceptive speed of the bulky fighting man, and his black hair shocked in frizzed ringlets from beneath the high mitre of his authority.

Prince Galad had known Thonga since his childhood and knew the man for a roughneck, a bully, a man who served Gabal-ayin solely for money and position. There was a secret between them which Galad had never penetrated and about which neither man would speak.

When they were ensconced in the private apartments, the public ritual of greeting over, Galad still did not allow his alert stiffness of bearing to desert him. Gabal, calling for wine, said: "And the ruse went off successfully, my son?"

"Of course." Galad felt contempt for the need for the ruse in the first place. "We came up from Endal and passed through Eresh by the canal of our friends last night. Your chariots were waiting by the North Gate. We rode in as planned."

"Good. Endal have been beaten—yet again. But soon, now, my plans will see that at last Eresh goes down before the devils of Endal. Then, my son—then you will be king—"

"King?" said Galad. "King of ruins? Do you think Endal will cease once they enter the city? I question the wisdom of this alliance with the devils of Endal."

"You do not question the dictates of your father!" Gabal's face contorted. His eyes glared. He thrust himself up stiffly from the overstuffed cushions. Spittle flew. "I command and you obey! I will not countenance your insolence!"

Galad soothed his father, saying the right things, a little discomfitted by the old man's vehemence. At last he felt it the right time to say: "I have brought a new witch. She has great recommendations. She comes from Perar in the Persaran Bend. With your permission let her be called. She will find a way of spelling the king, of outwitting Master Kidu."

Gabal showed his interest. He leered up, as a slave wiped his mouth with clean linen. He did not notice the slave.

"Bring her in, my son, by all means. Perhaps she may succeed where Master Ubonidas, the master fool of sorcerers, has failed."

"Wizards and witches are an unholy tribe," said the

chamberlain, Thonga, his bulky body uncomfortable beneath his ornate robes of office.

Gabal did not even look at his chamberlain; by this time in their relationship Thonga had acquired a privileged place.

"You are right. But they can be used. They cannot make gold!"

Galad turned back from giving his curt commands to a personal slave. "That is true, father. But their gems—"

"Do not talk to me of a sorcerer's stones! They sparkle and glitter and cannot be told from the real thing—until they are removed from the wizard's body. Aye! And then they shrivel and turn into the dross they are." Gabal's thin face, so fallen away, turned eagerly as a black-cloaked figure entered his private apartment. "This is the witch?"

Galad smirked. He counted it a small victory to have so won over his father in this matter. "Aye, father. This is Amenti."

From the black-cowled hood a pair of shockingly blue eyes stared calculatingly at Gabal. A black veil hid the rest of the woman's face. Her shape suggested all manner of thoughts to Gabal. He frowned. He glanced up at his son, standing so tall and straight, proud and erect in his strength.

Vashti—memories of his dead wife ghosted in—Vashti who had murdered her husband so that she might marry Gabal, the brother of the king, because her own sister had married the king. Well, they were all dead, now. But in this Galad she had borne him there lurked much of her, much of her tempestuous yet deep-running darkness. Low and full, the face of Galad, his jetty hair cutting a black band low across his forehead, his cheeks compressed, his jaw short and jutting. Hard, like a nugget, this son of his. Hard and dark and feral, well-versed in the ways of The River, respected as a resourceful foeman, feared as a superb swordsman, probably loved by a few and hated by many. Yes, Gabal, who undertook to describe many a man's heart in terms of gold, understood well the desires and the vulpine hardness of this, his son, prince Galadayin.

With a gesture sharpened by his thoughts, Gabal commanded the woman to unveil.

The graceful movement with which she unlatched the

desert veil and let it drop might, in another, have been taken as an affront. Gabal caught his breath.

A white triangular face stared out at him, dominated by those disturbing eyes of the blue of the skies above The River. But the hair—the hair! A brilliant fiery red, that hair twined in long twisted ropes about the woman's shoulders she slipped the cowl free. No hint of color showed in the cheeks; all a deathly white, that sharp face, except for the mouth which, ripely crimson, curved as a fruit curves, dripping honeyed juices, ready for the sucking.

"Well are you called Amenti," said Gabal. His hoarseness of voice displeased him. His mouth had dried on the instant.

"I am here to serve your son, prince Galad-ayin, may his name be revered. From whence I come is of no matter."

"Ah, but," said Gabal, his composure restored by reason of the instant decision to which he had come. "I think you are the miscegenation of a barbarian and a woman of The Salt Sea far to the west."

"This is true. But my barbarian blood holds no power in me."

"By Zadan!" said Galad, moving impatiently. "They are a fey people down in the southwest."

"Since the course of The River changed, in ancient times," said the witch Amenti, "we have learned much of the occult arts and of the forbidden lore of the Worm People."

Everyone—except Amenti—in the chamber shuddered at her words.

Gabal and Galad both, father and son, felt the inescapable wings of destiny beating over them. Each felt he must restore his own dignity, his own power.

Harshly, Gabal said: "You know why you have been brought here?"

"I know. Although gold was paid for me to the prince who had forgotten how to value my help, I came of my own free will."

At this Gabal again glanced up at the proud, erect form of his son, so brilliant in his gilded bronze, his harsh lowering face so charged with power. Yes, he could understand that.

The eerie feeling of immense forces wheeling away in spaces unknown to normal men fragmented his attention.

Those eyes—so blue, so blue—uncanny here in the dark-eyed land of Ea.

"Then you will begin your task at once. You will be afforded any help you may require. Master Ubonidas will be pleased to assist you. He can be summoned quickly from the Abode of the Bats."

At this Amenti smiled. Her lips widened, shining, red.

"Yes. We heard that Master Chaimbal had departed from Eresh. A hurried departure. If I have need of Ubonidas I shall call him."

"Yes," said Gabal. He swallowed. "Wine!" he bellowed, before his outstretched hand found the handle of the slave-proffered goblet. Drinking, he looked at the witch, and away. She was very different from Chaimbal and Ubonidas. And, at the thought, a strong glow of satisfaction coursed with the wine throughout his shrivelled body. Now, surely, he must topple the king his nephew, smash Neb-ayin-Ke utterly!

In his eyrie in Yellow Lotus Street, a somber place of mystery and terror to the uninitiated and a restful home to an old thaumaturge, Master Asshurnax pottered across to the desk where he was in the midst of mixing a potion to cure the inflammation in the foot of poor Nardu, who had somewhat foolishly allowed a wheel of a wain to run over that valuable appendage. The draught would bring a few copper coins. Asshurnax scraped a living casting a few simple spells for the folk of the huddled houses in his neighborhood and in caring as best he could for their poor abused bodies.

He passed Akheton, the skeleton hanging by the door.

Asshurnax paused and looked up.

The skeleton of Akheton was of sentimental value to him, being quite five hundred years old and reputed to be that of the notorious Akheton himself, and although Asshurnax could never be absolutely sure of the fact, he chose to believe it, for Akheton surely worked.

The lower jaw of the skull was tightly locked up against the upper, the gold-capped teeth rigid.

Instantly, Master Asshurnax placed the mixture for Nardu's foot somewhere among the clutter of dismembered toads and bats and parts of crocodiles on the desk. He struggled out of his working robes and bashed around until he found and donned his second-best robes. His cap of potency was, thankfully, where he had left it on the bronze nail driven into the brickwork of the door. He did not stop for a look around the eyrie.

Hitching up his robes and keeping his cap of potency balanced on his old head, he made his best speed toward the royal palace.

Such news!

The skeleton of Nebocar, who had been court wizard to the king of Eresh some eight hundred years ago, dangled with tightly clamped jaws in the eyrie of Master Kidu in the Tower of Relicts in the palace of Eresh.

Master Kidu sat in his chair of power, frozen, his spirit summoning, his ka prowling loose as he sent a grifting probing gently. Even as he sat thus, delicately sensing the tenuous threads before him in the shadow realm, he was aware of the excited approach of Master Asshurnax.

Well, the old fellow would know, also. Despite Asshurnax's perverted passion for working in horrendous conditions among the mass of the people, of performing small magics, he remained still and despite his own doubts a most prestigious sorcerer. Despite all, Kidu would welcome his old friend in a matter of this delicacy.

Out of politeness and, also, because the grifting was meeting increasing vagueness and directional loss in the quest, Kidu relaxed and withdrew and so was himself in his own body to welcome Asshurnax.

"Master Kidu! I give you greeting—you have read the bones?"

"Aye. A new sorcerer is in Eresh. This is, indeed, a matter of consequence. I was about to probe; but the spell works feebly. There are strong seals against surveillance."

"I will offer all my help, gladly—if you need it, that is."

"Come, old friend. Do not so constantly underrate yourself. Yes, we will join our kas and sally forth to discover what, if any, are the new dangers against which we must fight. As the king's wizard it is my duty."

"And I am with you. What with the worry over Odan, and now this—they are connected. I feel sure."

"Oh, they are connected. Ubonidas has kept so quiet of late one might think him a silent bird of the desert. But this new one—ah—this, I think, will prove entertaining."

For a space thereafter both wizards, comfortably settled in their respective chairs, joined and probed. The grifting drifted out, at once powerful and delicate, like the strand of a spider's web that floats so lightly yet traps and holds the burly blue-and-green flies. Together they probed—and, together, reacted.

Both men shocked back into their own bodies. Asshurnax could still feel the soggy thump of resistance. Kidu the sharper penetrative punch.

For a moment neither spoke. In the air about them a shadow danced, pirouetting, until Kidu irritably waved it away.

"There *is* a new one!" said Master Asshurnax. "The power!"

"Aye," said Master Kidu. "New and powerful—and a witch!"

Chapter Six

Of the Outcome of a Meeting in a Garden

In those days as the nobles of Eresh lazed away the brilliant days under the sun, delighting in all the goodness of life, giving praise to Zadan the All Glorious, and the working people stored up an abundance of wealth and produce, all, in their turn, giving praise to Zadan the All Glorious, and the slaves—well, the slaves did what slaves always did—Odan the Half-god meandered through life. He felt detached from reality.

Here he had saved not only the city but his own neck. He had proved to his own satisfaction that he was the son of a god. He had been told by that disgusting worm-woman, the Raven, that the old gods were not real, and that therefore the god he had thought to be his father,

Odan En-Ke, could not be real. But the god who had brought his mother Momi here to Eresh had been real. He had driven in his dream chariot across the sky, blazing with supernal fire. He had been seen. But, who he was, Odan did not know.

Ankidu, laughing, roseate with the glory of youth upon his limbs, snatched the quoit from the air and hurled it full at the princess Zenara. Here in the secluded garden with its trailing flowers and sweet perfumes surrounding the pool, they were perfectly safe, for beyond the bloom-crowned walls prowled armed and armored men, bronze clad, bronze armored, bronze armed, ready to strike down instantly any intruder.

Laughing in return, Zenara caught the quoit dexterously and returned it with such skill that Ankidu, reaching for the spinning circle, overbalanced and toppled with an almighty splash into the pool. This afforded both him and the princess great amusement. So great that Zenara, also, fell in.

Odan Crookback sat hunched with his massive shoulders against a palm-tree bole, comfortably padded with cushions, and scowled.

Zenara. There lay the problem. His sister—well, half-sister. And the both of them head over heels in love. It was not bearable. But—but he had borne it, by Hekeu!

The cunning taught him by the Hekeu, the dagger-tooth lion tribe of savages of Zumer, must aid him now, for his appeals to the gods had failed. Should he simply snatch her from the palace and drive away with her in his chariot? But that would shame her. No, that was not unthinkable, for it formed a very great part of his primordial thinking at the time; but it was not possible. At least, not for Odan the Half-god.

For Odan the god . . .

Ah!

Zenara's handmaids set up a great caterwauling as they helped their mistress from the pool. Her beauty as she rose caught Odan by the throat. He forced himself to look away. An unguarded expression had brought death many and many a time in the fetid warrens of the palace.

Ankidu wandered over across the grass and plunked himself down, shaking like a puppy. He glowed.

"By Zadan, my prince! Do not scowl so. Is not life superb?"

"Life is better than death, so 'tis said."

"Odan!"

Odan did not smile; but he half lifted a hand. "I have shocked you, my Ankidu. By Odan En-Ke! I stifle. Let us go out into the desert and chase these scrawny lions you have down here. Now, up in Zumer, we hunt the hekeu—and once you have hunted a dagger-tooth lion you can call yourself a hunter, by Hekeu!"

Ankidu cocked his head up. Odan knew. His young friend was surprised at hearing the taciturn savage boasting.

"No, Ankidu, that is not worthy—I am—"

"You are a damned unhappy man, my prince!" Ankidu broke in, as no one else, apart from his family, might, across the speech of a prince of Eresh.

Odan nodded. "But it will be settled—and soon."

Ankidu rolled over and regarded Odan closely. His fresh face seemed to the cunningly savage heart of Odan Crookback so naive as to be not yet weaned. "My prince—it is a woman?"

Odan had no need to reply. He was no older than Ankidu in years, even if a lifetime of experiences separated them.

"Then you must do as I do. I love, purely and unselfishly. But the lady is not for me. I know. Therefore I laugh and sing and drink and wench and reck nothing to it. Let us go and sample the fleshpots. When we are stupified, then let us see how great a hunter are the Hekeu—and from a chariot!"

"Why, you artful—" began Odan, and reached out one ape-like arm and, the next moment, somehow, both young men were wrestling and rolling over and over and laughing all the while. When Odan stood up, with Ankidu flat on his back, they felt greatly relieved. This was mere child's play. Odan, at the least, recognized that. He glanced across at Zenara, and—quickly—away. He saw Ankidu lifting himself up and, likewise, staring at Zenara.

And so Odan, at last, understood who it was his friend Ankidu loved.

The instant desire to slay Ankidu passed.

If anything, the bond between them was strengthened.

As a noble not of royal blood, Ankidu had no chance of marrying Zenara. Not unless the dynasties turned, as they did from time to time. But, love Ankidu as he did, Odan knew his friend was no dynasty toppler.

To turn their hearts from these dangerous subjects, Odan, at random, said: "I wonder how that oaf Numutef is coping with the army of Sennapur?" His voice husked far more gruffly than he liked.

Ankidu swung to regard him critically.

Then: "The prince Numutef, may his name be praised? He has able generals. And Ras Hillul, who yet a Ras will command the generals of the army, may he break an arm and a leg."

Odan looked about. His gaze was more appropriate to a primeval hunter of the Zumer hills than a soft secluded garden of a palace of The River.

"My Ankidu. As I love you—do not speak so fiercely of my enemies. The quantity of ears mortared into the walls of the palace of Eresh is of an enormity remarkable—"

Ankidu rolled over, bursting with laughter. His face grew scarlet with enjoyment and stomach pains.

"Oh, my prince! You are reputed a primeval savage. Yet you have picked up courtier speech so truly it is a joy!"

"Yet what I say is sooth."

Ankidu sobered.

"It is indeed sooth. And yet there is the other side."

"Oh?"

"Aye. My father, who is a good man and loyal to the king, as well you know, has a way with ears and mortar, also."

"Tell me."

At this Ankidu looked about, most conspiratorially. He bent his dark poll close to Odan's tousled brown mop, confined by the unbleached linen band.

"It is said that the prince Galad-ayin did not ride in from the north—"

"But he was seen to ride down the Processional Way! How could he not have ridden from the north? Ah!" Odan punched Ankidu lightly on the bicep. "I see. He hitched a ride on a sorcerer's flying carpet—or, even, in the dream chariot of a god!"

"Not so, my prince. He came from the south. He was ferried by boat through a canal of a family of adherents to his devil of a father and only pretended to come from the north."

Many thoughts jostled for Odan's attention.

But—"Gabal-ayin, the king's uncle—a devil, Ankidu?"

Ankidu's face crumpled. "I have said too much. May Zadan take pity on me. I should have known—"

"Now you have gone so far, had you not better finish?"

The distress disfiguring Ankidu's face was perfectly genuine. Odan felt all the harshness in him. Despite his love for Ankidu, a true feeling of friendship, man for man, he would brook no delay in answering his question. Ankidu saw this.

"You know how splendidly Gabal and the king are, together, in public? How the uncle loyally supports the nephew? No word spoken against Gabal would move the king to anger, save against he who was foolish enough to utter it. My father—"

"Aye," said Odan. "Your father who loves the king. Well?"

But Ankidu had sprung to his feet, his eyes hot.

"My prince!"

"Oh, sit down, sit down. I am still a savage—or so I am always being told. Even my mother chides me for my brutish ways. Look, my Ankidu. Say what you must say and then let us forget the matter. Hey?"

At that moment—with Ankidu cursing himself for his folly, with Odan half interested in what his friend had to say, half cursing his own folly and boorishness—a hail from the gate to the garden took their attention.

"Prince Galad-ayin, may his name be praised!"

And, hard on the guard's warning bellow, here came Galad, striding into the sweet-scented garden harsh in his armor, the gilded bronze scales catching the sun, his sword arrogant at his side.

With tiny make-believe screams the handmaids clustered about the princess Zenara like petals, scarves and veils fluttering in rainbow colors.

Slowly, Odan rose to his feet.

"There, you see," said Ankidu in an aside to Odan. "Here, in the private gardens of the palace where no ordinary man dare wear a sword on pain of instant death, and only members of the royal family may carry arms, all respectable royals put away their swords out of custom and reverence for family feeling—but this, this oaf flaunts his sword as though he marches off to war."

"Perhaps, my Ankidu," said Odan, mildly, "he does."

"I can scarce credit that—"

And then Galad had reached them and was drawing himself up and, hard and dark against the sunlight, was greeting them.

Odan returned the greeting as was prescribed.

He felt—instinctively—that Ankidu had somehow slipped out of the picture. Whatever there was of tension—if there was any tension—lay between himself and this Galad-ayin.

Confident in the magnificence of his own impression and the importance so thoroughly advertised by his jewels, his robes, his sash of power, his gilded scale armor, his jewelled belts and the costly sword and daggers, Galad flung his yellow-dyed cloak back over his left shoulder in a gesture clearly meant to establish his superiority.

His father had been precise. "You must tarry no longer, my son. You must marry Zenara—at once. Seek her out and pay court to her—a man like you—how can you fail?"

The plan would work. With the king dead and the puppy Odan with a slit throat, then marriage to Zenara must secure the throne, once the idiot Numutef had been pitched into the crocodile pool.

So Galad stared balefully upon the barbarian Odan— no. No, that was not right. Odan was not a barbarian. He was Odan the Khuzuk, a barbarian-slayer, from the tribe of primitives far away in Zumer. Galad felt no hint of resistance as he studied his rival.

But—but the look of the fellow came as a shock. He did not quite know what he had expected. The reports indicated that Odan was a fighter; but that would be a necessity. No—there was no gainsaying it, Galad was not prepared for the very breath of violence that clung to Odan Crookback. The man—he was scarcely more than a youth—presented a remarkable, a macabre picture. He must be a tall man, long of body and leg, yet he stood hunched over, his massive shoulders rounded, his incredibly long arms dangling. And that head, that face! Odan's head reminded Galad of the awesome sculptures he had seen, once, long ago in Lamenthoth, far to the east of Shanadul on the southern coast of The Sweet Sea. Regal power resided in that face, lowering, severe of profile, demanding. Truly, then, Galad realized with a horrified twinge of perception, this Odan-ayin *was* the son of a god.

The spell was broken as, surrounded by handmaids, the princess Zenara approached. The three men all made deep obeisances, for the moment seemed fitting for such gallantries. Zenara, with a composure that threatened to splinter as chicken bones splinter in the crocodile's jaws, greeted Galad.

For a fatuous moment conversation became general.

The purpose of Galad's visit was not made immediately clear. Slaves brought refreshment. They sat on the grass. For Galad the stiffness of his armor brought a dizzying moment of disorientation, as though he did not belong in this secluded and peaceful garden. The loose robes of the others mocked him.

He made his excuses as soon as he could in politeness do so, and left, the bronze flush along his jaw beneath the black stubble thankfully hidden by the smart dress beard.

"What did *he* want?" said Odan, carelessly. He had seen the strength in the man, the ruthlessness, the power, the accustomed attitudes to wealth and position. These attributes were becoming familiar to Odan in the people he was meeting. He had looked no closer. The presence of Zenara, so close, so close, unnerved him.

"He came, my Odan, to study you, to apprise himself of Eresh's mightiest warrior." Zenara crushed a grape between her fingers as she spoke, quite unknowingly.

"That is true," said Ankidu. "But, also, my princess, I think—I think he came mostly to see you."

"Me!"

"Aye."

"But I do not know him—his father has kept him out of Eresh for year after year. And when he has been here, for some reason I have been away—Shanadul, Dilpur, somewhere."

"I think," said Ankidu, "that was the doing of your mother, the queen, Momi of the bright countenance, whose name is praised among the gods."

"Then our mother did well," growled Odan the Khuzuk.

He stared curiously at his friend Ankidu. He was remembering what Ankidu had once told him, that Ankidu would kill without mercy any man who offered an affront to the girl he loved—the girl Odan now knew was Zenara. Grim danger lurked ahead in the infested relationships between these people.

"He—did look at me." Zenara lowered her eyelids. This

was no mock modesty. She had resented the cool appraising glance with which Galad had favored her. If the truth was known, perhaps she was more affronted that he had looked with such a cool and sexually-appraising glance *after* he had looked overlong at Odan the Half-god.

"By the Names!" snarled Ankidu. "One move—one step—" His right hand groped emptily at his beltless waist.

"My Ankidu!" said Odan, sharply, deliberately sharply. "He is a royal prince of Eresh. I will not have you dangling by the heels from the battlements or swimming in the crocodile pool."

"Oh, Ankidu!" exclaimed Zenara, and she clasped her hands together.

But, all the same, Odan Crookback saw that he must take heed of this swollen lump of pomposity, this Prince Galad-ayin, as he took notice of Prince Numutef and of the devils of Endal.

Two weeks later the three met once again in the quiet garden after Odan and Ankidu had spent a strenuous and exhilarating time in the western desert hunting desert lion. They had brought their trophies in. Ankidu had expressed himself as moderately reassured as to the ability of the wild Khuzuk to keep more or less inside a chariot at full career. They had tussled and sworn and boasted and drunk, and there had been a woman or two. Now, a little refreshed and looking out for more mischief, they greeted Zenara and were at once incensed.

"He dared?" shouted Ankidu. "He damned well dared?"

"He asked for the hand of Zenara," said Odan. "Surely the fool can ask? Our father gave him a short answer."

"Yes," said Zenara. "Father said he had—other plans."

"Do you know what oaf these other plans are, Ankidu?"

As a young sprig of the nobility, Ankidu would keep himself well informed as to the recommendations and eligibilities of other princes and nobles of the many cities studding The River like jewels.

Ankidu shook his head. He was still upset. "I do not know, by Zadan. No prince is worthy to lie in the mud for the princess to step across."

"No," observed Odan. "As to that I do not disagree. We must find out what my father has in mind. And, also, we must arrange a little happening for friend Galad. Something gentle, I think."

"Naked bronze—"

"Not so, my Ankidu! Come, now, would you slay your fool before you tease him a little?"

"Ah!" said Ankidu. The look of mischievous deviltry on his face mirrored—as a house cat mirrors in play the hunting of a hekeu—the dark and evil look upon the lowering face of Odan the Half-god.

Kufu the Ox blinked and swallowed with a vast nervousness he could make no effort to control. The splendor of his new robes dizzied him. The maidens had decked him in glory, and sprayed him with perfume, and, laughing, had tucked a dew-fresh rose behind his left ear.

"Brace up, man!" said Odan, mighty pleased with the effect. "You would be trampled in the rush down on Lupi Street."

"By Zadan the Sword, master," said Kufu, dragging in a straining lungful of air. "I made no bargain for this!"

"Well—you are to enjoy yourself. That is an order."

"Aye, my prince—"

"And you are not to get drunk on pain of—of something diabolically unpleasant I shall think of if the time comes."

"I'm too tight in the throat with all these gold bands to drink enough, by the Names."

The feast was a glorious, carousing, uproar of a success. Just what particular function the banquet performed in the loyal service to the king, Odan was not sure. Something to do with the anniversary of a new sluice system on the northwestern system of canals. The canals that, like suckling children, flowed between the loop of The River around Eresh and gave the city life, prosperity and a superabundance wherewith to celebrate.

The feast boomed along handsomely. Long tables had no place here. The guests in their best party robes sprawled everywhere on heaps of bright cushions, stuffed with the best wool of Eresh's finest sheep—the cushions—and with the best viands the city could provide—the guests. Animated conversations, the continuous sounds of harp and lyre, singing and dancing, the thousand aromatic smells of cooking food, the wild gyrations of the dancing girls whenever they could find a place to perform, the active darting of the slaves bearing in loaded platters and taking away empty platters—all this frenzied activity broke about Odan's ears with the strangeness of new tribal customs to an outlander.

Kufu the Ox, obeying orders, plunged into the fray. The banquet was held on the sloping lawns to the side of the king's palace, between encircling canals. Myriads of oil lamps cast their sheen upon the waters and the rioters, colored lights decorated the fruit trees arranged in careful geometries upon the lawn. The king and his entourage walked among his guests, smiling, extending his hand in greeting and blessing, the hand ritually decked with three rings upon each finger and a blood-red ruby upon the thumb. Neb-ayin-Ke smiled; but he looked forward to the time when he could remove the chafing rings and most of the cumbersome regal attire and go to join the small and private dinner party awaiting him within the palace.

The guests at the Sluice Feast were mostly officials concerned with the service of the canals and the palace, mingled with a sprinkling of soldiers and priests, scribes and artisans, and a goodly number of the farmers who held leaseholds at the hands of the king and his nobles along the canals and ditches of the irrigations. The fare was good—oxen roasted whole over enormous fires, spitting and spurting and arousing the salivary glands a hundred paces downwind; immense puddings stuffed with birds and game; incredible edifices of honeycakes and dates and almond-cookies; shellfish platters; birds' tongues preserved and used to add tiny dashes of piquancy to the gargantuan meals being downed by the guests. Yes, mostly the food was plain and no-nonsense; but good, very good.

At last the king could withdraw to his suite. What would go on now as the wine and beer was rolled forth by the slaves in ever increasing quantities needed no soothsayer to prophesy. There would be a few slit throats in the morning, a few more lives added to the population in nine months time. The king sat in the chair of libation and was thoroughly washed in perfumed warmed water. Freshly attired in a tasteful blue and yellow lounging robe, girt with gold belts, he entered the inner rooms.

Tasteful, the robe, and tactful. Blue for the priesthood; yellow for the army.

High representatives of both wings of his realm awaited him. The black hem to his robe represented a wing, too.

Both Master Kidu and Master Asshurnax had been bidden to the private feast.

Everyone rose and made the prescribed deep and reverential obeisance. The king motioned gracefully as he advanced toward the seat reserved for him. Here in the Jade Room designed for relaxation the seat was not referred to as a throne. A trifle of informality might intrude here. The guests seated themselves and the music struck up, concealed behind an ivory screen pierced and carved in the form of peacocks and lions. The first of the many sumptuous courses would be served once the initial warmed-honeywine had been consumed together with the honeyed fairycakes to accompany it. During this period Kephru-Ket would make a small sacrifice at the side altar. Knowing the sharp-set hunger of the company, the high priest would not be long about the ritual as the honeywine and cakes were served.

The king settled in his place and turned, first to his right to gaze with a smile upon the radiant face of his queen, Momi, and then to his left to smile upon the somewhat wan face of his queen, Fretti. He lifted his hands level with his face, palms together. Even as he struck his hands together as the signal for the sacrifice to begin, he heard a rustling noise at the side door, and a low voice, and shuffling.

The door opened and a man entered the private dining room.

"You're sure the bastard will come this way, Ankidu?"

"Yes, Odan—for the sweet sake of Father Zadan! You are treading on my heels and I've a blister there already."

Odan, trying to stop laughing, inched back. He had drunk too much beer, that was for sure. He had made a promise not to do such a stupid thing when he'd been with Nadjul the Quick; but Kufu the Ox seemed able to drink skin after skin of the stuff without any discernible effect. Odan's earlier warning now seemed, in retrospect, the foolishness it had all along been.

Now Kufu breathed harshly in Odan's ear. They were all stuffed up in a tiny slot of darkness by the Wall of Saffrons past which Galad was supposed to walk this evening of the feast.

The girl Kufu had found was most certainly a delicious piece. She said her name was Izi; but that could be a lie.

Her dark hair had been frizzed into ringlets about her cheeks and forehead. Her body really was splendid, lithe and well-formed, tigerish and loose within the folds of her green robe with its silver lace and copper ornaments. Her brown eyes were not trusting, although the lines at the sides of her mouth were practically invisible under artful cosmetics. Kufu had found her somewhere among the cushions of the feast in the park, and she had followed like a bird to its nest after the gold piece he spun under her nose.

"It must be done quickly," said Odan, quite unnecessarily.

"Aye, master," grunted Kufu. The Ox did not release his grip upon the girl's upper arm, just above the copper bangle.

"He comes this way to visit Sherahmi, who is a handmaid to Queen Fretti," Ankidu made a small noise in his nose. "This great prince who desires to wed the princess."

"Hush!" Odan's primevally-trained senses picked up the heavy tread of oncoming sandals. Even in informal gear Galad moved and sounded like a miniature army. They all shrank back. "Here he comes. Now, Izi, Izi of the fragrant form—perform!"

She giggled and stepped out into the lamplit passageway.

"Master!" This Izi acted well, heaving her breasts about and panting, rolling her eyes, throwing up her clasped hands in desperate supplication. "Master, have pity on me!"

Hurrying along to a pleasant night with Sherahmi, who although florid and spongy in places, yet knew what women existed for in the land of Ea, Galad hauled up short as a green-robed woman, very intense, very pretty, burst into view, the lamplight shining on her ringlets and in her imploring eyes.

"Help me, my master, or my mistress will stripe my skin all away—master, you would not want my skin sloughed from me as a snake skin?"

Saying this, Izi, with a sleight-of-hand that eloquently told she was not doing this action for the first time, slipped her robe off one creamy shoulder. Galad, already half-primed for the night's encounter, did not resist the beauty revealed.

"I care not for your mistress, wench—but, for you—"

"My mistress sighs for your arms, master, for your ardent caresses, your kisses—Come with me to paradise with her!"

Grasping the girl and feeling the exciting warmth of her in his hands, Galad said: "Your mistress? Can she be more beautiful than you, little charmer?"

"A thousand and a thousand times more, master! She is the princess Zenara. Come, I beg you, quickly, with me—"

Stunned, Galad gaped. Then: "I will go through the hellfire from those devils in Endal for Zenara—lead on!"

Watching from their place of concealment the conspirators saw Izi lead Galad away down the corridor. At the first turn they leaped out and raced through a cross-corridor to arrive first. In truth, Ankidu had picked his spot well; there was but a short distance for Izi to lure on the lustful Galad.

This close to the king in his own palace there was no chance that Odan with his as-yet rudimentary grasp of thaumaturgy could hurl a spell or bring any sorcery to aid them. Kidu had too tightly sealed all occult openings to the king.

"Hold, master—my damn beard!"

Odan spun about. Kufu was scrabbling about trying to hoist the massively ornate beard back under his chin. The beard was one of Ankidu's father's. Andan, like all nobles, possessed his cabinet of beards for all occasions. The gold thread, the jewels, the pearls, made this beard into a second-class regal function, day of sacrifice beard. Impressive, it glittered in the smoky lamplight, all askew under Kufu's ugly jaw.

"Here, Ox!" bellowed Odan, instantly shushing himself, and with Ankidu's practiced fingers they restrung the beard. "You look a noble of nobles, my Kufu. Remember to bellow!"

"Aye, master."

Into the tiny anteroom with a single lamp and behind the curtain, just time to still the tremble of cloth, when in came Izi, hurrying on tiny feet, scarlet-painted toenails agleam, beckoning on Galad. A muted hum and buzz came through the wall from the side, a distant noise that Galad drowned instantly by glaring suspiciously around the cramped room, and snarling out: "Where is this? Your mistress, girl—if this is a trap!"

"No, no, master. But we must pass—the women—you must not be seen. What the king would say—"

"So?"

Here was where Odan, in a rarely indulged in self-congratulatory mood, allowed he had hit the nub of the problem. He figured that sheer lust would overpower reason. Well—as he stared through a chink in the curtain at Izi he knew he had reasoned correctly.

With an indolent gesture of pungent sexual allure, Izi slipped off the green robe and stood revealed far more nakedly than had she been stark naked. Her body blazed beneath the gauze, a scrap of a garment half covering her breasts, barely reaching to her thighs. Galad looked. His face engorged.

"Put on the green robe, master—but, first, remove your clothes. There will be no betrayal then."

Watching her, Galad ripped off his own fancy robes, stripping to the buff, pulling on the green robe.

"My mistress, the princess, is fairer than I am as the moon is fairer than the morning star, my master. Imagine the joys that await you! Through that small doorway—there—lies paradise!"

If she's overdone it—Odan trembled with suppressed laughter, a commodity of which he had had precious little possession in his life. Galad, stark naked, wrapped the green robe about him, turned toward the door.

"You come with me," he said to Izi, gruffly.

"Of course, master. I shall guide you all the way."

Odan nudged Kufu.

At once Kufu the Ox, magnificent in all his borrowed plumage, the gorgeous robes, the golden bands, the gemmed belts and golden armbands, the rose at his ear, and the massively formidable black beard outthrust, catapulted into the tiny room. He pointed a dramatic finger at Izi.

"Wench! Faithless trollop! Now I have you, caught you red-handed with this impious sacrilegeous wretch! It is the ducking stool for you and the crocodile pool for him!"

"Oh! Oh! Oh!" wailed Izi, her feeblest act yet. She gave Galad a savage push. "Go, master! Run! Through the door!"

Galad did not wait for any more. With a great bound he leaped for the little door. He knew about palace intrigues. He had been wrought up, worked on, brought to

the boil. He would find his exalted rank would avail him
nothing in an imbroglio like this. So, Galad-ayin bounded
for the door.

Reaching out a long hand from the curtain, Odan
seized the end of the green robe and, as Galad crashed
through the burst-open door into the room beyond, Odan
twitched the green robe away from the splendid nudity of
the prince Galad-ayin.

King Neb-ayin-Ke was not amused.

Queen Fretti shrieked and covered her eyes.

An old crone loaded with gems and cosmetics sat up
very quickly from her cushions. "My!" she exclaimed.
"He's grown quite a big boy now."

Queen Momi threw her own scarf.

Galad caught it. His expression would have made a
dragon recoil.

"Guards!" bellowed the king.

Asshurnax had hidden his old head down, in the cushions. He nearly ruptured himself trying not to laugh before the king laughed. And it did not seem as though the
king would laugh. Kidu sent a most rapid grifting sniffing
everywhere in the immediate vicinity. He did not smile.
He did not call out: "Odan!" either. But he waited.

Odan walked in through the burst-open door.

Ankidu and Kufu had gone, back to dispose of the
props and to join in the revelry outside.

Odan put his hands on his hips and jutted that magnificent head of his from out of his hunched shoulders,
like a turtle. He glared around upon the company. He had
not been invited.

He said: "There is a report, my king, my father, to
whom be all the praise, that a naked man is prowling. Has
he been through here?"

But the king was not to be fooled.

The king, Neb-ayin-Ke, looked to his right, at Queen
Momi. He saw her flushed face and bright eyes, and the
mobile tremble of her mouth. And he remembered their
young days, when the god Odan En-Ke had brought her to
Eresh to his eternal gratitude, and he proved himself a
great king.

He smiled.

He stilled the guards as they surrounded Galad.

"Galad-ayin!" called the king. "You are heartily welcome to the feast. And you, my son, are welcome. Find seats. Galad, find some clothes. And, by Zadan, I cannot hold back any longer!"

And the king laughed.

The hilarity continued for some time. For, in sooth, it was a great jest.

But Odan the Khuzuk, lowering out upon the company, saw the way Galad regarded him. Galad had sense enough not to shout out for all and the king to hear. He did not declare with all the dark passion in him: "You are my mortal enemy, Odan! For this I will have your life or be damned to the seven hells!"

No, there was no need for flamboyance of that kind.

Just the tilt of that short squat chin, the deep gleam of hate within the dark eyes, the convulsive rictus of the jaws.

Well, to hell with the oaf.

Open enmity could be dealt with.

Let the fellow run in on his death an' he would . . .

Chapter Seven

Queen Momi Gives
Odan Advice

The royal palace of proud Eresh, at present ruled by king Neb-ayin-Ke, extended over a wide area within the city, a city within a city, cinctured by circling canals. A myriad towers rose from the sprawling many-levelled structure. In a high room, long and open to the sun and air along one side where the roof hung supported by an imposing row of columns, Odan-ayin, prince of Eresh, frowned in annoyance over his abacus and the clay tablet smothered with irritable calculations.

"Devil take it!" exclaimed Odan, hurling the reed stylus at Aladdu, whose bald pink head shone in the sun's rays like a copper shield of the desert spearmen.

"Prince!" said Aladdu, his old bones and sinews far too slow to dodge. The stylus stuck like a javelin in the clay tablet on which the chief of the household had just completed in his perfect script the details of salt procurement for the next seven years. Slaves would take the tablet and bake it into permanent form so that it could always be consulted, year by year, with the salt supplies received and consumed.

Aladdu was not without a sense of humor. He nicked the soft clay with a fingernail.

"Your assistance, my prince, will give us enough salt in five years time to preserve all the fish in The River and The Salt Sea, entire."

Odan grumped around. "I mean you no harm, Master Aladdu. But, by Odan! I am no clerk, no scribe. I understand how to run the palace, and my father the king knows that, also. And as for this abacus, this thing of grooves and clay balls, I know the answer to the figures in my head long before my thumbs trundle one ball from the next."

"You are to be envied the facility, my prince. It must come from being the son of a god. But the king, may his name be praised, has ordered that you be trained into kingship. Remember, Odan the Half-god, you begin late in life."

"I know, I know."

In these golden days in proud Eresh life was not all wine and dancing, hunting the lion from the fragile chariots, carousing with Ankidu, wenching and roaring from the night watch. Hard unglamorous work was required from a prince who would one day receive the suffix Ke to his name, and on the death of the king ascend the throne in his turn. Odan spent time with Momi, his mother, forever moved by her beauty, loving her in a way he could not explain. And, always, he would ask her: "And my father. He was really the god Odan En-Ke? There can be no mistake?" He would not say what blasphemous things the Raven, the repulsive wormwoman, had told him.

"Mistake? Of course there is no mistake—and do hold

your back up, dear boy. You do crouch over so. Your father told me himself, and his attributes were recognized by Mnenon-Ket, the high priest of Zadan."

"Mnenon-Ket—he died trying to save me. Or so I am told. I'd like to find out who did that."

"It is all over now, my son. And you are grown into a man, although I am sure those wild Khuzuks have no idea at all of table manners—and do sit up!"

The Raven had said the old gods were mere fantasies, dreamed up by frightened primitive men to stave off the horrors of darkness, the powers of the elements. Only the new gods were real, or so the Raven had said. No one else had offered that blasphemous theory. But—and Odan trembled at the implications—Odan En-Ke had never answered his impassioned cries for help.

A messenger entered the long columned room, bowing, holding out a baked-clay envelope. Aladdu smashed it open and removed the tablet, reading quickly, as the messenger, with great respect, said: "There is news from Dilpur. Your presence, my prince, is required at once in the throne room of the Hall of Reception."

With some relief Odan put aside the computations on the seed-corn ratios for the following year and stood up.

"Tomorrow, my prince," said Aladdu, with a sly mischief brightening his face. "Tomorrow we study the supply and warehousing of tin and copper so that a stready production of bronze is not interrupted by a failing on the part of the scribes."

"I shall, Master Aladdu, look forward to that."

A mass of courtiers and soldiers and nobles pressed forward within the Hall of Reception. Once he had been recognized in the throng an easy way was made for Odan. Sunshine slanted in past the painted columns, blue, gold, yellow, red, with their scenes of everyday life of Eresh in glowing colors. Fans of priceless feathers waved, jewel-entwined. Half-naked girls danced through the wide halls scattering scented water to cool the air. All a splendid glitter of wealth and power, the society of Eresh gathered to hear the news from Dilpur.

Narpul the Staff banged for silence.

A pair of doves, cooing on an eave high above, against the blue sky, emphasized the waiting silence.

A shiver passed through Odan the Half-god.

Reading from a heavy papyrus held by two slaves, Narpul's speaker intoned the message from Dilpur as though he read one of the ritual speeches of thanksgiving for ceremonial occasions. But the news, however Prince Numutef had wrapped it up, was not good. The army of Eresh had relieved Dilpur and a battle had driven the army of Sennapur back. But subsequent operations had gone less well. A battle had been fought. Because no relevant details were given, apart from a rodomontade concerning the numbers of strings of right ears collected from the enemy, everyone knew the battle had not been won. Sennapur and Dilpur now scowled, city against city, locked behind walls and battlements. Numutef had allowed a stalemate situation to develop.

One after another, high nobles stepped forward with offers to go—and this was done with infinite tact—and offer their services to Prince Numutef in his hour of triumph, so that these new forces might hope to share a little of his victory. The subterfuge was plain to Odan. He saw Nebayin-Ke frowning and biting at a corner of his robe. The deep shame would leave a scar.

No sense of elation or of crowing triumph at Numutef's failure moved Odan. He was growing, every day more surely, to love the city of Eresh. There was much that was evil and corrupt about the place, of course, and he well-remembered his youthful days as a bazaar pirate here—by Hekeu! What days those had been! But, also, he saw the ordered way of life, the respect for the gods, the harnessing of the power of The River, the bright sun-filled days of pleasure, the pride of the army of Eresh—yes, yes, there was so much about proud Eresh he would fight for, now.

To one side of the throne room fronting the Hall of Reception a space had been cleared so that Gabal-ayin's chair slaves might put him down, carefully. He sat propped on cushions, his wasted face more hawk-like than ever, glaring up at the king on the throne. He had kept hatred stifled within him for many years. Now the witch, Amenti, was working slowly toward the final moments, Gabal would not betray his feelings and thus ruin the work of a lifetime. He lifted an arm, supported by a slave, and, politely, the king in turn lifted his flail. The flail glittered as the king lowered it in kindly signal.

"My king, whose name be praised," said Gabal in his

hoarse, half-throttled voice. "My son, the prince Galad-
ayin, will gladly drive with a host to Dilpur."

That was all.

The baldness of the words shocked through the assem-
bly. But all saw what Gabal meant. The moment was one
for decision. Who better, then, than the warrior-swords-
man Galad? The king refused—and none knew why—to
send his son Odan. So let Galad go and redress the balance
and once more make the name of Eresh feared along the
central arm of The River. And, into the bargain, save the
bacon of the puppy Numutef.

The king spoke.

"My lord Gabal, my uncle, honored in Eresh, the light
of Zadan, you offer me words of great comfort. Let the
prince Galad drive forth. Let the prince Numutef greet
him and together let them finish the victory already be-
gun."

No one raised so much as a murmur. The king spoke.

"Let the two princes, like brothers, ride on to the victory of Eresh, to the greater glory of Zadan of the Sword."

On the cue everyone shouted, ringing voices making the
doves swoop and weave in darting grey flashes among the
high columns. And Odan felt Ankidu's hand constrict on
his arm. He saw his friend's fresh and open face stricken,
haggard, the eyes like coals.

"Aye," said Odan, with bitter harshness, his voice lost
and drowned in the uproar, so that only Ankidu heard.
"Aye! My father means to give my sister to that oaf
Galad!"

"Hold your back up, Odan! Now, come and sit here
beside me. Here is a honeyed date—tell me what you want
your mother to do for you—"

Scowling, Odan dropped awkwardly onto the cushions.
His mother's private apartments had amazed him for their
fripperies, their piled-up casual display of wealth, the hap-
hazard scattering of priceless objects. But her handmaids
seemed to know, more or less, where everything was. She
lived a soft comfortable kind of life, and was so good-
natured she could feel only puzzlement at Odan's savagery.

A slave, a copper-skinned half-naked sprite, reached delicately over Odan's shoulder and wiped his honey-trickling
chin with soft white linen. He noticed the slave. No other

of the nobles and wealthy citizens of Eresh—or any other great city of The River—would notice the ministrations of their slaves. No, not even Ankidu or Zenara.

The absence of immediate attention would be noticed. If the trickle of honey stained a tunic, say, then the lax slave would feel the rod, unmercifully striking along naked back, man or woman alike. That was the only way to treat slaves, so said the great society of the cities of the land of Ea.

"It's Zenara. Look, mother, does the king really mean to marry her off to that oaf Galad?"

"Odan! Why—why I do not understand you!"

"I think you do."

"Well—and if I did . . ." Momi would never forget how she had stood drooping against a filthy mud-brick wall while the villagers hurled bricks at her, hating her, wanting to hurt and kill her, and of how the god, Odan En-Ke had driven up so gloriously in his dream chariot, and of how the flaming car had driven high over the land of Ea between the Two Seas. She could understand that people liked to hurt one another; but it made a sad kind of sense to her, queen or no queen.

"I do not really," she began, twisting a scrap of gauze between her fingers. "No, I am not sure. Much remains to be decided—"

"Mother! You must make the king see reason. Zenara can never marry Galad. The man is—the man is—"

"He is a great prince of Eresh."

"And that may be so; but why have you always sent Zenara away when Gabal brought his son back to Eresh?"

The color stained along Momi's still unlined cheeks. She lowered her head. Her voice feathered out, soft.

"I—I felt—oh, Odan, why do you torment me so? And hold your back up! Very well. There is something in Galad, something I once saw—in a little village—I will speak to your father—"

"He is the king. My father is—"

"I will speak to the king who has been so good a father to you. There was talk of the prince of Kandalhur and Zenara—"

"Kandalhur?" Odan came quiveringly alive. "To the east of Shanadul on the north shore of The Sweet Sea! What kind of alliance would that bring to Eresh? Shanadul might resent it."

"You think like a statesman, already, my son. There are many enemies to Eresh along The River. Even the alliance with Karkaniz is in doubt. Old King Scofu-arbin-Ke has no son alive, although he has a young daughter. The king your father has the welfare of the city in his heart."

Odan realized—and not for the first time—that his mother the queen was no way as simple as she liked to appear.

He would have to talk to Ankidu about this prince of Kandalhur.

"But not Galad, mother."

"You must be careful he does not trick you as you tricked him. Oh, I know the king laughed. But when Gabal heard, he was so worked up, so wroth—"

Curiously, Odan said: "So your spies earn their bread."

"Of course." Momi accepted a sweetmeat absently. None of this rich sweet food appeared to coarsen her face or figure. "Now what is the trouble between you and your sister? You rarely see her now. It is noticed. If there has been some terrible argument between you I beg you, my son, let there be friendship again."

"I have not seen Zenara overmuch lately, mother, that is true. But I have been busy. The king makes me work. And I study with Master Kidu. And Ankidu takes me into the desert after lions."

How could he tell his mother the real reason? The proximity to Zenara, the woman who loved him and whom he loved, the woman who was his half-sister, drove him to distraction. He had been quite unable to bear the agony any longer. How he had managed to pass those sweet days in the garden he could not understand. They were rosy days, cut off from reality. Reality lay in fighting and scheming and in seeking ways of bypassing this hateful sibling relationship.

"Well, perhaps if you hold your back straight we will find a pretty young princess for you, along The River."

Astounded, Odan gaped. Then: "Yes, mother, Of course."

Momi sighed. "I just can't understand what those wild Khuzuks were thinking of. You were just a little boy, four years old, just a bright lovely little boy. And you return to me a great hulking man, a savage, a wild man of the hills—and do hold your back up, my son, or your chin will grow into your chest."

Chapter Eight

Five Answers to
Odan's Prayers

Survival. That was the key to unlock the secrets of the world, of all the land of The River between the Two Seas. As the fanatical shamans of the Hekeu totem in far Zumer had taught Odan Crookback, so he put their teachings to use, twisting the pain away from himself, avoiding the agony, laughing with the hollow corpse-laugh he knew so well, drowning sorrow. Zenara . . . Zenara was denied to him.

They had said farewell—said farewell more than once.

Now Odan went up in his finest raiment to the temple of Odan En-Ke, his divine father, went up with the price of three bullocks, gilded and garlanded, prime meat on the hoof, went up to pray and humble himself and seek for the proof, the understanding and the help he must have—or see his careful edifice of survival all smashed away in the red roar of madness.

The temple of Odan En-Ke had prospered in the days since the god had brought his pregnant mortal wife to proud Eresh to be the faithful consort of King Neb-ayin-Ke. The forecourt had been enlarged by purchasing an area of mud-brick dwellings and of levelling them to form the core of the courtyard. Low columned buildings surrounded the temple on three sides. No temple in a city might be built in the form of a ziggurat save that temple ziggurat dedicated to the chief deity of the city. Oh, there were cities with two or even three ziggurats; they were exceptions. Men would not utter the name of that depraved city that had built ziggurats to all her gods—truth to tell the lizard-infested ruins inspired forgetfulness.

As ever the sacred fire at the summit of the ziggurat of Zadan plumed a lazy column of smoke into the sky. That sight reassured all men of Eresh. But here, in the temple of Odan En-Ke, the sacred fire burned, also.

With all due solemnity Odan-ayin followed the rituals. Now he could shed the guise of Odan the Khuzuk, take on himself the full mantle of being Odan the Half-god. He genuflected as was required, was sprinkled with holy water, performed the rituals. The garlanded bullocks spasmed in sacrificial death. The rich smell of roasting meats wafted aloft to please the god.

Desiring to be alone within the shrine—a place reserved for the priesthood—he was granted this wish. Was he not, after all, the son of the god? Who had more right?

"Pray for us all, my prince," said old Nabozinadas, the high priest of Odan En-Ke in Eresh. He signalled with his great olive stave and the priests and acolytes in their blue robes filed out, backwards, bowing, in awe of this strange and enigmatic figure, bent and hunched, with the eyes of fire.

Odan knelt at the foot of the idol. Entirely objectively, Odan understood this colossal figure to be fabricated of men's hands. The noble head, the trunk, the splendid arms and legs, all were fashioned of wood. That wood had been brought down The River in the long ago, paid for by faithful worshippers, carved and sculpted into the glorious living likeness of the god. A profound peace characterized the features of Odan En-Ke. A breathing hush of reverence lived within the shrine. Guardian spirits, armed and armored, stood before the statue. Incense drifted into the air, prickling Odan's nostrils, a jarring factor in this place of awe. Incense stank—others besides Odan said this.

Odan bowed his head and prayed. The prayers were all the same, repetitions of what he so desperately longed for, demands and pleas he had made to the god his father before. He cast from his heart the vile suggestions of the Raven that only the new gods in their dream chariots were real.

Into his prayers a new note of urgency sharpened the intercession. Harder and harder Odan's heart pointed toward the fulfillment of his desires. A new sense of an urgency that must be answered, here and now, or take heed of consequences beyond computation, made of these prayers a harsher period of worship than ever before. Odan knew he was near the end of his patience, near the end of his rationality, near the end of trying to behave as his mother and the city and his king would wish him to behave—altogether far too near madness.

"I have prayed and you have not answered. If you are my father, why do you not answer me? What impediment stops me from taking my place at your side, as a true god, a whole god?"

The cloth of gold curtains covering the ark, to one side, shivered. On that ark the statue of the god would be placed on his feast day, to be paraded in all pomp through the streets of Eresh, to have the feet laved in the waters of The River, to pass by the palace and receive offerings from the king. Now Odan half glanced at the cloth of gold, and away, back up to the serene face of the god.

So ornate and heavy were the garments, the jewels, the gold and silver and bronze, clothing the statue, that cunning bronze props must be affixed within to hold the mass. Odan bent his head again and prayed.

"I do not challenge you. I care nothing for the prophecy that a god's mortal son must die if the god would be supreme in the pantheon. I do not believe the lies of the wormwoman. Grant me the godhood I crave, my father! I have done no sin in your sight—to you and to the city, this city that is Zadan's, I will be loyal, swearing it upon my life, if you grant me this boon."

Only silence and an empty echoing hollowness reverberated within the shrine of Odan En-Ke.

Tall curtains of crimson cloth swayed in the wall to the rear of the ark.

The candle flames swerved, all together, like birds in the airy spaces of the sky. The lamps smoked suddenly.

Was this a sign?

Odan half started up. His left hand rested on the golden rail guarding off the last few paces to the steps leading to the feet of the idol. His right hand lifted, the fingers clawed, as though he sought to rip away the last veils of secrecy.

The crimson curtains parted.

Men stepped through. Instantly, Odan saw they were men who had no business here within the most sacred shrine to Odan En-Ke.

Hard, predatory, businesslike, these men. They wore plain bronze-studded jerkins of boiled leather. Small leather skullcups confined their jetty hair. Their faces, seamed and brown, scarred, reflected perfectly in the blankness of their horror the trade by which these men earned their daily bread.

Bronze swords caught the light of the lamps.

Five men—a mere five men, sent by Galad-ayin, against Odan Crookback—five mere mortal men sent against Odan the Khuzuk!

But Odan took no joy from the pitiful miscalculation of Galad. He took the blasphemous irruption of these assassins into this most sacred of spots as a direct answer to his prayers.

There could be no god called Odan En-Ke!

How could there be?

Would a god allow hired murderers to enter his shrine when his own son prayed within?

With a snarl that drew sustenance from the snarl of a dagger-tooth lion, Odan the Khuzuk surged up, hurled himself headlong at the assassins.

The first of the assassins had been speaking, something about: "You are unarmed. Comport yourself to meet your death."

Odan took his sword arm in both hands, broke it into splinters, caught the sword before it struck the marble floor.

"Now you will see how a Hekeu fights!" he said. He said no more. The shamans, the teachers of the tribe, would have frowned and punished him cruelly for that waste of breath.

The remaining four were swordsmen of value. They fought.

The hollow spaces of the shrine echoed to the clang of bronze, the slur of sandal upon marble and upon priceless rugs. They foined with him, for they had been unable to smuggle shields in here. Nadjul the Quick—ah! How that fierce, quick, lovable swordsman would have joyed in this fight! So Odan the Khuzuk played these men, and struck first one and then a second down, and the two remaining backed away, sweating, their eyes starting from their heads, their faces showing the sickening realization they had hired out to their deaths.

The penultimate one shouted, high, and leaped, raked

his bronzen blade toward Odan's eyes in the same instant his companion slid in from the side, his brand seeking Odan's guts.

Odan jumped, sliced with a delicate touch, removed the first's right ear, landed on his feet, like a hekeu—like a hekeu!—and thrust through leather and skin and gut and blood.

He withdrew and the last, gobbling his fear, dropped his sword. He held both hands outstretched, his soaking face upturned, his dark hair matted across his forehead.

"Spare me, master! Spare me and I will be your man!"

Odan's bronze blade trembled. With a convulsive spasm of effort he held his sword arm. He did not slay the man as he ought to have done.

"I want no scum like you serving me."

"The prince, the lord Galad—he promised—I will be loyal."

"You do not know of what loyalty consists."

Odan lifted the brand. The fellow screamed, hugging himself, rolling in terror upon the marble, entangled in the sacred rugs.

Carefully, Odan sliced off an ear.

He lifted the assassin by the neck and ran him, blood-streaming, to the door behind the crimson curtain.

"Go back to your master, the oaf Galad. Tell him his life is in my hands. Tell him if he goes near the princess Zenara I will cut his living heart from his stinking body!"

"In all of Khepru, that is to say, in all of the whole world," said Amenti, with some display of temper. "I do not think there can be a sorcerer so wily as this Master Kidu of Eresh."

"I could have told you that for the asking," observed Ubonidas, somewhat nastily.

"Mayhap you could, master sorcerer. But without me, you would be a heap of dusty ashes now, or a little green toad jumping in terror from the snakes of the desert."

The two master mages, the wizard and the witch, wove their gramarye within the eyrie in the topmost chamber of the squat ebon tower known as the Abode of the Bats. Once, Master Chaimbal had practiced from here; now he sought a precarious refuge with Sebek-ghal in Endal.

Through an opened, half-curtained window in the thick wall, Ubonidas could see the racing, flittering, untidy forms of the bats. They kept up an unceasing chirruping. He found them a comfort. The moon silvered through the opening, gleaming on the pale naked body of the witch, Amenti. With a gesture of genuine anger, Amenti shrugged on a long scarlet robe, fastened the golden loops. Had Ubonidas—somewhat too fat, too bald, too short of breath—cared for such things, the body of the witch Amenti would have fired up his blood.

"I would like wine, Ubonidas—if it will not disturb you too much."

The lord Gabal-ayin had considered it prudent that Amenti should share quarters with Ubonidas. The arrangement caused friction between the witch and the wizard.

Neither showed the least concern at the ghostly servitor who brought the wine. Ubonidas said: "Here is your wine.

The ghostly servitor bowed and withdrew, with a clank.

Amenti sipped. "Again. But not finally. There must be a way of breaking through the sealings. But—and I own this fully and freely—I did not anticipate this Kidu would be
And so you have failed again against Kidu?"
so accomplished. It is remarkable."

"And you have then so great an experience?"

"I look young, Ubonidas. If you were not so bald and so fat and so uncouth you would look on me with burning desire. I *look* young, Ubonidas."

Ubonidas felt the need of a sip of wine himself.

A rustle from a high corner of the chamber, past the shelf of skulls, made Ubonidas rise.

"I must feed Urt. His dish of fat flies is a small price to pay . . . Chaimbal was foolish not to have taken Urt when he fled."

The spiders' webs trembled in their niches. Urt, the seeming-spider, shook with the delight of anticipation. His fears of Amenti could, while the flies lasted, be forgotten.

Amenti pulled a thin silver chain from the pocket of the scarlet robe. She twined one end around the forefinger of her left hand. She began to spin the silver links in a whirling circle, faster and faster, so that the chain became a spinning wheel of reflected light. Urt chomped on his flies. Ubonidas poured a second goblet of wine, contemplatively.

Around the spinning silver chain a miasma grew in the air, a cloud of silver dust spinning out of nowhere. The cloud thickened, grew outlines and furry edges, rippled and thickened and grew into an arm-thick caterpillar of glinting silver fur that coiled and twined about Amenti's own slender arm.

She let the chain cease from spinning and, lo!—the silver chain was fastened to a silver collar about the silver caterpillar's neck. Gently, sensually, Amenti stroked the bright fur, crooning softly, softly . . .

"Ah, my darling Vroo—my own Vroo who serves her mistress so faithfully—Vroo, my own sweet . . ."

Ubonidas drank some more. Nearly all the flies were gone.

Amenti sat herself upon a low settle, her movements serene and yet seductive. The scarlet gown moved against her body beneath. She stroked Vroo. All along the back of the silver caterpillar stretched a spinal flaunting of red fur, a red of exactly the same color as Amenti's hair.

"And tell me, Vroo—" Here the caterpillar coiled up and away from her arm, revealing many silver legs, and a pair of bright blue eyes on their caterpillar stalks. Amenti lowered her head and Ubonidas could no longer hear what the witch said to Vroo.

All the flies were gone.

Urt, the seeming-spider, emitted a puff of sound. Ubonidas summoned the ghostly servitor to remove the dish. With a clank, the dish vanished. And, on the instant, Amenti sat up and laughed, and Vroo disappeared as a puffball blows before the wind.

A black bat flew struggling into the ebon chamber, confused, bleating, fluttering. It flew madly about, from wall to wall. Ubonidas looked up, annoyed.

He moved his fingers and spoke a little spell—a little one only. The bat stiffened and fell onto a table between an alembic and the powdered brains of a crocodile, in a glass dish. The ghostly servitor picked up the bat and threw it out of the window. Even as the clank sounded, the bat recovered the use of its wings and fluttered up among its fellows.

"The princess Zenara," said Amenti. Her smile was rich and sweet, as rich and sweet as the aroma from the rotting vegetation along the forbidden banks of The River.

"What of the princess, may Nirghal rot her bones?"

"Precisely, Ubonidas! Through the princess we strike."

"The lord Gabal desires Zenara for his son Galad."

"Then all the better. We destroy two crocodiles with one cast."

"And I think, I think, you will go to the wormpeople."

Amenti frowned. "If I do, it will not concern you."

"That may be true. It may not be true."

"Men have consulted the Raven for many years. But now the Raven is dead. I heard. It caused great grief among the sisterhood."

"Chaimbal has consulted the Raven. He told me."

"He will do so no more. But I, I, Ubonidas, have many other sources. The sisterhood is well-loved by the wormpeople. Our strength, conjoined, will smash this Master Kidu, utterly. Very soon, very soon, the princess Zenara and the king and all their people will bow to the will of the lord Gabal."

"I pray Ulhu for the day."

"But, I think," said Amenti the witch, and her pink tongue crept out furtively to toy with her red lips. "I think I shall maintain this Odan-ayin for a space, to play with, as a plaything. I think this Odan the Khuzuk will afford me many pleasant hours."

Urt, the seeming-spider, shuddered.

Chapter *Nine*

Of a Proposition from the Goddess of Love

The secret of Balniodor's Invisibility was one thing. To put it into practice was another. And to ensure that he remained invisible long enough to accomplish his nefarious plans was quite another thing altogether.

Odan swore and skipped behind a garlanded pillar in the multi-columned vestibule in the southern end of the palace. So many doorways, so many colonnaded arcades, so many courts and stairways and rooftop gardens, had the palace that their names occupied roll after roll of papyri, to know them all was the work of a lifetime, and only a few of the higher chamberlains under Narpul the Staff would care to stake a copper coin on the extent of their knowledge.

Halfway through he had seen his shadow, hunched and malevolent, fall across the parquet. So Balniodor had failed him again—well, to be fair and accurate, his grasp of the sorcerous spells had failed himself.

Yet Odan had thought this entranceway easy enough.

He hunched down and thought and rumbled out a fresh casting.

The shadow vanished. H'mm . . . He peered around the pillar and then strode with a jaunty swing for the double valves of the entrance, their wooden leaves bound with bronze. A sleepy guard in his brown and yellow rested on his spear. Almost—almost but not quite—Odan the Khuzuk kicked the spear butt away. That would have been a capital jest. But such a demonstration of sorcery—as the guard would surely know at once—was like to bring Kidu or one of his new and fresh-faced assistants running. Then Kidu would smell the grifting and know.

Even now Odan could not be sure that Master Kidu was not carefully watching him, all the time, and no doubt weighing up just what deviltry the young prince of Eresh was up to . . .

Odan remembered the time Kidu had watched over him, with a lamp, in the dungeons of the palace of Eresh.

So, with a second thought, Odan passed the sentry and set foot outside the palace. The sentry belonged to the King's Guards, a regiment of three or four hundred or so, depending on circumstances, a body of men separate from the regular army. Odan strode out into the sunshine and made his way around to the chariot area. The work of a moment secured a fresh-shone rig, with two curvetting horses and an outrigger. They had been prepared for some courier or other, and there would be a fuss at their disappearance. They vanished out of sight as he flung the cloak of Balniodor over them.

With a lashing crack of the long whip, Odan the

Khuzuk sent the chariot rolling out, heading southwest over the irrigations, heading for the ruined site that Asshurnax, mightly perturbed, had at last told him of.

"But, my lad, my prince, beware!" Old Asshurnax had said, breathing hard. "The ruins are accursed!"

"But they are the site of power?"

"Oh, aye. They are the site of power."

So, accordingly, Odan the Half-god drove invisibly on in the sunshine, rolling out to this fabled and accursed site of power.

Flowers grew profusely everywhere over the site. The ruins leaned greyly over sheets of daisies, with white hearts and yellow petals, and yellow hearts and white petals, over glowing chains of golden buttercups, of blue swathes of forget-me-nots. Creeping vines bowered the old columns and broken walls. Odan unhitched the team and let them graze. The chariot glimmered splendidly in the sunshine. He went to explore.

The demon-driven obsessions forcing him on were being seduced at every turn in life. Just to relax and be a prince, to study to be a king, to take a laughing girl to wife—take the whole four the laws allowed—to laugh and drink and be merry and forget all about this maniacal desire to be a god!

But he could not forget Zenara.

He came at last to a crumbled courtyard where tiny green lizards ran. The eastern wall's rim just cut off the last faint wisp of smoke from the tip of the watchtower on the western marches of the bounds of Eresh. Insects buzzed. The courtyard contained a pool that was a pool; the water shone darkly up, like polished silver, still.

Water was the source of life. Here, if anywhere in the desert, he would find the source of power.

The River curved in an enormous bow from Dilpur east to Eresh and round towards south-southwest and then due south to destroyed Tubal and then south-southeast to vile Endal. Thence The River turned west again and ran undulating toward the great Persaran Bend, where it reversed its course once again to travel, with many curves and branchings, to the Delta in The Sweet Sea.

To the northwest right around to the southeast, The River looped, out of sight, around this lonely desert spot.

There was sweet water here. But, there remained only ruins.

Why did not people at least stop by here, if they did not live? What made this spot accursed?

Asshurnax had said, uneasily, that the cursed spot was called Nir-Bal-Thaps.

Odan prowled around the pool. Brick facings, crumbled in the heat, penned in the still water. Lily pads floated, quietly. A sense of oppression grew. The quietness, emphasized by the long droning of dragonflies, drew tightly down around the shattered courtyard and the forgotten pool.

Old Master Asshurnax, who had once been Odan's thaumaturgical mentor, had not once questioned the reason for this visit to Nir-Bal-Thaps by his ex-famulus. He knew. He it was who had first put into Odan's savage heart the idea he might one day be a whole god.

Odan felt a tremble in the air. A shimmer of coalescing light above the pool caught and refracted colors. Odan lifted his head, jutting grotesquely from his hunched shoulders.

"Hear me, Odan En-Ke!" he called. He spoke in a clear, deep voice, composed, holding the screaming excitement in. In this place of accursed power he should reach the god . . .

"Odan En-Ke, my father—if you exist—answer me! Show your face to your son! If you do not exist then let what powers there may be stand forth—rise up, stand forth—let me, Odan, see what manner of being or spirit infests this place!"

So spoke Odan, and waited, his shoulders hunched, his head jutting forward.

On the left of the pool grew a wide and massy clump of the sweet-scented blue lotus. On the right of the pool grew an equally dense bed of the rose lotus. Sacred, the lotus, designed to give delight and comfort to women and therefore to men.

All the lotuses, every blossom, turned upon their stalks, and inclined inward, to the center of the pool.

The lily pads moved on the surface of the water, swaying like smooth-sliding dancers, this way and that, as the shining ripples broke away from the center, plashed against the ancient brick.

For a wild primeval savage the forces of nature existed.

They were to be used—placated, every now and then, of course, with a juicy sacrifice—but they were to be feared only if a man's spirit quailed before them. No man can stand against the lightning, no man halt the onrushing flood, no man shout against the burning desert sandstorm; but a man, especially a man of the Hekeu, can learn to live within the fiercest manifestations of the elements.

Odan the Khuzuk stood, calmly watching the pool, expecting he knew not what—nor cared—so long as he received an answer.

From the center of the pool a shining oblate sphere rose, lily pads entwined like vine leaves around the forehead of a carouser. Smooth, shining, round, the globe of water rose swaying into the air, swaying upon a long gemmed column of water that writhed sinuously this way and that, that dipped forward and back like the dancing of a snake.

Odan felt his muscles jump and his bronze sword came halfway out of its sheath. He thrust the blade back. This was no occasion for swords, not even for swords fashioned from Zadan's metal.

The shining sphere of water runnelling with multicolors, like oil streaks upon the liquid surface, swung closer. The globe changed in outline. What blasphemous shape it might be that swung upon the column of water, dripping, Odan did not know. That it must be an elemental not of this world of Khepru he felt sure. He held his position. He glared up, malevolently.

Water dripped and splashed and the awful thing swayed above him, shining, wet, viscous, pulsing with power.

"What manner of being calls upon me, with little understanding?" The voice sounded like the dregs of the sewers that run, at last, through bronzen grilles into the waters of The River.

"I am Odan! Odan the Half-god! What manner of being are you?"

"My name is washed away with the years. I remain here, within this desert place, dry, dry, dry."

"Yet are you fashioned of water."

"Fool! Of water—this little puddle? Water? When I crave all the sweet waters of The Sweet Sea? *Fool!*"

"If you require my pity, thing of water in the desert, you have it."

How clearly Odan saw! A water elemental, desiring

above all things in the world water, fresh, sparkling crystal water—chained within this parched desert, anchored forever to a tiny forgotten puddle!

A golden vessel in the form of an amphora appeared on the mouldering brickwork of the pool. The watery thing's voice gushed on, pleading, begging, threatening.

"How I long once more to roam the wastes of The Sweet Sea! How many fine galleys there are for me to devour! Take up a portion of my substance, mortal! Fill the golden vessel. Take it to the shores of The Sweet Sea and there pour it out, into the deeps, let me once more take up my destiny!"

"That is not my provenance—"

"But it is mine! Fool! You are a puny motherless son of a mortal! What know you of the mysteries? You shall be drowned, your nostrils stuffed up, your lungs flooded! I tell you, I warn you! Take up my substance within the golden vessel and travel as fast as you may to The Sweet Sea, lest a worse fate befall you!"

"I will not let you loose upon The Sweet Sea," said Odan.

He jumped back. Water splashed where he had stood.

"Fool!" The gushing voice spurted with an anger at once obscene and liquidly ludicrous. "Take me up—"

"Here is for you!" said Odan the Khuzuk.

He bent and his right hand scraped dry sand from the courtyard. He flung, an underhand spraying throw. Only a tiny amount of sand he threw. But the sand spattered against the column of water, against that blasphemous misshapen watery globe. Dry, the sand. Dry, dry . . .

As though the rains over the mountains of Zumer had burst in one cataclysmic hail about his ears, the water globe broke.

Water showered back into the pool. Lancing lines of water, blobs and drops and puddles of water, plopping back in a hail of whitely-shining silver spurts. Water to water, pouring down, flattening once more into a mere still pool within an abandoned courtyard amid a tumble of forgotten ruins.

The desert forged unbreakable chains.

Odan, breathing deeply, advanced to the edge of the pool.

He threw more sand upon the water.

"Sleep on, poor foolish elemental. Your sins are not yet requited of the gods."

For, to Odan, a man of the land of Ea between the Two Seas, it was clear the gods had chained this water elemental here so that it might no longer harm honest seamen upon The Sweet Sea.

A last expiring wave plashed against the rose-red brick-work, crumbling dust away, that stained like blood across the dark surface of the water.

Had there been horror in this for Odan? Had he felt the supernal wings of the divine or the damned? He did not think so. He felt cheated. He sought his father the god. Twice, in days, he had been cheated. He had called on his father before and not been answered. Now when he called he was requited by armed assassins, and by malicious water elementals.

The madness simmering in him grew dangerously close to the surface. He could not support the demands of a life that meant he might not have Zenara. He felt the blackness closing in around him.

He staggered. He fell onto the dust of the courtyard.

His hands pressed against the sand and dust. He felt a paralysis in his legs. His heart thudded against his chest as the ram-headed beam smashes against the proud battle-mented walls of a besieged city.

He would deny this Odan En-Ke. Perhaps the Raven had been right. Perhaps the old gods were only figments of the desperate and fearful imaginations of primitive men. Perhaps only the new gods in their dream chariots were real.

Well—Odan staggered up. He presented a wild and ma-cabre figure. His brown hair swirled about him. His unbleached linen fillet was caught askew, so that he brushed the hair from his face and it fell back again over his eyes. His enormous body hunched grotesquely. His arms lifted, the hands like claws. His magnificent head jutted forth, proud, intolerant, strained back. He shouted to the heavens. He challenged fate and the gods.

"Do you listen to me, you gods in your dream chariots! Do you hear me you old gods away in your garden? I am Odan! I am Odan the Khuzuk! Is there no god who will grant me the boon of godhood, saving my father who is not known to me? Is there any god who will use me as the prophesy says, to gain the crown, to gain all? Come, you gods of the heavens! If you have the courage of mere mortal men! I challenge you! I, Odan the Khuzuk! I challenge you!"

Panting, gasping for air, his face alight with the passions burning him, Odan stared into the bright empty sky.

"I know the story of Abak! I know a man may be a god! And I am already half a god! Come, I challenge you, let one of your number prove your courage, you gods who play with men's lives and destinies!"

Over the land of Ea between the Two Seas where rain falls perhaps once in the lifetimes of ten generations a vast sheet of lightning flashed. A long jagged stroke of lightning slashed down from the heavens. High, high, a cloud grew. A cloud, there in the land of The River, where clouds were never seen from generation to generation.

Odan stared up. The cloud grew. Over the mountains and valleys of Zumer the clouds hung, black and massed, and the lightning struck and the thunder rolled. One small cloud, one stroke of lightning, one clap of thunder, would not impress a wild savage of Zumer.

Staring, Odan saw the cloud grow roseate, grow gold, glow with supernal fires around the edges. He saw the long radiant arms of fire reaching out across the heavens. He knew this vision was vouchsafed him alone; this was not visible from proud Eresh over the horizon.

"Come, you great god!" he bellowed. "Let me see you and your chariot of fire!"

He was mad. He was quite mad by this time. He must be insane, thus to stand, head jutting, glaring up as a god descended in fire and glory from the heavens.

In a great burst of maniacal frenzy he had conjured a god.

A god had answered his call and his challenge.

"And if you're the devil Nirghal En-Theus come back to taunt me, you can take yourself off! I am Odan and I am of Eresh! Show me your attributes, show me your face, if you dare! For I am Odan the Khuzuk and my father is a god—*is* a god!"

The cloud coalesced and vanished and now only the radiance was left, a blinding brilliance that leached all color from the desert and the ruins and washed Odan's face with fire.

Water stung his eyes. He blinked and fought away the

pain that lanced his eyes. He glared up, maniacal, proud, glorious in his insanity, grotesque.

A dream chariot appeared, a chariot of fire, swinging down low toward him.

A voice spoke. Not the majestic booming of a godvoice he had expected. This voice husked sweetly, soft, mellifluous, honey-sweet from the shining radiance of the dream chariot.

"And would you slander me so, Odan the Khuzuk?"

Odan gaped.

The chariot hovered. He could see. Surrounding the central radiance reclined beautiful women, languorous, wanton, transparently clad in flowing chiffons. Rosy-limbed, they sang or played on lyres or flutes. He saw the flowers, the fruits, the goodness of the earth heaped up about their feet. Within their protective circle and lasciviously reclining upon a gilded couch in the form of a desert lion—a goddess!

The goddess smiled and lifted a rounded arm, beckoning to him. Odan took a dazed step forward.

"Tia," he said, swallowing. "The goddess Tia Nin-Apsish."

"I am Tia. And you are Odan. You call upon the gods, and I answer you. Your desires are known to me, the secrets of your heart like an unrolled papyrus. Why do you hesitate?"

"I seldom if ever visited your ziggurat in Karkaniz."

"I know. You were never zealous in your offerings to me—and yet am I not here, come in answer to your prayers? Do I not seem fair in your sight?"

"You are exceeding fair."

"You say you are the son of a god. I am inclined to believe you, for no mere mortal man would stand as you do, so glowering and rude when a lady speaks."

"I am what I am, my lady."

"Ah!"

"You answer my prayer. Will you aid me—will you—"

"Softly, softly! I know what it is you seek. Because you desire love am I come to you. Because you desire godhood for the sake of love I bow to your prayer."

"You—my lady—you will aid me?"

"And yet it is not only for the love of a mortal woman that you seek godhood. I can see that, too. There is in you a hard dark core, Odan the Khuzuk. You are the son of a god, that is so; but—" Here Tia's voice dropped away. Odan thought she had said, half to herself: "But which god!" But he could not be sure.

The moment gave Odan a chance to try to see what this Tia, the goddess of love, the patron deity of the rich city of Karkaniz, looked like. He found he could scarcely focus his eyes long enough to make any impression. A hint of Zenara? Yes, of course; all men said that Tia looked like their own love. Beauty, fairness, a glowing radiance, the hint of rosy rounded limbs, flowing draperies, braids of thick hair, coils of flowers, gems—he became aware she was speaking again.

"You know the prophecy concerning the son of a god?"

"I do." Then, because of a feeling that this goddess was a deity of a different stamp from Nirghal, with whom he had last dickered, with disastrous results, Odan added: "My lady."

"Then if I am to use you well, I ought perhaps not to say I wish to become supreme among the gods." Her laughter tinkled, free, full-throated, spine-tingling.

"I do not fear the prophecy. But all men and all gods own you as supreme, my lady Tia. Love conquers—"

"Do not say it! I am tired of that foolish expression. Love is love, and love is what you make it. What I make of it is something else again."

"Nirghal En-Theus, Nirghal of the Fire, lied to me. What he made of fire was something else again. My lady, he said Odan En-Ke did not exist—"

"And did he not trick you? Is not his son, Nirghi, destined to fulfill the prophecy?"

This interview with a god provided lessons; it proceeded on lines very different from Odan's interview with the devil Nirghal.

"You have visited my great city of Karkaniz, Odan Crookback. That I know. Like vermin you crept through the bazaars, you and your Terrors of the Souks."

Odan said nothing.

"Away to the west on the shores of The Salt Sea are many fine cities—none so great or proud as my Karkaniz. My king and my priests cow the little cities with whom they do business—and yet, and yet the many few go up against the lonely great."

"The ants will eat the lion, my lady."

"No! Not whilst the Lady Tia Nin-Apsish guards her own! You know the city of Zemlya?"

"I have sailed down The River through Zemlya—"

"And you saw how her citizens worshipped so abjectly at the shrines of the ziggurat of Mut? How they puff up with pride this Mut, this earth goddess, this fecund cow, many-breasted, full-bellied, slobbering?" Here the radiance shimmered into a rainbow brilliance, a coruscation of light that forced Odan's eyelids shut, the tears squeezing thick under the lashes, like thickened honey. "Mut! She shall be brought low! In the houses of the gods she shall wail at the doorposts and not be admitted! Against me, against my love, against my wonderful city of Karkaniz, has this vile Mut conspired! She shall rue her transgressions against her sister!"

Privately, Odan had always considered Mut as a jolly goddess, fat and comfortable, happy, providing food and all good things. But it was perfectly clear that no sisterly love extended between Tia and Mut.

He understood the nature of the purely divine problem. Now the economical problem was presented to him, in starkly simple terms. Zemlya lay some one hundred sixty miles east of Karkaniz, upstream. Due south of Zemlya, distanced about 60 miles, stood the city of Sennapur. The desert crossing could be made with good beasts and sturdy wains and full water skins. Light and easily-transportable goods, expensive, costly wares, were being carried across the desert south from Zemlya direct to Sennapur for onward transmission down The River.

Odan saw the consequences instantly.

And yet—"Surely this small traffic does no real harm to so wealthy a city as Karkaniz, my lady?"

"Harm? My despicable sister, Mut, tricks me out of what is my due. Perfumes, gems, spices, all things that may be slung into a wain and carried across the desert—costly items, Odan! Still the timber and the stone and the corn and hides, the beasts, go downriver through my city. But I will have a stop put to this contraband traffic."

It was scarcely that. But Odan felt an argument on the point would prove unpleasant—at the best.

"But Karkaniz is powerful, wealthy, her army can—"

"My army campaigns along The Salt Sea, teaching the cities there that the lion will not be devoured by ants!"

So the proposition was put to Odan the Khuzuk.

Maybe the traffic between Sennapur and Zemlya was not so small, after all. Maybe it was hurting Karkaniz and the other cities cut out from their expected dues-gathering in the bend of The River. Zemlya must be taught a lesson.

Every Bend and every Reach of The River possessed its own name, of course, and the cities within The Salt Sea Bend were all being hurt by the traffic over the desert between Zemlya and Sennapur. Kheru, to the south of Karkaniz, and Erlash to the north were two subject cities, entirely dominated. Upriver east of Erlash stood the declining city of Kigal, in whose dusty courts the merchants chaffered for bags of barley where once they had handled barge loads. Instinctively, as he turned the problem over in his heart, Odan saw through to the turning point of the goddess Tia's plan.

"Yes," she said in her light, mellifluous voice. "You called for aid and I have answered. You are my choice. Men will follow you, Odan the Half-god."

There was a point on which Odan desired information. A god—or a goddess—would know what was happening on the other side of the land of Ea long before the fastest means of mortal communication could bring the news.

"And Sennapur? If this traffic persists, then how fared the army of Eresh against the army of Sennapur?"

The answer he did not want to hear fell about him—fell yet with a welcome sound!

"Sennapur drove back the army of Eresh. Now, in Dilpur, under the princes Numutef and Galad, who quarrel, the might of Eresh frets away."

Welcome, yes—for, had Eresh conquered Sennapur then the goddess Tia would not have called on Odan for aid. Truly, the misfortunes of one were the blessings of another.

The brightness dazzled. Was this how his life would be, once he was a god?

Zenara—the total hopes of godhood meant only Zenara . . .

Although, Tia, the goddess of love, who understood the secrets of men's hearts, had said there were other and darker reasons for the insane desires driving Odan on.

"Begin, then, Odan the Half-god. Serve me well. We shall be good friends. Very good friends. And your godhood shall serve as a beacon light in the heavens, drawing you on to glory."

"I shall begin at once, my lady."

"Go to my temple in Eresh Minor. The high priest will give you all things needful. I shall honor him by a visit not in dreams but in person—and thus will he do your bidding in my name."

Rising on wings of flame the dream chariot rose into the air. Tia's maidens began singing songs of such loving sweetness they dizzied the senses. Tilting his head back so that his enormous hunched shoulders creaked, Odan watched until the dream chariot vanished in the firmament.

Once more he trod a path that would lead on to godhood—and this time, this time by Ke the Creator of All Things, he would not be cheated. This time, he, Odan the Half-god, would become Odan the god!

He turned away from the pool to seek his chariot. He saw a scattering of spots of water drying in the sunshine, thinning, drying, vanishing until only the dust and sand remained.

Chapter Ten

A Girl and a Snake in a Garden

Odan the Half-god's magniloquent, almost maniacal, challenge to the gods had given into his hands another chance. He faced life with a fresh zest. There was much to do, and great ventures to set afoot. He worked. The high priest of the temple of Tia in Eresh Minor, surrounded by acolytes and handmaids of the goddess, served him well. Gold and silver were provided of the bounty of the goddess. Mercenaries were hired. Many men in Eresh and

Dilpur were anxious to march with Odan the Khuzuk, pressing forward in blood to glory and booty.

There would be other warriors to be taken up, men like Nadjul the Quick who could see in a quick and successful campaign under a renowned prince greater profit than in many year's hard work guarding crawlers and barges along The River. The main army of Eresh was not touched. Anyway, Neb-ayin-Ke took counsel of his chief men. Should they send reinforcements to Dilpur? Or should the usual state of armed truce be allowed to reestablish itself?

Kephru-Ket, the high priest of Zadan, counseled caution.

"We have sent half the Leopard Archers, half the Tiger Archers, and four Kisraens of the Wasps. We have sent half the Wolf spearmen and four Kisraens of the Bullocks. We have sent the entire regiment of Hawk chariots. Plus many slaves and laborers and shield bearers. We extend ourselves. Endal is beaten back, but she is not beaten to her knees. Always, we must guard our southern approaches."

"Kephru-Ket speaks with words of wisdom," said the lord Andan, Ankidu's father. "Let us hold what we have."

"Yet would I dearly love to see a triumph over Sennapur," said the king, fiercely. "With my son Numutef driving in glory at the head."

A growl from the cripple's chair, and: "And, my king, whose name be praised, my son, prince Galad-ayin, driving in his chariot with him."

"Yes, my lord Gabal-ayin. Yes, of course."

"And this, I think," said Andan, with a slow, dignified look toward Master Kidu, "is what the king's wizard would counsel also?"

As always, the king relied on the three arms of his service, the army, the priesthood, the sorcerers.

"The omens fall crookedly, my king, whose name be praised. I can fend off Endal for a space, aye, and defeat the wiles of the mages of Sennapur. But, in time, we must deal with an eye to the future. In addition," added Kidu, not without a little relish, "this war plays havoc with trade."

At this there was a grave nodding of heads.

"Then so let it be," said Neb-ayin-Ke. "The king has spoken."

So it was that Odan the Half-god, the king's son, was able to leave Eresh with a light heart. His own plans were all that mattered to him. Ankidu glowed with the thoughts of the glory ahead. Kufu the Ox, taken into service by Odan, went methodically about his duties, still a little surprised that he, a willow-worker's son, a shield bearer should find himself in the position of Ras to a regiment of mercenary archers.

"Our plans call for speed and surprise," Odan told his assembled officers. He, too, could feel the strangeness of his position. But he, a Hekeu, a savage warrior well-versed in raids and vicious surprise ambushes and attacks against the yellow-haired barbarians of the north, knew exactly what he was about. "We move fast and we move silently."

The little army passed upriver by night, avoiding Sennapur's spies by a subterfuge involving Odan's casting of a spell culled from the second book of Abimalaikal the Abhorred. The sentries in their bronze and leather found their eyelids as heavy as the granite monoliths shipped down The River from the mountains so far away. The flotilla of boats passed, ghostlike upon the smooth dark waters.

Such was the power of Odan the Half-god, supported, he felt sure by a sending from Tia, that the flotilla was well away upstream before the mages of Sennapur awoke to the certain signs that thaumaturgy unlicensed by them had been used in their city. That would, in the nature of the everyday operation of spells and griftings along the central arm of The River, take time.

In like manner Odan passed Zaylit, Igash and Garsh-Haviz. The next city, Kheru, lay in fief to Karkaniz and his army could proceed openly. Kheru conjured a happy memory for Odan, a bittersweet memory of a meeting with Nadjul the Quick. When Odan and his men at last reached Karkaniz they were immediately struck by the bizarre appearance of the place. Odan had run with the Terrors of the Souks here. He was accustomed to a bustling, prosperous city with everywhere lavish evidence of enormous wealth. True, the city still bustled; but there were more slaves than usual, and they were herded about their tasks in chains. The army, both the regular army and the vast bulk of the reserve militia, was away fighting along the shores of The Salt Sea. Children were performing tasks their fathers had left. Still the traffic flowed; but gangs of women worked on the docks, as well as slaves.

Making the customary sacrifices at the outer altar of the temple of Tia in her Ziggurat, Odan sought audience of the king. He was granted an immediate interview, another result of the divine intercession of Tia, who had appeared to the king the previous night in a dream, and had left him in no doubt as to what to do to please her.

"You are welcome, prince Odan. The great goddess, the Lady herself, has spoken. Enter and take barley and salt. Then we may hear some pleasant music and watch the dancing girls—"

Odan sized up this old buffer.

King Scofu-arbin-Ke presented a plump, genial appearance, swathed in costly robes, a gilt-bronze dagger forever tangling up his chubby legs, his face smooth and unlined and perfectly barbered. He had plundered his beard cabinet and selected a massy creation of gold thread and seed pearls, and no doubt this did the visiting prince of Eresh great honor.

Odan said: "There is no time for music and dancing, king, live forever. I have a task and I cannot delay."

"Yes, yes, of course. Yes, well, I understand that." Old Scofu bumbled on, struggling to keep his pleasant smile. "But, surely, prince, you will need to rest and refresh yourself? And your little army will relish a night in the fleshpots of Karkaniz—"

Odan did not miss that word "little."

"One night, king, that is all." Odan turned to glance back at Ankidu at the head of his small group of commanders. "And if any man is late reporting for duty his back shall be striped a hundred times, fully and with force."

"Aye, my prince," said Ankidu. This was, after all, merely army custom, tradition and simple common sense.

Even the mercenaries understood that. No army could function without discipline. That, as Odan the Khuzuk knew, was why the naive and stupid yellow-haired barbarians always came to grief between the millstones of civilization to the south and complete savagery to the north of them.

Truth to tell, the women of Karkaniz were pleased to entertain a brand new army of men, even if a small one, and Odan felt that there would surely be a few bloody

backs on the morrow. He could feel no sorrow over that.
A proper example, early on, worked miracles for morale
as well as discipline. These men he had garnered, a fraction under three thousand of them, archers and spearmen,
they would follow a great and glittering princely figure;
but, also, they wanted to know that their commander was
a man who knew his own mind, a man able to make a decision, a man of the army. Odan's experiences of the army
were all too short.

"Obeying my Lady's instructions in all things, prince,"
said King Scofu, pulling a gold thread in his beard, "I have
gathered up a chariot force for your disposal." He
mumbled on a little, not anxious to come to the point.
Then: "I have been very fully stretched—those devils
along the caravan routes, along The Salt Sea—they drain
my resources. But I have found a little over a squadron
for you."

A squadron of chariots usually consisted of forty rigs.

"Oh, I know it is not as many as I had hoped for,
indeed, prince, there is hope that Kheru will scrape up a
half-squadron extra for you. But we need our strength to
the west—"

"I shall need no chariots," said Odan. He spoke firmly.
He heard the stir of surprise in his group of officers at his
back. A glittering bunch, they were, in their bronze and
leather, with their yellow cloaks and scarves, the feathers
bright in their helmets. "No chariots," he repeated. "Until
perhaps we have the walls. Then a show of chariotry,
trailing branches in the sand, might accomplish wonders."

King Scofu pulled his beard, straining the clasps; he did
not understand.

"King, may you live forever, you may order the chariots
forward to Erlash, there to wait my orders."

King Scofu nodded. His mind was on the wine and the
dancing girls—and some part of his attention was, perforce, directed to his army battling in the unfamiliar ter-
rain along The Salt Sea. If Zemlya was to be broken, then
this haughty creature of the hunched back and fiery eyes
would do it—the goddess had said so.

"Then, prince," said Scofu, clearing his throat. "Let us
spend a pleasant night before you depart."

He clapped his hands and the audience was at an end.

Odan threw down his armor with a grunt. The high priest of Tia in Eresh Minor had presented it to him, scale armor with each bronze scale in the shape of a heart. It was highly showy, glittering, imposing, and it weighed a fair two thousand shekels. That was not a great deal for a Hekeu; but Odan had his doubts as to the gaudy armor's efficacy in battle. He would wear his own harness, made to his specification in the armory of the palace of King Nebayin-Ke.

Clad only in a loose white tunic he strolled out onto the terrace leading to one of King Scofu's secluded gardens. Water tinkled refreshingly somewhere and the sun cast long blue shadows from trees and bushes. Birds flitted past, after insects.

On the morrow, early, the army would be on the march.

How pleasant, in the cool of the evening after the sun has lost his burning power, to stroll in a shadowed garden, green with beauty, watered with life!

And, on the morrow, the army would march out . . .

Odan saw the girl where she sat upon a brick seat, a gauzy wrap of yellow chiffon drawn loosely about her white tunic. Like his, her feet were bare. For a single heart-stopping instant he thought she was Zenara. Then she moved her head, lazily, watching a butterfly and he saw that her hair, although lighter than the jetty locks of folk along The River, was not as fair as Zenara's. Her face attracted him at once, soft and yet not simpering, young—very young, not more than fifteen—with a sweet curve to her lips that held more than a hint of sadness. He stopped still, on the grass, watching her.

She turned and saw him.

She stood up, a hand to her breast, caught unawares. Odan became powerfully aware of her beauty, a beauty that was not as Zenara's beauty, as though a rose and an iris should stand, side by side, and claim attention.

"I did not wish to startle you—" began Odan.

She pointed at him. For an instant Odan thought she would cry out against him, call for her friends, for guards, perhaps, have him cast down in chains; but her expression showed only a sudden and urgent fear.

"Do not move! Stand still—Whoever you are!"

"But—" said Odan. He did not move.

"By your foot—creeping over the grass—a scorpion! You will be bitten if—"

Odan looked down. The scorpion was almost upon him. There was just time to move, to bend, to crush. Just time—for a Hekeu.

"Oh!" she said. The color flooded painfully into her face. He saw her surprise. "You are mighty sudden in your wrath—whoever you are."

"I am Odan—"

"Oh!" Her surprise was entirely genuine. She put her hand to her lips—she turned like a gazelle and was gone.

"Well, now," said Odan-ayin, prince of Eresh. "Was she real, or a figment sent by a mage to torture me with visions of Zenara?"

That hair, that tinge of lighter color, heritage of some old mating with the barbarians of The Salt Sea. Yes, men and women along The River called that fairer tint in the hair a touch of the gold brush.

Odan put his thumbs into the belt of thin gold links that supported his dagger. The girl seemed to him unreal, fey, an apparition. And yet—and yet—a rustling in the bushes ahead of him told him she lurked there, spying on him. The sound would have gone unremarked by a mere man who had never hunted along the thick valleys of the hills of Zumer where every sound had a meaning, and most meanings meant death.

Keeping his somber features composed, his massive head hanging a little, thumbs in belt, Odan strolled as though casually past the bushes. At their end he appeared to all human sight to vanish. One moment he was lounging along; the next he was gone. Another Hekeu would have seen him move, perhaps. He crouched on the far side of the bushes, immobile, barely breathing, and watched the girl as she hid behind her bush, holding the branches so as to see better, trembling, reminding him of a young doe come falteringly to the water hole to drink.

She turned her pretty head this way and that, wondering where he had gone. Odan saw the long sweet curves of her body, young and not quite formed as yet, saw the way her thigh pressed against the white tunic. He saw a squat, triangular head lift against that whiteness. He saw the coiling sinuous motion in the same instant that the girl became aware of the snake creeping at her side.

She turned her head, paralyzed, unmoving.

Odan moved as a hunter of the Hekeu moves when he grapples with the dragons of Zumer.

The dagger ripped free of its sheath. He poised and threw. In a single fluid drive of motion Odan's throwing arm powered the dagger in a streaking glint of flame through the darkling air.

The snake thrashed insanely. The broad-bladed bronzen dagger sheared the snake's head clean off.

The girl looked up and saw him. She did not scream.

Then, together, they watched the severed head of the snake.

The triangular shape tumbled onto the rich dirt beneath the bush. It changed. Two sinewy arms and two sinewy legs grew from the head. The severed snake's head transformed itself into a bulbous toad, breathing like a bellows, which leaped agilely beneath the leaves and was gone.

Odan refrained from hurling a spell after the thing. The thaumaturgy had worked here, in the palace of Karkaniz, to the benefit of the sender. His poor magics would falter. He turned to look at the snake's body for some clue and, lo! the body was vanished and only a thin straggling line of blue powder lay on the rich dirt and fallen leaves.

"By my Lady Tia!" exclaimed the girl. Her color was up and her eyes, fine and long-lashed, looked exceeding fierce. "I will to Master Boaz. He will explain this."

"You had best—" began Odan the Half-god.

"I thank you, Master Odan, for your courage and skill with your dagger. It seems we are requited, one for the other."

Odan looked blank. Then: "The scorpion—yes, my lady."

The conceit amused him, driven as he was by demons so far beyond tragedy.

She ran fleetly off. Odan was acutely aware of the litheness of her form, the fleeting splendor of her legs, the trailing yellow scarf a glory about her. Well, whoever her mistress was, she would not part with the girl easily. And yet—why should Odan, so enamored and drunken with Zenara, worry his fierce head over a silly half-grown girl in a palace garden?

Yet she had not been silly—and she was splendid, by Hekeu!

Chapter Eleven

The Sack of Zemlya

Zamaz the sun shove bravely upon the tall battlemented walls of Zemlya, picked out the colors of the flags and standards, glittered from the bronze spearpoints of the sentries unflaggingly pacing their beats. Odan took off his helmet and wiped his forehead with a cloth. He was still not used to having slaves petting and fussing with cloths around him.

"There, master," said Kufu the Ox, resplendent in his bronze and leather, a great yellow cloak thrown back to reveal his girth, his armor, his belts and swords—and his sash of power he wore at the insistence of Odan himself.

"I see them, my Ox."

From the southern gateway of Zemlya a caravan was passing over the canal on the narrow brick bridge. This bridge bore no comparison to the great Bridge of Eresh that spanned The River. Chariots flew along before, and fanned out to either side of the long plodding column. Wains were heavily loaded, their onagers and oxen hauling into the traces. Much of that weight would be water.

"We seize a caravan coming to Zemlya from Sennapur," said Ankidu, in his fresh, eager way. His face showed his joy at the prospect. "And we march in, like wolves among the sheep. Aye, my prince, it is a noble plan."

"It may be, my Ankidu. But it is not my plan."

Kufu and Ankidu stared at their leader. It was quite plain they were more than nonplussed.

"But—my prince—" said Ankidu.

100

"And when is a caravan due in from Sennapur? Tell me that, my Ankidu, strong with the bow, tell me that."

"I do not know—by Zadan, I do not know!"

"I shall open the gates of Zemlya to you. When they open you must enter as though fire stalked your heels. It must all be done swiftly and silently until we have the main gates and the walls. Then we may cry havoc to your heart's content."

Odan felt again that grotesque lick of amusement at his friends' reactions. How could he, a man debarred by so cruel a trick of fate from the woman he loved, ever find humor in any situation? His own vicious nature, sharpened by the years of grinding training with the Hekeu, yet found increasingly opportunities for a black humor that appealed to him. By Odan! They would play these conies of Zemlya!

He considered his little army.

Two thousand archers, he had, and a thousand spearmen, more or less. Of these, fourteen hundred archers came from Eresh. Of the spearmen, five hundred were from Eresh, four hundred from Dilpur, and the rest were mercenaries hired from their posts with merchants along The River. Of mercenary archers he had but fifty or so, and these he had placed with the regiment from Dilpur.

The bowmen from Eresh were divided into two regiments, one under Ras Kufu, the other commanded by Ras Enidu. Enidu's men were crocodile archers. The habit of naming regiments was common all along The River; but almost all cities called those regiments of archers whose men worked in pairs, instead of with shield bearers and gerrhons, crocodile archers. Crocarchers. They were highly trained and valuable. Because of that Enidu's regiment consisted only of six hundred men.

Odan glanced up at the brightness of the sky.

"We will make a sacrifice to Tia," he said. "She will secure us from observation, throwing dust in the eyes of Mut, her sister. As to the sorcerers, my work will be done before they see the jaws of their skeletons move."

"And you may leave the army to us, my prince!" growled Kufu the Ox.

Odan nodded. "I shall do that, my Ox. And, in return, you must promise me to heed Ras Enidu. He can teach you much."

Enidu laughed, showing his broken teeth above the harsh dark strip of beard beneath the helmet rim.

"I can teach him much of what being a Ras is, my prince. But few men can teach him about fighting, or of how to make men fight, by Zadan!"

Sharply, Ankidu called: "A chariot comes!"

Odan snarled bitterly in his throat.

"See how the fool kicks dust! Surely they will see that from the high walls of Mut's city!"

The oncoming chariot swerved and disappeared from view behind a rolling billow of sand. Due south from Zemlya the ground rose for about twenty miles, then it extended for a level plateau before descending again to the course of The River at Sennapur. That long lifted tongue of land running for near a hundred and fifty miles westward provided the reason why The River looped in The Salt Sea Bend.

The chariot swirled down toward the army. Its driver saw the group of officers beneath the crest and lashed his tired horses up the slope towards them. He leaped down and saluted with a great crashing of his fist against his armor.

"Great news, prince! The army of Karkaniz has gained a glorious victory! The cities of Ittoral cower before the might of Karkaniz and of Tia!"

"Humph," grunted Odan. "And how many men will the king spare for our enterprise here?"

The messenger gulped for air, clearly put down at the reception of his news. "The king, whose name be praised, will send regiments of archers and spearmen, clouds of chariots, and—"

"Yes, yes," said Odan. "That will be excellent. They can hold the city after we have taken it."

Kufu picked his teeth. Ankidu clutched his sword hilt.

No one suggested Odan wait for the soldiers from Karkaniz. Odan's men hungered for booty and wine and women. Odan hungered for the promise he felt he had exacted from the goddess Tia.

Anyway, as Odan clearly saw, in subduing the cities of Ittoral, that eastern portion of the coast of The Salt Sea, Karkaniz would still require many men. He could expect a few regiments. To take Zemlya in any other way than by means of his plan would require an enormous army and a siege train.

At the grandiose conception that the word "plan" brought to his mind, Odan's harsh mouth curved in a deprecatory grimace. The plan was merely that suggested by Nirghal against Eresh.

But it must work. By Ke and by Hekeu, it must work!

Cloaked in Balniodor's Invisibility, Odan walked into Zemlya by the last of the light, just before the gates were closed for the night. He chose the southern gate, and he observed everything as he walked quietly in. In an hour it would be dark enough for his purposes. His little army had eaten well of the provisions supplied by Karkaniz. They would wait until after the success of the surprise attack before they drank—and even then Odan intended to have Kufu alert to providing full sentries and suspicious patrols.

As the sun at last sank and the shadows dropped down over the mud-brick houses, Odan emerged from his concealment. Still careful, he had switched back to visibility the moment he was under cover. Now he once more cloaked himself with the magic of Balniodor and made for the western gate.

Zemlya lay on the southern bank of The River. With the three main land gates opened, he could dispense with the riverine gate. The western gate afforded no trouble. The guards went to sleep—or slipped into death—their skulls stoved in.

Odan lifted the enormous bars, using the cunning levers and pulleys with their glistening fatty lubrication. The gate was left shut; but unbolted. Like some long wolfish shadow in the night he sped to the southern gate and, in like fashion, released the careful bolts and bars.

The eastern gate provided a hitch.

The sorcerers of any city of the land of Ea, supporting their king's majesty, must be prepared for any occult attack against the safety of king and people within the walls. Attacks might come in many different ways. Invisibility was not unknown, it had been used so often in the past, as the stories told, that most modern thaumaturges regarded it as outmoded. The use of flying carpets was another well-known device for surprising a city, as was the employment of various monsters of horrific appearance. The mages of Zemlya awoke and knew that in their city a new sorcerer had appeared. Skeletal jaws closed sharply. The clicks sounded like notes of doom.

The mere knowledge that a new mage existed would not of itself reveal the source or the intention of the new warlock. That must be discovered.

Staring with hungry eyes across the mud-brick court toward the strongly bolted and barred eastern gate, Odan became aware of a tingling all along his limbs. A sorcery was being practiced upon him. By virtue of his half-godhood he could withstand much of the high gramarye; but he had his limitations still.

Instantly, he shed the cloak of invisibility, and stepped deeper into the shadows.

A pair of sentries patrolled, back and forth, their spears over their shoulders, their helmets mere dark lumps in the moonless night. When the moon came up . . .

The tingling vanished. A cat loped into the starlit darkness beyond the edge of the wall. It stopped and looked about. Odan knew, as he knew he stood within Zemlya, that this was no mere mortal cat.

He remained as still as a Hekeu hunting a hekeu.

Give the infernal thing fifty heartbeats . . . If it had not removed itself by then—Odan did not need to loosen the sword in its scabbard.

A noise began over at the western end of the city, a noise caught and re-echoed from the southern. Odan frowned. The cat's tail went up like the mast of a ship setting sail on The River. It padded off, heading south.

The two sentries had not heard the noise; they continued their measured pacing. They did not possess the ears of a savage from Zumer—or the occult power of a sorcerer.

Odan ran at them. Two flat hard blows stretched them unconscious on the bricks. He dashed for the bolts. From the other side of the gate he could hear the harsh breathing of men thwarted in an attempt of consequence. He heaved at the bars, turning the great many-spoked wheel, exerting all the physical force that had broken the necks of lions and oxen. He would not open the gate with sorcerous means now; let the mages of Zemlya wonder for a space longer . . .

Groaning on its hinges, the gate swung open.

Ras Fernahu stepped bulkily through, the starlight aglitter on his sword.

"My prince!"

"Carry on, Fernahu—make sure your spearmen secure all the entrances."

Ras Fernahu ran swiftly up the stairs along the wall followed by a line of his spearmen, feral, swift, deadly.

Satisfied that the eastern wall would be in his hands within mere moments, Odan ran fleetly for the southern gate. Here Enidu should already have entered. The walls there should be secured. The city slept on as the wolves entered.

"All secure, my prince," said Ras Enidu. He smiled. He was a great gut of a man; but he could fight.

"Pen the soldiers in their barracks. Make sure they are safe. Leave the wine and the wenching until after."

"My prince!"

Odan ran fleetly for the western gate. He could trust these men, for in the military system of Eresh they had been trained up in the regular army from the age of sixteen. After their period of service they would return to civilian life and form a permanent militia, ready to be mobilized instantly. Also, among his little army, particularly among the spearmen, Odan had younger men who had been outside the military system, and were therefore a trifle suspect. He would train them up, though. Material goods might provide the best incentive for a man to do well in the army; when a city called every man capable of bearing arms must fight—and die if necessary.

Even the sons of slaves might aspire to a decent life, even the citizenship, if they served well. Not of the army, they would be used by the army.

Here was the western gate. Odan looked about. It was very quiet.

A voice hailed, hoarse and rasping: "Tia!"

Odan rapped back: "Odan!"

Men stepped forward and their nocked arrows held on his chest. Then one said: "It is the prince!"

"Is all secure here?"

"Aye, my prince. Ras Kufu has gone with the lord Ankidu to the riverine gates. We hold here."

"Make it so. Once the city is ours—then, my lads, then!"

Odan found the riverine gates and walls secured and the garrisons boxed in their barracks. The moon had not yet risen. Kufu and Ankidu had done their work well. Zemlya was held in a grip of bronze.

After that it was a matter of confining the king and his people in the dungeons of the palace, of burning the ziggurat, a task in which Odan had little joy, and of removing the statue of Mut. Two sorcerers were unfortunately killed by panicking spearmen when their amulets failed them and their arms began to shrivel. The third sorcerer, seeing the king confined and the goddess humiliated, came in voluntarily and surrendered to Odan.

"For I see you are a mage, also, prince. I will do nothing against you, being so reduced in power, if you will spare me."

He was given his life.

The moon rose to shine down upon a city shattered. Fires gouted from the ziggurat, for this had been the goddess Tia's command. Even so, Odan made sure his men had plenty of time to remove objects of treasure. These men were here for booty and what they could plunder; they were not here to settle a quarrel among the gods.

He went away from the scenes of looting and drinking and sought Ankidu. But Ankidu was busy making sure Kufu kept some men sober and standing guard. Only stupefaction would halt the sack of Zemlya now.

The day after tomorrow the regiments promised by the king of Karkaniz should be here. The traffic with Sennapur was stopped. There was here in this city a small temple to Tia, for her worship was widespread. Thither Odan took himself. He told the high priest what had chanced, and brushed past him and his frightened priests into the inner shrine. The statue was not overly well-made, but it was rich. A guard of archers stood duty outside to prevent desecration of this temple.

"Tia!" called Odan, bowing. "My Lady! I have done as you commanded. Zemlya is yours. Your sister, Mut, has been humbled. Grant me now the boon I crave—as you promised me."

The statue's coral lips moved.

"I promised you, Odan, nothing save my friendship."

"Yet in friendship, then, grant me—"

"There is yet Sennapur, Odan the Half-god."

"What of Sennapur, Lady?"

But Odan knew. He saw. It was clear enough.

"You have served me well and faithfully." The carven

statue with the silvered face mask and the coral lips and the gemmed eyes looked down on him with infinite sweetness. "You have done some of what I desire of you."

"Sennapur—?"

"Yes, Odan the Half-god. Do to Sennapur as you have to Zemlya. Deal with Farbutu as you have dealt with Mut. Burn his ziggurat! Desecrate his statue! Place Sennapur in the hands of the king of Karkaniz—and much will be yours, Odan the Khuzuk!"

Chapter Twelve

Across the Desert

"Your advice, Master Boaz," said King Scofu, chomping juicily on a pomegranate, the syrup running down his shaven chin, "is as always sage counsel. Do what you will with this treacherous mage. Let the villain suffer for his impertinent attempt upon my dear daughter."

Boaz bowed. "The king has spoken," he said in his crow's voice. "Long life to the king, may he live forever."

Withdrawing from the private audience chamber, a cheerful, garish, fussy place much used by the king for affairs of state, Master Boaz took himself off to confer with his fellow mages.

They met in Boaz's luxurious suite of apartments in the tallest tower of Scofu's palace. Here opulence paraded itself. The gathered wizards, all five of them, greeted Boaz with great satisfaction.

Boaz, himself, preened. A fine, tall man, in the prime of life, he had that vulpine look about his head, that constriction of nostril and shine of cheek, that spoke of great ambition allied to ruthless determination.

"The king's faith in his mages is fully restored," said

Boaz, sitting in his chair of power. He arranged his heavy cloth of gold robes fussily. Not for him the dusty arcane robes of your common wizard. "The sending of the snake convinced him he must trust us absolutely. It was a capital scheme."

"And this young prince Odan, this whippersnapper. The princess said he was very quick with his knife. Very quick."

"He possesses a few minor powers. The goddess, may her name be revered above all others, will dispose of him in her time."

"But can we be sure?" The mage who intruded this note of doubt looked surely as fierce as Boaz; but about him the aura of fear was compounded by one of decadence. "We control the king. This is sure. But can we trust the priests?"

"The priests of a god may defy a sorcerer, Luanu, that is known. But the high priest shares our aims. With the army, the priesthood, and us the sorcerers, Karkaniz is ours! All ours."

"I pray Ulhu it be so," said Luanu. "We have slain or disposed of all the king's children save this one princess, this princess Eshta. We cannot fail with her. She must trust us absolutely—"

"Yes, yes," cried Master Boaz, peevishly. "We shall control her as we control her fool of a father. Make no mistake. And now, let us have wine. The dupe Odan has taken Zemlya and marches across the desert on Sennapur. Is this not a time for rejoicing, brothers?"

Odan the Khuzuk drank the red-tinted water from the goatskin bag with the habitual caution of a Hekeu. All around stretched the desert, burning, rolling, a waste of desiccated sand and dust. He lowered the bag to watch a chariot spurting dust haul in from the southward.

"Aye, my prince," said Kufu, whose broad face was caked with sweat-soaked dust. "And if he doesn't say Sennapur is over the next ridge I'll cut his liver out and fry it."

"We have water and supplies for two more days, my Ox."

Odan spoke gently. They would reach the city and The River. It was written in the tablets.

The army tailed on, marching in long columns. Their

heads were down and their backs lumped in mockery of
Odan's own. Their throats were dry and their armor and
weapons weighed on them and the sun shone. They did
not sing.

More than the original three thousand there were, now.
King Scofu had sent two full regiments of archers, and another of spearmen. And he had sent two regiments of
chariots. The army of Karkaniz was at full stretch. Yet the
city was great and wealthy, more rich even than Eresh.
She could afford a large army of mercenaries as well as
her own regulars and militia. Odan was as pleased as he
was ever likely to be.

The chariot wheeled in with the green and white plumes
of Karkaniz flaring bravely and the horses sweating and
shivering as the driver lashed them on. He hauled up and
the chariot warrior leaped down. He flung up an arm in
greeting.

"Sennapur, prince! Over the next two ridges lies The
River!"

"Halt the army, Ankidu," said Odan. "We rest until a
glass before nightfall."

"Your command, my prince," said Ankidu, in the form,
and was off bellowing orders to the various Ras and their
regiments.

Odan dismounted from his chariot and stood, stretching,
summoning up in his mind the bird's-eye view of this
stretch of The River. Sennapur. Well, this was somewhat
different from Zemlya. They had captured one caravan, to
the soldiers' delight; but the small costly items would have
to be sold and the proceeds divided fairly. Already most
of the men had cast away into the sand the bulky and precious loot they had taken from Zemlya. Of what use
golden candlesticks, silver tripods, massy chests of gems
when all you wanted was an honest drink of water?

A chariot remarkable for the amount of gilding lavished
upon its basically fragile framework spurted up. The
slightest movement sent up a stinging cloud of dust. Odan
waited for the driver to haul up and the officer to alight
and approach. He studied this man with the watchful eye
of a hawk.

Slim, wiry, with the dark shock of hair customary to
people along The River, this general Jonnu moved with
the cat-like power of a fighting man. His face, burned
brown by the sun and the wind that blew forever in the

face of the chariot warrior, revealed a lively intelligence.
He habitually wore a short, forked black beard, threaded
with a single row of silver wire. This general Jonnu in-
trigued Odan. The man had brought up the reinforcements, commanding them as their general, commis-
sioned from the king of Karkaniz. Yet he had made no
attempt to exert command over Odan.

Why should the king employ a foreign prince, with a
ragtail of a little army, when his own general brought up
more men? Yet, if this thought occurred to Jonnu, he had
not voiced it to Odan, he had placed himself under Odan's
command and served loyally.

There was a mystery here.

All generals habitually fought to secure the supreme
command for themselves. The likeliest probability was,
considered Odan, that the goddess Tia had appeared to
General Jonnu in a dream and ordered him to place himself under command of Odan the Half-god.

And, even if Jonnu did not realize it, Odan learned
much from the general.

Obscurely aware that he might be acting like a statesman, or like a king—or like a rascal—Odan put himself
out to be polite and courteous to Jonnu. It might pay divi-
dends later.

How the savage tribesmen of Zumer would mock him if
they could see him now! Their every instinct was to run
headlong on to danger, and by courage and skill and the
will to survival, to conquer all. Now Odan deliberately dis-
simulated in his dealings with General Jonnu of Karkaniz.

The men fell out and Jonnu and Odan walked a little
apart.

"You have a plan, prince?"

The truth was, Odan had only the same hoary plan. But
would it work again?

"I will open the gates of Sennapur. We seize the gates
and walls, confine the soldiers, and that will be that."

"I welcome your confidence, prince." Jonnu evidently
wanted to come to the point; but the point was sticking.
He kicked sand. "Dilpur," he said, at last, and stopped,
looking at Odan.

"Ah!" said Odan Crookback. "Dilpur."

"There is an army of Eresh there. It is known along
The River. Would not they serve you—and thus serve my
Lady Tia and, also, Zadan of the Sword?"

"More likely Redul, god of Dilpur. But that would serve Zadan, also. I take your meaning, general."

How much did this dark, intelligent man know? Had rumor carried along The River news of the quarrel between Galad and Odan? Everyone must realize the aspirations of Numutef. Both rested in Dilpur and because they quarrelled so much nothing was done about Sennapur. Odan, well aware of what Neb-ayin-Ke had decided, yet considered that any general worth his salt would strike at Sennapur and thus save his honor.

They were all hard men with Odan, here in the desert. Hard, dark men, with dust and sweat on their faces, with hard bronze armor, and sharp-edged weapons. The flames of a burning city, the shrieks of dying soldiers, the screams of women, the rending crash of falling walls, all these things were a part of these men's lives, their experiences, their expectations. Of them all Odan was, surely, by far the most savage, the most fierce, the most predatory. But his experience of this so-called civilized warfare was abysmal. He had taken a city by trickery. He had fought well and helped to save Eresh.

But, compared with the soldierly experience of these hawks with him, what was Odan the Khuzuk?

Yet they trusted him and followed him.

For, was he not Odan the Half-god?

The decision was made for him. Out of foolish pride— no. Out of self-interest—assuredly.

"We shall take Sennapur," said Odan the Half-god. "We shall not require the help of the two princes of Eresh sitting in Dilpur."

To any priest, any mage, any soldier with brains—to any simple ditch worker of the irrigations—it must have been clear as the stories flew up and down The River that the gods were in tumult, one with another. All men knew the gods struggled continuously, as men struggled on the earth beneath. Various garbled tales told of olden times, and of how the gods fought, and of how their dream chariots flamed across the sky, putting Zamaz to a ruddy-ochre shade of himself. Ever since Ke created all things, one struggled against another. And now, it was said, the goddess Tia, the goddess of love, sought for the pre-eminent position, sought it and looked set fair to gaining the crown of heaven.

Priests in their ziggurats of the cities strung like jewels upon the winding glory of The River offered up burnt sacrifices, consulted their deepest mysteries, sought advice and consolation from their gods. For if the god's city fell and his ziggurat was thrown down and his shrine violated, his statue defiled, was not the god's power destroyed, also?

Into her soft warm hands the Lady Tia had taken the cities of Kheru and Erlash a generation ago. Now her power extended east and west along The River. Right to Zemlya, her power overawed. The goddess Mut was thrown down and her people, her beasts, her wealth—her city—passed over and resided in the shade of Tia.

Now, men whispered, where next would the goddess of love strike in her power and glory?

Odan the Khuzuk, grim of face, lay on his belly peering over the last ridge and down onto The River and the city of Sennapur. As the wolf gazes on the sheepfold so Odan the Khuzuk glared down upon Sennapur.

As a hunter of the Hekeu desirous of gaining coup and of attaining to the mysteries of his totem gazes upon the wolfpack so Odan the Khuzuk stared calculatingly down upon Sennapur.

The city presented a fair sight, with many towers with banners flying, with sentries patrolling, with commerce beetle-like upon the smooth flowing waters. This city would not easily fall. Numutef and Galad had discovered that.

At Odan's side, Ankidu coughed as sand bit into his throat. He stood in great awe of prince Odan-ayin. He recognized that the demigod possessed awful powers. Yet he had to say what lay heavily in his heart.

"The mages of Sennapur are of a fearsome reputation, Odan, my prince."

"So I hear, my Ankidu. Yet must I test their skill, or we will moulder here in the desert."

At Odan's other side Kufu the Ox grunted and almost heaved himself up, to relax as his own military training caught that betraying movement. Instead, he swore, and said: "Over there, my prince. By Zadan of the Sword. What is that chariot doing?"

A chariot cut a line of dust from the desert, haring straight as an arrow for the northern gate of Sennapur, for the main bulk of the city was built on the north bank of The River, with a sprawling mud-brick suburb on a narrow island near the center of the flood, reached by ferry, and a cluster of shacks on the southern shore. The chariot bounced and reeled, and only one occupant drove like a maniac for the city gate. The watching men saw the guards at the gate snap to attention. The chariot smoked up the long incline and vanished into the shadows beneath the battlemented walls.

Odan inched back and stood up. He did not look pleased.

"It was a chariot of Sennapur, by the horses' plumes. So we have not been betrayed by one of our own."

General Jonnu met him. The wiry man looked wrought up. His cheek twitched under its coating of dust in the sunshine.

"My prince," he said, formally, and so Odan knew the news was bad. "A patrol from Sennapur. Two chariots." They mounted up into their own rigs to drive back to the army, waiting out of harm's way—or so Odan thought,

"Yes, general."

"One of our patrols spotted them and chased. One of our chariots was shot up and crashed. The other caught one of the Sennapurians and shot the driver of the last. But, as you saw, the warrior took over the reins and escaped. Our men shot and missed."

"I see," said Odan. "And it is sure the Sennapurian saw our army?"

"It is certain, prince. They know we are here." Jonnu pulled his forked beard so that it sagged from his chin, the gesture of a desperately angry man. "I have had our patrol impaled. That is routine. But the damage has been done."

"Impalement is too good for them, by Zadan!" said Ankidu.

Kufu the Ox said nothing.

Odan felt nothing about the patrol one way or the other. He could see the disastrous collapse of all his plans. Impaling the guilty charioteers might be routine, tradition, in Jonnu's army; it would not help Odan now. And they had lost four men, also.

The shamans of the Hekeu would know what to do . . . Odan the Khuzuk said: "Listen to me. All of you. This is what we must do."

Chapter Thirteen

Tia Rules

With the exception of the two regiments of chariots, the whole little army commanded by Odan the Half-god marched. Behind them in the sand they left the wains, the near-empty water sacks, the provender, the fodder. They left cumbersome cloaks, tools, anvils, all the impedimenta so necessary to an army. Scattered and abandoned in the sand lay the equipment of Odan's army.

Drawn a little back from that scene of hasty flight, to the rearward face of a long sand dune, the chariots of Karkaniz waited. General Jonnu commanded them. He had been given strict instructions as to what to do, and he knew his head depended on his success.

Odan marched his men. They were not Hekeu. But he marched them without heed of complaint or sickness. Due west he drove them, forcing them on. He marched afoot himself. He sent Ankidu and a handful of chariots on ahead and to the wings, just in case. On and on over the burning sands they trudged. At the rear of the column men with cloaks wiped out the footprints of the army, smearing them as clean as they could, destroying evidence that an army had passed here. No man threw down any spare equipment to lighten himself, for all had been left with the chariots.

Odan did not look continually at the sun. He knew how old Zamaz was sinking. This was a gamble, hardly even a calculated risk. But he felt sure of the pride of the army of Sennapur. They had defeated Numutef and they had held Galad in check. Not tonight—no, on the morrow—they would sally out proud in their strength.

Straight to a confrontation with this small army that had come up against them they would march. Formed, powerful, confident, regiment by regiment, they would march out to give battle and destroy.

Long after the sun sank and with minimal rests, Odan kept his army marching on. Toward midnight they curved in toward The River, and when the water was reached, in total silence, the men flung themselves down, to drink and slake their thirsts and to gain what rest they could for the morrow. For the morrow for them would start long before Zamaz had completed his journey through the twelve hells beneath the earth, driven in stately majesty out to rise again in the east.

"No trumpet calls, Ankidu."

"Aye, my prince. I doubt if any wight has the puff left to blow a single call."

"They'll have puff in the morning. By Hckeu! They'll fight!"

Just before the sun rose in Zamaz's dawn manifestation of burgeoning power, for each glass of the sun's progress across the heavens bore a sacred name, a small group of workers, farmers, beast handlers waited in the lightening shadows for the western gate of Sennapur to open.

Most cities of the long central arm of The River in the land of Ea between the Two Seas refused to allow the dead to be buried within the walls. Necropoli were built out in the sands, beyond the last ditches of the irrigations. Some of the tombs of the kings were vast indeed. Sometimes one particularly memorable man who had performed prodigies of valor for his city might have his tomb built on precious land near to the city's walls. The group of laborers waited by just such a sepulchre, not speaking, huddled close to their clumsy carts. Their eyes were often directed to the topmost pinnacle of the ziggurat of Farbutu, god of Sennapur. The first beams of sunlight would strike down the ziggurat, tier by tier, past the balconies and the hanging gardens, the tinkling fountains, the serrated tiers of decoration. When the shadow line sank below the level of the walls and the sun burst fully onto the eastern gate of the city, all the gates would be thrown open.

That was the usual daily routine.

On this day the northern gate had opened early, long

before dawn, and, strong in their might and power, pompous, marching with banners and chariots, the army of Sennapur had gone forth, silently, a host bent on chastisement.

The light grew stronger. A dawn wind blew, gently, and the smell of the blue lotus scattered a fragrance upon the cool air.

Hidden by the bulk of the city, the sun must be up, over the horizon. Still the western gate did not open. The soldiers pacing the walls glimmered to more solid life, silhouettes against the golden glow.

In the olden days the fierceness of the scorching summer sun used to dry up the fields, turn them into mere ochre continuations of the surrounding desert. The River flooded season by season; but the falls varied and no man could be sure that his painfully cut ditches would fill and last enough for him to crop his fields with green and so gain sustenance to last another year. Then the new gods came in their dream chariots. They it was who had shown men the true way of irrigation. They had placed in men's hands the shaduf, the waterwheel, the cunning slope of irrigation, canal engineering cunning with gradients—very cunning, the new gods, in their assistance to humble men. The wormpeople had been vanquished as the old legends told. And so now with the new crops from the new gods, the fields stood green all the year around, field by field, ditch by ditch, and the silver and gold shimmer of water threaded far from the banks of The River, far into the desert to the limit of the irrigations.

So this sepulchre, whitewashed, clean, could be built here on land that might otherwise have provided barley or wheat, root crops, or fodder. The shadows grew shorter.

With a soundless clap of thunder the sun, Zamaz, burst above the battlemented line of walls. Day had come and the gates of Sennapur remained fast shut.

"May all the imps of hell damn and blast them!" growled Kufu the Ox, shaking his farmer's hoe.

"Aye!" said Ankidu, hitching up his coarse ditch-workers kilt. "The devils know we are here! Else why do they not open; why are there no other workers, coming forth to their daily toil?"

"They do not know we are here," said Odan, and at his voice the little group around him quieted. "Did we not safely bind those wights from whom we took these

clothes? Has any man spied on us? No! Then Sennapur
does not know we are here. They do not open because
having sent their army out into the desert they are
naturally cautious. It is plain common sense. It shows one
reason why so far they have not been subdued."

"But, my prince—we are here, outside, and how may
we gain entrance?"

Odan repressed the scarlet fury. His plan to break a
way in by a subterfuge, eschewing all sorcery, had seemed
to him fine and wonderful, a true plan a Zuman would relish. And now simple military routine had defeated him.
No, by Odan! He would not thus lightly be shamed before
his army.

There was a way.

He turned to glare upon Kufu the Ox.

"The moment the gates open, my Ox, do you and your
men rush in, shouting, making a great cry." He swung on
Ankidu. "My Ankidu. Go back to the army. Tell the Ras
to begin to march up now. By the time you have gone and
returned, Kufu will be happily smashing skulls within the
open gates."

"I am gone, my prince." Ankidu turned and raced away
among the lotus blossoms, following the narrow trails with
ease.

Odan the Half-god shut his eyes.

He had travelled through Sennapur with Nadjul the
Quick, between that happy encounter in Kheru and that
tragic parting in Eresh. They had been good times, with
the Swordsman . . .

The life of a hired guard along The River was not a
bad life for a hardy young man, quick with the sword,
deadly with the bow. There were perks to be had, pretty
girls in each city, a foaming jack of beer, a gambling
game at which to win or lose.

In Sennapur Nadjul had collected a hatful of copper coins from those wights chaffering around the western gate
who had been gulled into betting against the power and
accuracy of Odan's throwing arm. The flung spear had
smashed through the piled bricks, slicing like a wire
through cheese. Renewed bets had taken up another hatful
of the little copper coins as Odan's mighty cast sent the
keen-headed spear slicing with finicky exactitude to halve
a pomegranate.

Yes, he remembered the little brick-paved square by the western gate of Sennapur.

He focused his powers, conjuring the names and the dread spells culled from Master Asshurnax's murky tomes. The baked clay tablets yielded sinister griftings—away went Odan's ka, drifting into Sennapur, allowing him to see and seize the guard standing idly by the levers of the gate.

The bricks felt hard under his sandals, where one of the bronze studs had broken free and left the others to dig into his sole. His cheap bronze armor chafed his shoulders. His mouth was already dry, although he had been on duty for so short a period. May Farbutu send a rapid release from sentry duty!

With the eyes of the guardsman, Odan saw. He saw his fellows watching some children playing hopscotch. The shouts shrilled. The guards were not sure if they were pleased or sorry to miss the battle sure to be won to great glory in the desert.

Slowly, Odan forced the guardsman to bend to the lever. He moved it. It moved silently in its greased channel. Up it came. The gate was barred by this single great baulk of timber, floated down from the northern hills. It rotated upright. Casually, Odan sauntered toward the gate, his hand on his swordhilt, feeling the dim, panic-stricken strugglings of the ka of the guardsman like a mouse scrabbling in a darkened chamber.

"Hey! Jaipur! What do you with the gate? The orders are clear. Hey! Jaipur!"

Swiftly now, this guardsman, Jaipur, controlled by the grifting sent by Odan the Half-god, set his shoulder against the gate and pushed. The gate opened. Harder, Jaipur pushed. He felt rather than heard the rush of bodies at his back.

"Come away, Jaipur! Close the gate!"

These men suspected no real danger. They thought, probably, that their comrade Jaipur had some genuine reason for opening the gate. Jaipur, possessed by Odan, showed them differently.

The gate swung back. A swift look out showed Odan the fearsome sight of Kufu, wielding his sword, bounding forward and at his back the others of the advance party. Odan turned back, quelled a despairing attempt by Jaipur to regain control of his body, and drew his sword.

The fight was short, quick, and bloody.

Kufu and the others burst in.

Quickly, Odan said: "Kufu—away up the walls!"

The guardsman, Jaipur, collapsed. Odan opened his eyes back by the white sepulchre, all blue-green in the shadows, and stood up. He started to run for the gate and heard the hard slogging rush of his army at his back, led on by Ankidu.

They roared through the western gate and on into the city, column after column, archers and spearsmen, raging in to take a city. With the main army of Sennapur absent, the few guards left had no chance. In a kind of repetition of the events of Zemlya, Odan and his men secured the city.

A nasty moment was averted as a party of soldiers, racing up the winding stairway to the eyrie that was their target, fell back, paralyzed. Odan leaped ahead and hurled his spear. The heavy bronze point tore through the heart of the wizard at the top of the steps, his powers wrenched away by the powers—still only half-formed—of Odan the Half-god. So died one mage of Sennapur.

A Kisraen of spearsmen were stretched with crocodile legs in a row in the street of the next eyri. Once again, and with the sustaining supernatural power of Tia to assist him, Odan forged ahead. Another mage of Sennapur died with a bronze blade destroying his heart.

The soldiers, restored to the use of their own human legs, set up a shaky caterwauling cheer. Sorcery was a deep, frightening, unknown area of human life, to the ordinary soldier.

When the ziggurat of Farbutu began to burn, sending sparks and smoke shooting from the galleries along four of the tiers, and the king and his retinue were rounded up in a welter of the blood of their personal bodyguards, the other mages of Sennapur chose the easier course.

Odan looked on them, brooding.

"You have fought well for your city. But now Sennapur is fallen! Farbutu bends the knee to Tia. Let no thaumaturge's hand or spell be raised against my men, and you may retain your lives."

They swore, by Ulhu and by Lorghimu and their own sorcerous gods. Also, Odan made them swear by Tia and Zadan. For, as he said: "It is meet you know who has overthrown you."

Odan the Khuzuk stood on a shady terrace of the royal palace of Sennapur. The afternoon sun gilded the columns and set a dancing golden coinage in the leaves of the trees above.

Odan quaffed deeply of good beer, from a golden vessel, and he felt the pride bursting in him, enormous, tempestuous, luscious. Alone, with his small army, he had taken the city of Sennapur that had defied Numutef and Galad. How he would crow over them! How they would be humbled in the sight of the king, Neb-ayin-Ke, and all the might of Eresh!

"We did it, Ankidu! We did it—and no thanks to Galad and Numutef. By Hekeu, this is a day!"

"Aye, Odan, my prince. This is indeed a day. But should we not send word to Dilpur? The two princes will hasten here—they will—"

"If they come they will come to bend the knee to me as their superior! Have I not conquered where they failed?"

"Yes, my prince." Ankidu looked troubled. "But the army of Sennapur. They ring us here, waiting. They will have a say in what transpires."

"No, my good Ankidu. They will have no say. Their city is fallen. The god's shrine has been destroyed, his ziggurat burned, his statue taken out and defiled, ready to be transported to Karkaniz. Tell me, Ankidu, my friend, you who understand the ways of civilization in the land of Ea. When all that happens to a man's city, where does his allegiance lie?"

"You mock me, my prince!"

"Not so. I am a Zuman, a primeval savage, one of the Hekeu totem. I do not understand civilized ways. If a Zuman's totem is crushed, if another totem gains ascendancy over his, I know what will happen then. Tell me, Ankidu, what power has the god of Sennapur now? How can that army out there break in against us? Are not the walls tall and strong? Will they break in against my wolves?"

Ankidu shook his head. "We can hold them—for a time. But what you say is true. They are as dead men, for they have no god to sustain them—"

"Aye! And no mages, either!"

"True. An army of Karkaniz will take them under command. Sennapur is known from henceforth as a city of Karkaniz. Tia rules here."

"Tia rules. Aye. Sennapur serves Karkaniz, now. Perhaps, one day in the future, the god Farbutu may reestablish himself, find a city to honor him. But not Sennapur. Sennapur is Tia's."

Ankidu bit his lip.

"And what of Zadan, my prince?"

"Zadan and Eresh have been well served this day. Now Sennapur poses no threat against Dilpur." Odan quaffed more beer. His brown eyes were very bright. "Who commands the army of Sennapur, out there, beyond the walls?"

"The king's son, the young prince—"

"Send him up to me. Take his weapons away. Yet treat him with courtesy. I have a mind to tell him his fate."

"Yes, my prince."

Odan clapped a rough arm across Ankidu's shoulders.

"Remember, Ankidu, remember. There is a treaty of alliance between Eresh and Karkaniz. This day we have served the king my father and Zadan the All-Glorious exceeding well."

"Yes, my prince."

And Ankidu took himself off to escort the young defeated prince of Sennapur to his destiny, which was held in the palm of the hand of the young prince of Eresh, Odan the Half-god.

Chapter Fourteen

"Look, Odan the Idiot, Look!"

Odan had the young prince of Sennapur loaded down with chains and incarcerated in a deep and dankly dismal dungeon. Then he freshened himself up, put a flower behind his ear, and, dressed still in his armor and carrying his weapons, went off to the temple of Tia within the city. This temple, wealthy and in a good position, was closely guarded by four Kisraens of Kufu's archers.

The goddess of love boasted a temple in most cities. It was natural. Here came the strong young men, lusting after fair young maidens, seeking advice and amatory help; here came the fair young maidens, lusting after strong young men, seeking strong potions.

"All quiet, my Ox?"

"All quiet, my prince."

"We showed them this day, did we not?" Odan was still stuffed to bursting with pride in his achievement. His glee devoured him with self-esteem. "How those two oafs will be green when they hear the news!"

"Yes, my prince."

"Keep a sharp watch. I go to converse with the goddess. She will decide what fate will befall these miserable wights of Sennapur."

"Yes, my prince. And—I think Zadan of the Sword will—" Here Kufu the Ox halted himself. His face grew red under the tan. He shuffled his heavily sandalled foot.

"Yes, my Ox? Zadan the All-Glorious will—what?"

"Will—be pleased, my prince."

"But of course!"

Laughing, Odan the Half-god strode into the ornate entrance of the temple of Tia in Sennapur. Laughing—Halfgod—had he not every right to laugh? Would not he soon be a whole god? Would he not, though!

The shaven priests of Tia greeted him with a maladroit mixture of pride and humbleness. Male gods were served very often by priests hairy to excess; goddesses usually were served by shaven priests—and by charming little votaries and voluptuaries of the sanctuary, girls who would solace a man after the strife, for a suitable offering to the goddess, of course. Odan pushed through them all, unheeding of their querulous cries for him to comport himself seemly, and to remove his big brutal weapons. He had been discarding his sword and spear, his bow and shield, too often of late.

Through them he pushed, through into the inner courts and across brick pathways between gardens of sweetly scented flowers, past fishponds filled with carp—the priests enjoyed a juicy fat carp, nicely cooked, with onions—past whispering fountains that cooled the air and soothed the ear, on through long colonnades of trailing vines, and so, at last to the tall bronze-bound valves of the outer shrine.

Here two men, shaven, armed with spears, stood guard. Odan glared at them.

"Begone!" growled one, grinding his spear butt on the brick path.

"If you do not bow to the goddess first—" said the other, twirling his spear so that the heavy butt lifted, ready for a blow.

How he would have finished the sentence neither he nor Odan would ever know. One sentry Odan struck along the temple, the other he struck upon the chin. He used no other weapon than his fist. He stepped over the two unconscious men and shoved the tall narrow doors open.

The thought occurred to him that there might be some being who could halt him from his destiny—but he could not think who or what that might be.

A long columned vista of blueness met his gaze. High in each wall a clerestory admitted light and air. At the far end stood two more doors, closed. These Odan kicked open, for he wore the heavy studded sandals of the soldier.

He stood, dwarfed in the portal, on the threshold of the goddess's inner shrine. Her statue towered up, high, higher than any statue of a goddess not in her own city had any right to tower. He tilted his head back, straining against the stoop in his shoulders, and he brushed the long hair from his face.

Doves cooed and flew high in the dim-sunlit blue light. The scent of the blue lotus hung heavily. Statues of naked girls wielding huge swords and spears, clad in helmet and sandals only, guarded the sanctum. The statue of Tia glowed. Her eyes, her lips, her whole face, exuded that carnal air of supernal calm wisdom. What the statue of her back in her own ziggurat in her own city of Karkaniz must be like, if this was her statue here in this city, staggered the imagination.

The coral lips moved. There were lines in the silver forehead.

"Who are you, impious beast, who bursts in thus! On your knees, dog of a mortal! Lest your insult to the goddess may never be healed!"

Odan the Half-god remained standing.

"Tia!" he bellowed up. "Tia Nin-Apsish! How can the

eyes of a goddess be blinded or deceived? Have I not delivered over into your hands the cities of Zemlya and of Sennapur? Have not the ziggurats of Mut and Farbutu burned, their effigies defiled, packed ready for transport to Karkaniz, to await your pleasure? Have I not done all those things commanded by you?"

"Odan the Khuzuk! You presume upon a goddess!"

"I presume nothing!" Odan began to feel as though he stood upon a yellow sandbank in The River as the floods undercut his footing. "We are friends—good friends—as you yourself said. I have done as you commanded and have kept my part of the bargain. Now, Tia, my Lady, do you keep yours!"

"I made no bargain with you."

Odan put his left hand around his right wrist. He squeezed. He squeezed as though he choked the life from a marauding wolf. He must retain his sanity—such as it was—or all was lost.

"I am the son of a god! Odan En-Ke may or may not exist—the devil Nirghal said he was not real. Do you say he was not real, also, my Lady? Do you agree so well with Nirghal—for, as you know, he, too, betrayed my trust in him."

The obliqueness of his criticism of the goddess was surely not enough . . . Tia laughed. Her spine-tingling laugh tinkled in that tall space, making the doves whirr in grey and blue serrations of beating wings.

"I own you are a man, at the least, Odan the Khuzuk, whether you are a god or not."

Odan released his wrist. He glared up, as best he could, forcing his stooped shoulders back.

"You are sworn to make me a whole god, Tia—"

"Softly, softly, Odan Crookback. There is yet more for you to do in serving me before that can even be discussed."

Well, of course. Shouldn't he have known? Who dickered with the gods dickered with more than fate and death.

"What shall I do for you now, my Lady? Drink The Sweet Sea dry? Water the desert with The Salt Sea? Change the course of The River?"

"All these things may be done, Odan—aye! *And will be done.* But not through your mockery."

Distinctly, Odan felt a biting chill strike through him. He shuddered. What the goddess said—she *knew*.

"You made a bargain, as you thought, with Nirghal. He betrayed you. I shall not betray you, in like case."

"No!"

Odan's high shout crashed against the roof, set the doves into a maelstrom of motion.

"No, my little mortal, no?"

"No. Find some other way, my Lady—I beg you!"

"What is the way you imagine?"

Odan would not answer. Nirghal had demanded in return for making Odan a whole god the treacherous betrayal of the city of Eresh into the hands of his army of Endal; and Odan had agreed. He would not repeat himself—would not.

"Look, Odan the Idiot. Look!"

One of the statues moved. The life-size naked girl moved. Odan stared, his left hand resting on his sword hilt. The girl lifted her sword. He saw her face. It was Zenara. He had never seen her fully naked before—and, with a savage burst of sullen fury, he knew that Zenara need not look at all like the indecently voluptuous body below that glorious head.

"Look at what you throw away, Odan."

And, weirdly, another statue came to life, naked, lascivious, beckoning to him, rounded forms glowing with desire. And it was the girl in the garden who had rescued him from the scorpion and whom he had saved from the snake.

The two beautiful naked forms glided about him, swirling their swords, their red lips pouting with passion, their eyes melting upon him, their breasts, their thighs, their hair enough to drive any man berserk with lust. Odan stood, looking at these apparitions, feeling what any man would feel, yearning—and yet wondering, for he was the son of a god. He looked at the phantasm of Zenara and he felt his heart turn over.

"Do you recognize her, Odan the Oaf?"

"No."

"You lie!"

"If you can read my heart, you know I speak truth."

With a flash of blue fire, spitting, feral, vicious, the naked statues were mere naked statues once more, upon their pedestals, immobile, cold.

The voice of Tia, the goddess of love, dripped sweet as honey in the shrine of her temple.

"And you do love your Zenara, the princess of Eresh, your sister?"

"My half-sister. Yes."

"Think of her, then. Think of her as she really is."

Odan could not stop thinking of her.

"It is not a great thing I ask of you. Think of Sennapur. Has the city been harmed? Have my men slaughtered her people? Now that the city acknowledges me as its god, will anyone suffer?"

Odan knew this to be at least three quarters true.

"But," he said. "Eresh—"

"Ah!" The coral lips smiled. The statue did not move; but it seemed to Odan that the statue of the goddess bent sweetly down to him. "I can show you your Zenara, in all truth, an' you will—"

He could not stand that.

"No."

"Then it is settled? You will know how to proceed. You are gaining a fearsome reputation along The River, Odan, the Khuzuk. Men will follow you. You will find a way. When my statue stands in the ziggurat of Zadan in Eresh —then, Odan the Half-god—then you may ask your boon of me again."

Chapter Fifteen

Flames along The River

The ghostly servitor, with a clank, brought forward the long scarlet robe. With a little shiver Amenti slipped the cool stuff over her body. She was soaked in sweat, sweat in globules about her forehead and upper lip, running in trickles down her body, between her breasts, over her belly, down her legs. She gestured and the ghostly servitor produced a golden goblet with warm wine laced with honey. Amenti drank gratefully.

"You have succeeded?" said Master Ubonidas, anxiously. He glanced at the curtain-shrouded window in the thick walls of the Abode of the Bats. The moon silvered through, the ragged shapes of the bats wheeling and flittering across the glowing silver orb—as was proper—and he looked back. If the witch could not succeed in summoning her friends among the wormpeople's familiars on a night like this, then the lord Gabal might as well have her strangled and slipped into the rolling waters of The River without more ado.

Mind you, that task was probably beyond even Ubonidas' strength in sorcery . . .

"I shall need a bath, Ubonidas." Amenti licked her lips on which the warmed wine shone. "And if you take a potion I shall allow you to scrub my back. It has been a long time. And my familiars, although dear to me, do not always provide the best companions in the bath."

Ubonidas nodded and the ghostly servitor withdrew. Urt, the seeming-spider, trembled his webs; but he had far too much sense to venture to intrude upon the wishes of the witch Amenti.

"And the wormpeople? My gramarye foretells much there."

"Yes. Yes, for a mere man you have some powers. But the sisterhood is well loved by the wormpeople. I have seen and spoken with one who is known to this later world as the Sapphire. She will aid us in smashing the sealings of this bastard Master Kidu over the princess."

"And her price?"

"That need not concern you!" Amenti flared up, her colorless face drawing down into a white mask of contemptuous anger.

"Very well, Amenti." Ubonidas felt he was cowed; but he also thought of the potion he would take, and of the long white back of Amenti, and he betrayed nothing of his feelings. "The news along the gutters is that the prince Odan has gained a high reputation as a warrior prince. He is a great leader of men. So is said."

"He is an oaf. He will be brought low—when I have my hands on him he will never lead men again—ha!"

"He shames the princes Numutef and Galad. My lord, Gabal, is wroth at the slight put upon his son. He grows impatient at the delays in our work."

"When the wormpeople ruled all Khepru there was rich grassland where now the desert covers all. There are places known to the sisterhood—and a few high sorcerers—which contain power. The Sapphire will make such a place available to us. The princess will be safe there. Then will your lord Gabal-ayin make his terms with Neb-ayin-Ke. And his son, the puissant prince Galad, will have his way with the princess Zenara."

Ubonidas chuckled. The ghostly servitor came in with the stoppered vial with the potion, a crusted, violet draught.

"The bath is drawn, Amenti."

"The plan will take time. There is a girl—a handmaid—who must be trained and taught well. But the plan will succeed and nothing Master Kidu can do will halt it."

"I will bring oil, also, for your back—Amenti—"

"I do not like to be thwarted, even for a day. This Kidu. I will teach him the power of the sisterhood, once your lord Gabal has seated his son upon the throne of Eresh."

The two horses of the messenger's chariot staggered and fell against the shaft. The messenger, his yellow cloak flaring, fairly knocked Narpul the Staff out of the way as he ran shouting up the great staircase. The enamelled spearmen of the King's Guard regarded him with blank painted eyes. Through the bronze-bound doors, through the silver-bound doors, and bashing straight on through the gold-bound doors, the messenger burst into the Hall of Reception, and so on past to the small withdrawing room.

Kephru-Ket, the high priest of Zadan in Eresh, staggered back from his priestly pose before the king's small throne. The messenger threw himself to the carpeted floor, panting and heaving; but shouting out his message.

"Oh king live forever! News from Dilpur!"

"Speak," said the king, adjusting instantly to the obvious gravity and importance of the message.

"The prince Odan, your son, king live forever! He has taken Dilpur by a trick! He is leagued with Karkaniz and the goddess Tia, against Dilpur! It is treachery, my lord the king, whose name be praised, said by all, in sorrow—

Prince Odan takes Dilpur by a trick and marches on Eresh!"

"Impossible!" said Neb-ayin-Ke, brusquely. "Odan—no, it is unthinkable. I think, captain, your head will roll after you have been impaled—or maybe dangled by your heels from the battlements."

"My king, glorious in the sight of Zadan of the Sword. I knew this would be your word, and it is why I volunteered for this task, for many were afraid to tell you, seeing the fate that overtakes the bearer of bad news."

"Yes, well, I have long since ceased that vile practice," said the king, testily. "But, captain, you lie."

"May Zadan strike me down! Do I not pray to Zadan that I do lie! But it is the truth, oh king live forever."

Neb-ayin-Ke looked at Kephru-Ket. The high priest looked stunned.

"Send for Master Kidu! By Zadan! Am I served by dolts, by traitors! Why do we not know? Heads will roll—aye! Heads will roll!"

"Oh king, I will to the temple," stammered Kephru-Ket. "I will seek guidance from Zadan the All Glorious. If the goddess Tia truly means our great god harm—it is unthinkable, unthinkable—the goddess of love!"

"And we have a treaty with those cunning devils of Karkaniz. Oh, this is not the work of King Scofu, for he is a genial old idiot. This is dark and deep. This is the work of his mages and his priests—and his army chiefs, too. But Odan! Odan!" The real sense of grief began to strike at Neb-ayin-Ke cruelly, then. He groaned. "Have I not loved you as my son, Odan? Odan?"

A call of that strong nature within the palace brought Master Kidu at a run. His long mournful face with the two black down-drooping moustaches showed a deep concern. He passed Kephru-Ket and the high priest panted out: "Disaster! Disaster! The mad Khuzuk means to destroy us all!"

As he ran into the withdrawing room, Kidu sent out a preliminary grifting. He had been fighting a stern battle of late, against the new witch in Eresh, and he was deeply drained of psychic energy. His new famulus was of some help; but Kidu knew he was up against powers that possessed a horrific potential for occult destruction.

"King live for ever."

"Kidu! You have betrayed me! Down on your knees! Tell me why I should not have you impaled."

"Tell me first what is the news."

"You are condemned out of your own mouth. You, my court wizard, my master mage, stand there and confess you do not know!"

Kidu, beside himself, burst out: "Know what?" Then, quickly, he added: "King live forever."

"My son, prince Odan-ayin—he has taken Dilpur by a trick and marches on Eresh—" A look at the messenger who had shrunk back. "With an army of Karkaniz?" The messenger nodded.

"A moment, my king."

Kidu sent a powerful grifting. He drove hard and surely toward Dilpur. Below him the sand blurred past, the green strip of irrigation beside The River. He winged on—and then he was standing on the rich carpets in the room with the king glaring at him, shocked back into his own body. He breathed deeply, through a pinched nose, and his long face grew longer and more mournful than ever.

"There is great thaumaturgy practiced before Dilpur. Many mages conspire. I must work at this, seek a way to see through and thus—you must excuse me, my king. In my eyrie are things needful—"

"You had best bring us a full report, Kidu. You have sinned grievously in your laxness. I am displeased. Your head depends on this."

"It is difficult to believe Odan—I must hurry."

Kidu ran out before he realized the horror of the moment had forced all the obsequious parting words away. He shot a swift grifting toward the eyrie on Yellow Lotus Street. Old Asshurnax would have to help in this, aye, and all the other mages of Eresh. They were in for a ferocious battle on all the occult planes and spheres there were. He did not stop to summon Master Ubonidas. He knew which side that bastard was on. As for the witch, Amenti, she could strike hard, now, if she chose. But the king had commanded. Kidu and his fellow mages of Eresh were in deadly need of comfort and assistance.

He shot a grifting toward the ziggurat. Kephru-Ket might be able to assist. The great god Zadan must defend his city. Normally, Kidu refrained from using sorcery in the vicinity of any temple and particularly of the zigguat. But this was a genuine emergency. He circled down, easily enough, and saw Kephru-Ket kneeling outside the middle shrine. Kidu frowned. Why did not the high priest enter the inner shrine, as was his privilege and duty? He lowered in the invisible air and whispered in Kephru-Ket's ear.

The high priest did not look startled.

"Kidu! Listen to me. You are the court wizard and it is to you the city and the king must turn. I have prayed, I have ordered sacrifice. I shall pray and I shall sacrifice—but there is a hollowness, and emptiness—oh, Kidu, I fear, I fear! I fear that Zadan of the Sword, Zadan the All-Glorious, has left us, has abandoned us and the city of Eresh to the awful fate that will overwhelm us!"

At the head of a motley crowd of fugitives, King Norgash of Dilpur, with his grandson, Prince Numutef, the second son of King Neb-ayin-Ke of Eresh, threw himself into the city and sought sanctuary with his son-in-law. The two kings met in a private chamber of the palace, with Numutef and Galad-ayin. Gabal-ayin had been summoned. The weary, dispirited soldiers were quartered about the city, and people went about with worried, pinched looks.

"Great sorcery was used, king," said Norgash. He looked shrunken. "A chariot of fire was seen in the heavens. By what trick the young prince Odan scaled the walls and opened the gates is a mystery."

Neb-ayin-Ke bit his lacquered fingernails. "And the fighting? Was—was Odan wounded?"

Numutef glared at the king. Well, if he took offense, a king was a king and a son was a son, and Neb-ayin-Ke was prepared to demonstrate the difference.

"There was no fighting, Neb-ayin-Ke," said Norgash. "The trick with the walls, the open gates, the sorcerous spells, all conspired—" He made a vague gesture, as though flies clustered before his face. "The soldiers did not fight. They were duped. There was no bloodshed."

"And it is certain sure that Karkaniz and the goddess Tia are involved—"

"The chariot horses wore green and white plumes. No offense was shown to the ziggurat of Redul, although—" And here Norgash panted, and licked his lips, and went on with a visible effort. "Although the great statue of the god was removed, and the statue of Tia from her temple in Dilpur was blasphemously placed in the great god's stead."

"I just do not understand it," said Neb-ayin-Ke. He looked about, seeking reassurance. He met only the blank, wolfish, almost hostile stares of those in the room. Would they feed so on his misfortune?

He was a king. He had been a king for some time, and the habits of his heart were more ingrained than he knew.

"We will array the army of Eresh. The militia, all the forces. If these devils of Karkaniz break the treaty then they will be slaughtered, to a man, and their ears shall dangle in long chains from the eaves of the ziggurat of Zadan of the Sword." He was aware of Queen Momi entering the room, tears staining her face. She moved like a pale ghost. He went on, remorselessly.

"If my son Odan cannot wait for me to die—if he seeks out of the evil in his savage heart to slay me and take the crown—I know how to hold my city."

Momi uttered a little cry, and tottered forward to fall in a heap at the king's feet. He stared at her. His compassion was not inexhaustible.

"Odan is the son of Queen Momi and of Odan En-Ke. I have treated him with all honor. But he has lived with the Zumen. He is a primeval savage, scarlet of fang and claw."

"Oh, Neb-Ke!" whispered Momi. "My Odan—"

The lord Gabal-ayin entered, borne on his great carved chair.

The gathering immediately braced up. The lord was known as a man hard above ebony, a man who would tolerate no wrong, forgive no slight, a man who would harbor a grudge to the tomb.

He made obeisance to the king and then stared with hard, bright, intolerant eyes upon his son, the prince Galad.

"And so you ran away from Odan the Khuzuk!"

Galad's face would have melted cold bronze. He did not speak. There was nothing he could say.

Like a boar facing the hounds Gabal swung back to the king. "The goddess Tia, the goddess of love, king—she and all the gods of The River do not forget. Their memories are long."

Neb-ayin-Ke went to stroke his chin in his favorite gesture and his beringed hand felt the gold wire and the hot-iron ringlets of a state beard. "True, my uncle. Zadan the

All-Glorious truly earned that title of honor—and the other gods do not forget."

Well, the story was old now. About five hundred years ago Eresh had extended her power westward, up The River, taking over the dominion of Dilpur and Sennapur and reaching out tentacles of power to the very gates of fabled Karkaniz itself. In the reign of one king, and his lifetime only, had this occurred. When the jealous gods had banded together, with Tia at their head, and pleaded with Nirghal to drive daggers of bronze into the exposed back of Zadan, the king had died. King Nu-ayin-Ke had died at the assassin's hand. And the gods had driven the army of Zadan back, compressing Eresh back and back along the winding length of The River until her people were once more masters of one city and one city only.

No, the gods in their dream chariots did not forget.

Since then the treaty with Karkaniz had kept each end of the central arm of The River, between the seas, away from each other's throats—save for occasional flare-ups. Now that Endal, the city of the devil Nirghal, to the south, had reduced and destroyed the city of Tubal, all attention in Eresh had been focused to the south—until Dilpur by the marriage of her princess with the king of Eresh had brought Eresh once more to confront the western reaches.

And Odan-ayin, prince of Eresh, led an army strong with banners and chariots against the city of his father and his god.

"The son of Odan En-Ke does not justly requite me," said Neb-ayin-Ke. He spoke with great bitterness.

"The army—" began Gabal, scowling up from his cripple-chair.

"The army will fight," said the king. "I shall speak to them. And my words will not be of rewards but of punishments." His hearers shuddered, for a king in the land of Ea between the Two Seas wielded enormous and frightening powers. "Before that, we shall go up to the temple of the great god, Zadan of the Sword, and sacrifice and make obeisance to him for the victory."

But in the ziggurat of Zadan Kephru-Ket, the high priest, knelt up from his beseeching prayer and knew with soul-scorching horror that Zadan the All-Glorious had forsaken his city of Eresh.

Chapter Sixteen

General Jonnu Risks his Head

"But, master!" said Kufu the Ox. His massively corrugated face furrowed as he struggled to find expression.

"It is because I trust you and the lord Ankidu, my Ox. There is trouble in Kheru. Ankidu and you will lead the men of Eresh against them and chastise them. You will show them the error of their ways."

"But, master—" said Kufu, again. He sweated. Under his yellow and brown robes he sweated. His massive leather armor, scaled with the bright bronze, creaked as he moved. Armor must forever be oiled. His sash of power, many-fringed, bright with colored threads, held in place by the white wide belt, and the metal belts supporting his daggers and his sword, swelled as he breathed. His ox-features looked as stubborn not as an ox but as the miscegenation of an ass and a horse. "But, master, not one man of Eresh will go with you on your next enterprise!"

"We guard Dilpur for the goddess Tia," said Odan, somewhat off-handedly.

The trick by which they had taken the city of Norgash still pleased him, although he suspected the presence of Dilpurnians in their ranks had pulled the trick through. But Ankidu, Kufu the Ox, Ras Enidu and the others of Eresh—they would never march on Eresh in so gullible a way.

"You must, my wild Khuzuk," the goddess had said, "you must separate the men of Dilpur and Eresh from my soldiers of Karkaniz. You will go up against Eresh with my men."

And, of course, it made sense.

Here, it was, here in Dilpur that he had seen Zenara after the devasting discovery they had made that they were half-brother and half-sister. The agony of those days remained with him, a permanent scar on his heart. But, so near he was, so near to the glorious outcome of all his hopes!

He managed, in the end, to convince Kufu and sent him off to superintend the transfer of his regiment to the boats that would convey them upriver to Kheru. Ankidu would be more difficult to hoodwink, far more difficult. Odan the Khuzuk, Odan-ayin, prince of Eresh, ordered up a fine two-horse chariot, and driving himself, went off to the desert to hunt lions with some of General Jonnu's staff. He left orders that the contingent of men from Eresh must be away and upstream within two glasses.

Jonnu would see to that.

The wiry, intense general had done well with his chariots in the desert, bamboozling the army of Sennapur. Now, with more and more reinforcements coming down The River from Karkaniz, so that a sizeable army grew in and around Dilpur, the general was still content to take his orders from prince Odan.

Driving out in a swirl of sand, hunting lions, Odan found he brooded upon the enigma of Jonnu. The mystery must have an answer. Odan through his experiences had grown to distrust the gods. He distrusted Tia. She had not promised his godhood in so many words, not even as far as the foresworn Nirghal. He fancied that Tia had given orders to her high priest in Karkaniz, and he to the king, and he to General Jonnu, that all honor and obedience be accorded Odan the Half-god. Once Eresh lay in her hands, perhaps she might reveal her true face.

But, no! Odan would not allow these thoughts to enter his heart. Once he had delivered Eresh over into her hands, Tia must—she must!—grant him the godhood he craved.

She must!

The lion hunt went well. The beasts fought and snapped as the arrows pierced their sides. But Odan's heart was not in the sport. Anyway, what of challenge was there in shooting arrows from a chariot into a mere desert lion to a Khuzuk who had stalked and slain the dagger-tooth lion afoot?

They trailed back to the city, with the slaves bringing in

the carcases of the lions, as the sun dipped swiftly to the horizon rim. The men of Eresh had left. A report was given Odan that the lord Ankidu wore the face of a skull as he went aboard his boat. Odan brooded. He watched as a fresh contingent of mercenaries sent down by Karkaniz disembarked. They were slingers from the Island of Dinos in The Salt Sea, eight Kisraens of them, near four hundred men. He watched them, small, copper-skinned men with curled hair and ragged teeth, with wide-lipped crafty smiles, their bags of sea-washed stones slung over their shoulders. When all their stones had been expended they would use leaden bullets. Odan looked at them, foreign, dark, vivacious men, and he thought of his archers of Eresh he had banished upriver.

He forced himself to dwell on the glorious prospects opening ahead of him—all those things he had dreamed of—godhood, Zenara, the golden glory that would be theirs. So why was there this leaden feeling? Why could he take no joy from food, from music, from the skirling dancing as the girls shed their veils in the banqueting hall of the palace of Dilpur?

Odan had had little truck with slaves. He had found young Inki, a bright-eyed imp who served him well enough, and who could be trusted to shave him and clean his clothes and polish his weapons. Inki had grown into the habit of always being near his master without being noticed. Well, all slaves developed that habit when they were chosen as body servants, of course, otherwise they went back to the fields or the pits; but Inki possessed a cunning sleight of hand that fitted Odan's mood. Slaves had been placed into the world by Ke and Creator, when he had fashioned the world, along with women and beasts and the crops of the fields and the birds of the air and the fishes of the seas. All, Ke had placed under the hand of man.

All the same, Odan felt some slight sense of relief when he could leave the banquet and retire to the chamber he had chosen for himself. A small suite of rooms, the apartment was the one Zenara had occupied when she stayed in Dilpur.

The sense of her nearness comforted him a little.

The sense of her nearness only in the walls she had seen, the tables she had touched, the bed in which she had slept.

Odan did not sleep well.

In dreams he felt he ought to receive some sign; but his dreams seldom vouchsafed the grandiose confrontations with the gods claimed by other mortals.

Certainly the cloak of well-wrought sealing the mages of Karkaniz, aided and abetted by the sorcerers of the cities freshly owing the sway of Tia, had cast over Dilpur would not halt a god. It would confuse the mages of Eresh. The sealing was powerful.

Odan fretted and tossed and turned on the bed. Old Master Asshurnax and Master Kidu—they must be trying to fathom out what was going on in Dilpur. Surely, they must have some idea by now that Odan, whom they had helped so powerfully, had turned against the city they loved?

Tia was using him. Yes, he could see that clearly enough. But he was using her. As a goddess her powers were aweful. But he was a Half-god. His powers were puny; but, all the same, he was making use of the powers of the goddess of love to further his own desires. And those desires would joy her heart, also, for she was Tia Nin-Apsish, the goddess of love.

It was no use. He could not sleep. Rising, he walked naked to the balcony and stood looking out over sleeping Dilpur. The stars formed a swarm of fireflies in the dark. Night scents rose from the gardens beneath, the tinkle of water soothed; but Odan stood there, tense and angry and resentful.

Was he not a Zuman, a wild primeval savage from the mountains and valleys of Zumer? Born a demigod and given into the hands of the king of Eresh as a son, he had known four babyish years of princedom. He was a Zuman, of the tribe of the Hekeu! Survival was the key to all life. He wanted Zenara. She wanted him. Then surely anything he did—*anything*—must be good in the sight of the shamans of the Hekeu? Anything to gain Zenara. Yes. His father—Odan En-Ke—would agree. He was an old god and, despite all, Odan still felt convinced that the old gods were real. The Raven, the disgusting wormwoman, and the devil Nirghal En-Theus, had both said the old gods were figments of primitive man's imaginations, created out of fear and awe and terror. But Odan was the son of a god. If not Odan En-Ke—then who? Not Nirghal. He stood on the balcony and in the cool of the night he sweated.

In the land of Ea there were many gods, each day saw
the celebration of the days of four or five gods. Were they
all mere shadows? Were only those gods who owned a
city, whose ziggurats rose to the sky rich with the smells of
sacrifices and incense, heavy with prayer, the real gods?
Odan knew of no city dedicated to Odan En-Ke.

There were many gods and many temples to the gods.

The gods fought, one against the other, for supremacy.
There were prophecies, stories. Once again, as he so often
did, Odan thought of the story of Abak . . . That gave
him hope.

He would do anything for his godhood and Zenara.

He would even destroy the city he loved.

He was, after all, at heart a primordial savage.

Odan blinked.

It was the middle of the night, when the sentries cried
one to another about the walls, and the city slept. And yet
a monstrous golden glow filled the sky and drenched his
eyes with light. He glared up with streaming eyes and saw
the radiance pulsing, high, sublime, a gigantic comet that
crossed the firmament and filled the heavens with fire.

The light swayed and swerved, swooped low toward
him.

He shut his eyes. He felt no heat, he heard no startled
cries, and so he knew that this chariot of fire appeared
only to him. A voice spoke, low, sweet, mellifluous—and
sharp with the tang of rotting fruit.

"Odan the Khuzuk—you have served me well."

Odan squeezed his eyes open. He stood upon the high
balcony in the palace of Dilpur and he looked upon the
divine form of Tia, the goddess of love, reclining in her
dream chariot, surrounded by naked girls, and all laughed
at him, mocking, deriding, contuming.

"My Lady?"

"You have taken Zemlya, and Sennapur, and Dilpur.
And now you would be prepared to take Eresh—in my
name."

"And?"

Her voice sharpened. "You are a mortal—oh, yes, there
may be somewhat of godhood in you. But do not
presume."

"I do not presume against the gods. I would be one of
them."

She laughed. The mocking tinkle chilled Odan, so that the sweat dried on him.

"You have served me well, so that I shall let you live—"

"Our bargain! Tia! My Lady! You promised—"

"I promised nothing. I release you from my service, for you are a hindrance to me now. Begone from Dilpur, lest worse befall you."

Sheer, blind, absolute panic hit Odan. Bewilderment engulfed him. He stammered. "I served you and you will make me a god! It is a compact! Would you be foresworn?"

"I have no need of you now. And guard your tongue."

"But—"

"Do you think a goddess would stoop to bandy words with a mortal—and a man at that? You mean nothing. Go and crawl with the beasts of the field for all I care."

The light pulsed, fading and growing.

"Is this the honor of the gods!" Odan burst out passionately. "You owe me, Tia! For all I have done—you cannot turn me out, like this—is there no honor among the gods?"

"There is honor such as you could never understand."

Odan could not understand what was happening. He stretched out a hand imploringly. "My Lady! Do not abandon me! Zenara—my Zenara—the goddess of love would listen to a lover's plea!"

"Forget your Zenara. Anyway, she is taken from you."

"What do you mean?"

"Zenara is taken away from Eresh—rogues, rascals, men who bear you and your father no good will. It means nothing. The girl was at best a simperingly pretty face."

Odan reeled.

He grasped the brickwork of the balcony, grinding it between his fists. He must fight. Survival. The Hekeu . . . *Zenara!*

"You need me to take Eresh. I am a prince of Eresh. You need me! You will find Zenara for me, help me rescue her—you need me, Tia Nin-Apsish! You need me!"

"I need no puny help of mortals. I do not follow the foolish prophecy. I held Eresh in the palm of my hand, Odan the Idiot." The light began to fade. Tia's voice lisped fainter and fainter. "For Zadan, the great god Zadan of the Sword, is thrown down, and his ziggurat in Eresh lies empty, waiting for me—waiting for me!"

The dream chariot faded and was gone.

Insanely, Odan shouted into the night sky.

"I curse you, Tia the Foresworn! Goddess of Hate! I curse you until the death of all the gods!"

Only emptiness and mocking hollowness answered him.

Odan staggered from the balcony. All his hopes had been blasted. He was ruined. But Zenara—Zenara! What had chanced? He struggled across the bed as though he waded through the marshes of the lower reaches of The River. His bronze sword in its scabbard lay there. He glared at the blade, owlishly, his head paining him, the agony knifing his heart. Zenara!

A noise in his bedchamber aroused him, and he turned to see General Jonnu, fully accoutred, march in at the head of six officers. They were all Ras, all commanders of regiments of Karkaniz.

"Prince Odan," said Jonnu, speaking in his clipped, nervous way. "It is my duty to—"

"You will stand aside, Jonnu. Or you and those with you will die."

Jonnu lifted his empty right hand. His face looked ill with a pain that Odan could not comprehend.

"I took my orders, prince. I thought you a boor, a mere savage. But I now know you to be a prince. You are to be arrested and chained—these are the orders from the priests of Tia, who have command in these things."

The six Ras remained silent. They did not draw their swords.

"Yet?"

"Yet I cannot ill-treat you. It may mean my head. But my commanders agree. We wish you well, prince. Now, go before it is beyond our strength to assist you."

Odan began to put on his robes and his armor and belt up his weapons about him. He dressed as a warrior of Ea dresses.

"I have been badly treated, general. Yet I misjudged you. I crave your pardon for that. I will take my life, that you give me, and I will pray Ke and Hekeu that your life is spared. As for what may follow—"

"Go swiftly, Odan the Half-god. May your gods go with you."

"I wish I could say and yours with you."

"I serve My Lady Tia. But there are things—the gods

are not to be understood by mortal men. How, then, to grasp a single inkling of a goddess?"

Odan went to the door, past the line of commanders, and looked out. He knew what they risked. Yet he did not make an attempt to throw a spell of protection over them, for the mages of Karkaniz would sniff it out directly. They could use their military wiles to deceive the priests, and perhaps the mages; he wished them well. He felt the wonder of these men's conduct. This was a thing difficult to understand. Would Tia understand?

The corridor was deserted. He stepped out and flinging his yellow cloak over his left arm, half-turned.

"May Ke go with you."

And Odan the Khuzuk went stealthily away from the high palace of the king in Dilpur.

Chapter Seventeen

In the Eighth Hell

Toward morning Ankidu lifted himself groaning from the hard uncomfortable bench on which he had spent the night and went out on deck. He knuckled his back, yawning, staring about as the stars paled and the sky flushed with the coming glory of Zamaz. The River flowed as sweetly as ever. He looked critically at the lines of slaves toiling at the oars, for the wind was dead foul and the broad rectangular sail lay furled slantwise across the deck. All speed, Odan had said. Well, Ankidu had kept the slaves working all night and if the wind did not veer soon he'd have to rest them, if he wished them ever to work again.

The sounds of water splashing, the whisper of the dawn breeze, the smells of The River all about, awoke a lighter feeling in him. Odan had been beyond himself at their victories. That was understandable. But Ankidu had felt deeply hurt that the prince had not stayed to wish him godspeed with Zadan—or any of the gods to which the savage Khuzuk owed—but instead had gone off into the desert on a lion hunt.

He yawned again and looked back at the following boat. Kufu was plainly visible on the raised aft deck, sniffing the morning air. Well, military habits died hard in old soldiers.

These boats were the clean-lined craft, slender through the water, designed for passage up as well as downriver. They would reach Sennapur, Ankidu supposed, and then on to Kheru and a brisk little dust-up with these foolish rebels. The cities in between would provide food and water. He yawned again and saw a vulture circling high in the air. Enidu, Ras of the crocarchers, came on deck, groaning and stretching. The vulture descended and perched on the boat's rail.

Ankidu looked surprised. Enidu grunted and, picking up a chunk of mud dried by the rail, went to shy it at the big bird.

Ankidu, mildly, said: "Isn't that bad luck, Enidu? Suppose some mage, or some god, inhabits the bird?"

Enidu guffawed, but he lowered the mud.

The vulture opened its beak. Its beady eyes looked about the deck, fastened upon a crocarcher snoring with his head shoved up against the side, his cloak swathing him, his mouth open. The vulture gave a kind of convulsive hop and the crocarcher opened his eyes and sat up. He turned to Ankidu.

"Ankidu!" said the crocarcher."You must—"

He said no more. With a ferocious roar Enidu bellowed.

"Oaf! Idiot! You do not address the lord thus! Stripes it is for you, my lad! A hundred at the least!"

The man's face struggled, as though he fought a battle in the quicksands of The River. "My Enidu—my Ankidu—I speak to you through this crocarcher's mouth. But I am Odan! Listen."

They gaped. Then Ankidu gasped: "The vulture! Odan sent a grifting with the bird. It is the prince—he speaks to us!"

"Aye, my Ankidu. Listen well, for I am tired and have much to do. We have been betrayed. The ruse of Kheru

was to get you and the men of Eresh away. The devils of
Karkaniz march on Eresh."

At this Ankidu took a step forward, his hand half jerk-
ing the sword from its scabbard.

"Aye, my Ankidu. You must turn about at once. Use
the wind to retrace your passage down The River. But
march through the desert around Dilpur, for the mages
would descry any attempt to pass directly. March back to
The River and take boats—get to Eresh as fast as you
can."

"Yes, my prince, yes!"

"Tell the king—throw yourself at his feet. Tell him I
was betrayed. We were ensorcelled. Tell him we give our
hearts and our swordarms for Eresh."

"I will, my prince. And you?"

But the crocarcher yawned and stood up clumsily and
looking up, saw his Ras and the lord staring at him as
though he sprouted horns.

"Go on, go on!" said Ankidu.

"My lord?"

"He is gone." Ras Enidu growled it out. "The prince has
returned to his body and left us with this husk of a man."

"Ras!"

Ankidu leaped for the helmsman. He kicked the skipper
of the boat, who lay wrapped in his grey cloak on the
deck. "Turn the boat about! Back downriver! Hurry!" He
shouted across to Kufu's boat, following. In a flurry of
breaking water and sprawling oars, the boats turned. The
sails were hoisted. As the sun broke free of the horizon
rim the small armada of boats spread their wings and hurried back, downriver, toward Eresh.

Coming back to his own body from that of the crocarcher, Odan whipped up his horses. He had breathed them
in the desert east of Dilpur, for he guessed chariot patrols
of Karkanizan soldiery would be securing the irrigations.
The dawn broke golden about him. He had judged his
place well, far enough away from the sorcerous sealings
clamping Dilpur, placed there by the mages from Karkaniz.

Only jumbled images, scarlet memories, black night-
mares, remained to him of the past night. Catastrophe had
overtaken him. All he could do was react as a Hekeu
would react. Self-reliance was taught by the shamans of

the Hekeu. Self-reliance and survival. He would win
through, and the goddess Tia might go and drown herself
in her carnal love, he would have no more truck with her.
The sunlight brought no lessening of his madness; but it
brought, as though symbolically, a clearer light to bear on
his problems.

First he must find Zenara.

Nothing else mattered for the moment.

If Ankidu convinced the king that Odan was not a traitor, all very fine. If not—the world of Khepru was wide.
They would find a place to live, Zenara and he, somewhere.

This was a problem. It was no different in essentials
from a problem he might have faced as a Zuman. The
quality of personal horror involved had unmanned him,
and an unmanned Zuman was a dead Zuman. If he was
hunting a dagger-tooth lion, as, after that first hekeu kill,
he had been forced to do on his perilous journey from Zumer to Ea, he would know how to go about it. Now he
sought the girl he loved. There must be tracks, spoor, signs
he could pick up. Sorcery? Most probably.

He would make one last attempt to seek the help of his
father. His contempt for this god who had sired him was
not so great that he was blinded by filial scorn. He did not
understand the ways of the gods. By Hekeu! That was
true.

He held the gods as beneath contempt. Twice he had
been tricked. That was twice too many for a Hekeu. But
he must open every gate in this search for Zenara. Perhaps, now, his father would answer .

Cunning entered the heart of Odan the Half-god. A new
cunning, wrought of Zenara's love. If the gods mocked
men, he would fail absolutely. But—if some gods mocked,
others might take pity on him. With the cunning of the
Hekeu reinforced by the sophisticated cunning of Ea,
Odan the Half-god made his decision.

In the midst of the desert, as the sun rose to burn and
scorch every living thing, Odan dismounted from his
chariot. He threw his yellow cloak back. His splendid head
thrust aggressively forward from his massive stooped
shoulders. He did not stare up challengingly into the sky.
He bowed that head of his, his shoulders stooped, he
bowed in deep obeisance and he called, called from the

agony of his heart, called to what there might be of ordinary mortal love in the heart of the god his father.

"Odan En-Ke! If you hear me, take pity on me now! You are a god and must know of my love for Zenara! This is a love denied me by the laws of men. And yet— and yet she is in peril, and I must save her! My father! Odan En-Ke! Hearken unto me!"

With bowed head and hunched shoulders, Odan waited.

A tiny wind ghosted across the desert. He could see the little sand grains blowing at his feet, in desiccating streams, reminding him of the fresh streaming becks of Zumer as they broke pouring through the rocky watercourses as the snows melted.

He did not lift his head. "Odan En-Ke! My father—my father the god who brought me into this land of Ea through Momi, my mother—hearken unto me! Help me now! I ask your help for Zenara, my love, Zenara, the daughter of Momi—help me now, I pray you, lord god my father!"

The wind spattered him with sand.

He looked up. The chariot horses tossed their heads, their bits and harness aflame in the sunshine. The chariot rolled as the horses turned their backs to the sand-laden wind. Odan half-closed his eyes. Damn the chariot! Where was his father, the god?

Willy-willies grew in the desert, running in erratic, gyrating circles. The sky turned yellow. He stood now in the center of a square formed of four tall columns of sand, whirling, rustling, tall swaying cylinders of yellow sand spinning and spinning at the four corners of the square.

The ground lurched.

The ground moved under his feet.

Now four more spinning columns of sand formed diagonally with the first four so that a ghostly star was marked out upon the floor of the desert. The wind screamed past above and sand stung his eyes, his lips, his cheeks. The ground swayed as though weighed in a goldsmith's balance.

Odan gasped. The ground fell away beneath him. The lip of a precipice in far Zumer, collapsing under him, could not have hurled him down more rapidly. Yet he retained his footing. He still stood, hunched, his hair blowing about his face from that unbleached linen fillet, his fists gripped onto his sword and dagger hilts, glaring up

with that leonine head thrust defiantly forward from his
stooped shoulders.

He did not cry out. He gave no sound of surprise or
alarm as the ground plunged away beneath his feet. The
yellow sky vanished. Yet still the sand-laden wind stung
him. He blinked his eyes, feeling the grittiness, and
clenched his teeth. Was he being dragged down into the
underworld to view the sights of hell viewed nightly by
Zamaz in his journey under the earth?

The plunging earth steadied. A bruised purple sky shone
with green runnel tints above him. Colossal ebon walls
shut in all sight to the left. And to the right—to the right
a lake of molten lava glowed and burned and shot sparks
of orange flame into the jetty night sky.

The stink of sulphur and pitch wrinkled his nostrils.
Like the outpourings of the volcano, Mount Wusuv, the
infernal stench and heat blasted at him. He flung his yellow cloak across his face and it was as though the strong
cloth did not exist. The supernal baleful fires burned and
glittered, the lake of molten lava burned unquenched.

He was slipping and sliding down a slope strewn with
volcanic detritus. The air scorched his lungs. He could
scarcely breathe. He plunged on down, almost falling,
flinging his arms wide to keep his balance. Almost to the
lip of the lake he tottered. Almost headlong into the lake
of fire he pitched headfirst. He staggered, gasping. A hole
in the ground snatched at his feet—the hole moved, scuttling across the black ground like a gigantic hungry spider.
Down the pitch blackness of the hole fell Odan, toppling,
spinning, helpless.

Down and down he fell. Heat blustered at him, forcing
his mouth open with a furnace blast. He struck an ebon
floor, and rolled, and struggled up, glaring about, baleful,
malignant, seeking some foeman at whom to strike with
keen bronze. His sword was in his hand. He did not
remember drawing.

"You will have no need of bronze here, my son."

He stood in a narrow cave of obsidian, glinting with
fire-reflections. The roof pressed down in jagged razor-
sharp protrusions. The floor bruised his feet. He looked
about, the bronze blade a bar of glittering gold in his fist.

"Who are you?" he called. And—"Where are you?"

A ruby glow grew against the wall. He saw as though

he looked through imperfectly blown glass, thick and clouded, red with mist.

For a few heartbeats he could not understand the scene he saw, like a tableau, etched within the confining rock.

A figure lay stretched upon a black basalt stone. A man—a man?—stretched and bound with chains. The chains glittered in the brooding light with a strange silvery-greyish sheen, unlike silver, unlike lead. The man lay face upward but Odan could not see his face. From a cleft in the rock above a drop of yellow fell. It dropped upon the face, and it flowed and as it flowed so it melted and fumed and scarred the flesh. Another drop followed, furrowing down the eyesockets, gouging past the nose, dripping fuming past the tortured lips.

But Odan scarcely saw the golden dripping torture drops.

The man's skull had been opened and an eagle darted its sharp beak within the cranial cavity and plucked savagely at the grey convolutions of the brain.

The man's abdomen had been opened and a vulture gripped his intestines and shook its predatory head from side to side, its sharp beak dragging out the guts, yard by yard.

Odan's eyes remained wide open. His heart did not falter. Other things were being done to this man stretched upon the black basalt altar, and Odan saw them all, and stored them up in his heart.

The man spoke.

"Put up your sword, my son. I have little time today before I shall be unable to speak to you."

"You will be dead within a half glass."

"Not so. Each day the eagle and the vulture and the dripping gold destroy me, and each morning I am born afresh to be destroyed again. Over and over."

Odan swallowed.

"You call me son. Are you Odan En-Ke?"

"No."

Rocks fell with a clatter at the side of the chamber, and a ruby glow pulsed through, turning everything to blood.

"Are you my father?"

"Yes."

Odan took a half step forward. The sword trembled. At last—at last he had found—and, like this, like this!

"Why are you chained up—tortured—are you not a god?"

"I am a god. As you are half a god. But when other great gods league against a single god, much may befall."

Now that he had—now that, at last, he saw his father—no it was happening—now—Odan felt so many words jumbled and constricted struggling to be uttered that he could say no word at all. He tried to speak, and the god his father said: "Let me speak, my son, and listen. For if you wish to save Zenara there is little time."

"I listen."

He had expected to vilify his father, to call him to account for treachery, and neglect, for all the wrongs done in Odan's lifetime. But the sight of this chained and tortured god wrought a profound unease within him, more than an unease, a grief, sharp and poignant, that came to betray him to himself.

"Then know my plans for you were thought of before you were born. I know of the prophecy that a god will father a mortal son upon a mortal woman, and through his agency will the god secure the supreme power in the pantheon. That was nothing to do with my plan. I love your mother Momi, as only a god may love. I wished her nothing but good. And, you, likewise, I wished only a long and happy life. I did not seek to make myself supreme at the cost of your sacrifice."

Odan believed.

The god continued, his voice husking a little as the eagle and the vulture twisted their beaks, avid, greedy, pulling.

"I love your mother Momi. I would not allow you or her to be harmed, and if the gods knew I had fathered a son, they would assume I had done so to fulfil the prophecy and you would be doomed. So I called myself Odan En-Ke."

'Nirghal fathered a son, Nirghi. That is known."

"Speak to me of Nirghal and you speak of a deadly enemy. He and Tia, between them, they have conspired with the other gods conquered by Tia, and have laid me low. Even Hoveuz could not gainsay their demands that I be forced into chains and confined here."

"Where is this frightful place?"

"This is the eighth hell, the hell below the seventh."

"So you are in hell, because Tia conquers along The River?"

"Yes—but do not blame yourself. You do not understand the ways of gods. Our ways confound the cloudy mind of mortal men—and yet in humanity is there much to instruct the gods."

Odan wanted to know so much, and he could not speak his thoughts, so jumbled and confused the clamor of his heart.

"Odan En-Ke—do the old gods really exist? Is there an Odan En-Ke? Did Ke really create the whole world?"

"I believe the old gods are real; but many deny them. As for Ke, someone created the world, for the gods I know found this world and took it for their own."

The eagle and the vulture tore and pulled. What agonies his father was enduring, endured every day, Odan could not comprehend. He spoke, sharply. "And will you make me a whole god?"

"A god like me?"

"You will not stay here forever."

"Why not?"

Odan did not know why not—not then.

"I will tell you where Zenara is held. It is a place beset with peril. The people hold sway there."

"I have had dealings with the wormpeople. Tell me, father, tell me. But first, I beg of you, make me a god and I will save Eresh and drive the army of Tia back and thus you will be released from hell."

"Would you not do all that, for your father, out of love? Would you do all that only as a reward to me for making you a god?"

Odan did not hesitate.

"Make me a god and I will help to release you from hell."

The vulture and the eagle were tearing this god to pieces; his voice husked, softer, fainter. His agony was repeated each day.

"I will not make you a god."

"You fool! You torture yourself."

"I loved your mother Momi for her sake alone. I did not plan to become the supreme god. I may do so one day, not now. Because you are my son, and the devil Nirghal discovered this when I succored you against him, they believe I try to make the prophecy come true. But I will not make myself supreme and I will not make you a god."

"Even to escape from hell?"

"Even that."

"The story of Abak——"

"Is a pretty story."

"You, who say you are my father! How do I know? Tell me where Zenara is——"

Even as he spoke so a location in the desert, a name, a sign, formed in Odan's thoughts, so that he knew.

"I give you thanks, my father! You may stay in hell, for you have been unknown to me all my life. I see you are chained not with bronze, but with Zadan's metal. Truly, you must be powerful among the gods, to be thus chained and brought low!"

No cry escaped the chained, tortured god. He tried to turn his head, and the eagle dragged viciously back. Odan took a step back, involuntarily.

"Odan—for that is your name now, my son. Odan—will you for my sake save Eresh?"

"Your sake?"

"I am chained with Zadan's metal."

Odan saw. It was not difficult. He should have understood before. It made little difference, so he thought then, blinded by grief and urgency and desperate fear for Zenara.

"Let me go back to the desert, to the land of Ea, Zadan my father, Zadan of the Sword, Zadan the All Glorious! For you are chained in hell and I must be about my business."

"And will you not be about your father's business?"

"If my father remembers me and makes me a god."

"That I will not do."

"Then release me from this hell!"

Zadan of the Sword moved against the dripping molten gold that ate away his face, moved against the eagle that pulled out his brains, moved against the vulture that drew forth his intestines. He moved against all the other things that were done to him, day after day. He lifted a fingerless hand and he said, in a voice that grated like Zadan's metal itself: "Go back to the land of Ea between the Two Seas, Odan my son! Go back and do what you must do. There will come a day when your eyes shall be opened—now, for the sake of Momi whom I love and her daughter, Zenara—go!"

Chapter Eighteen

Into the Caverns
of the Worms

Littly placed the beautiful mask upon a side table out of reach of the scented steam that rose from the wide bath of warmed water. The mask had been cunningly fashioned by Master Bitori of the ivory workers, with help from his confreres the potters, the weavers, the silversmiths, and animated by a deeply sorcerous spell cast by Kidu. The mask concealed the leprously hideous face of Littly when visitors called. Now she stepped into the bath, all her lithe voluptuous body naked and receptive to the warmed scented water. The green and jowly monstrosity between her shoulders, with its scarlet eyes and jagged fangs,, its warty lumps and excrescences, had become a burden to which she was almost reconciled.

She sat up, the water running down her body. She put her slender hands on the bath sides, and stood up. Her body gleamed with the perfumed water. Then she stepped out of the bath and walked steadily into the passageway and so through the eyrie in the Tower of Relicts into the mysterious chamber of Master Kidu.

Kidu looked up from the incredibly ancient baked clay tablet filled with the small precise lines of writing used by the wormpeople.

"Littly? You will catch cold—" Kidu felt a start of surprise, as he always did, at the beauty of that body and the sordid hideousness of the head and face.

"Kidu," said Littly, and Master Kidu bristled. He

151

started to speak sharply to the naked girl, to remind her that he was the master, and she the servant girl.

"Kidu—I need your help! I have been wronged! Zenara has been taken away and I need occult help to free her."

"Odan?" said Kidu. His mournful face hardened. "Odan! Ingrate! What do you require of me, traitor?"

"I can help Eresh beat back the forces of Karkaniz. But first I must rescue Zenara. I am going to the Cave of Jewelled Sleep. The sign is Yrn. Yrn. Support me, Kidu, I beg you—"

"Odan—you requite the city of your birth in foul fashion! Odan En-Ke the god your father entrusted you to—"

"My father is Zadan of the Sword. I know that now. Help me, Kidu—help me—"

Littly said: "Oh!" She turned, her naked body still steaming, running water, and ran from the master's chamber.

Kidu was left, drumming his knuckles upon the table, torn between wonder, fears for the safety of Eresh, and a desire to send a particular nasty grifting to cause young Odan a peck of discomfort.

The sandstorm snatched Odan up as though he whirled helplessly in a boiling pool of bronze.

Circling horizontal streamers of wind-driven sand spun about him. He flung the yellow chariot scarf about his mouth and nostrils, gasping for air, feeling the gritty sand grains chafing at his skin, his eyes, clogging his nostrils. He spat. He stuck that arrogant head of his down and slogged on, pumping his feet into the yielding wind-blown sand—and his feet struck nothing solid.

He yelled. He felt the whirling sand devils snatch him up, carry him into the air, blown around and around so that the blood roared in his head.

"By Hekeu! The gods have a hand in this!"

Around and around, up and up. The yellow murk about him whirled faster and faster, bearing him up.

He saw streaks and veils of yellowish blue appearing within the swirling horizontal lines of sand. He could see a little. He was enclosed in a funnel of air within the enormous whirling column of sand.

There seemed to him more than mere sorcery to this. High he was carried, high and higher. All below spread the desert. The whirling column of sand raising a long

streaming wake of lifted and pummelled dust and sand
trailed away to the south. Over The River shot the sand,
boiling the water into a yellow and white maelstrom. No
boats traversed the riverine highway; the damn'd war had
halted traffic and the merchants of The River chewed their
fingernails and their beards and mumbled of ruined con-
signments and lost profits, and sacrificed to the gods.

South and south, swinging to the east. Soon the shores
of The Sweet Sea rose into view over the horizon, and
greeness took the place of the everlasting desert.

Down to the ground the sandstorm stretched, its towering column tottering and thinning. As good rich earth with
the green growing vegetation halted the onward march of
the sand so the column out of the desert dwindled and
shrank and collapsed.

Odan pitched onto the ground, rolling over and over to
fetch up in a bush from which he emerged, cursing, shaking himself to rid his hide of the sharp spines.

He checked his weaponry with the unthinking profes-
sionalism of a warrior of the land of Ea or a Hekeu of
Zumer.

The magical wonder of this sudden transportation
through the air meant nothing to him. Aflame with the
desire to find Zenara, tortured by thoughts of what she
must be going through, obsessed with his love for her, he
knew his father must have a hand in what had just happened. Zadan must! Nothing else made sense—unless—
and at the traitorous thought he felt a cold chill of horror.
Unless those who leagued against him had thus forced up
divine or sorcerous help and banished him to the shores of
The Sweet Sea—driven him like a stupid sheep out of
what was going on, what really mattered, in the land of
Ea.

Zadan his father had retained power enough to summon
his son to his presence. Did he have the power to hurl his
son miles through the air, caught up in a whirling sandstorm?

Fervently, Odan believed he had.

Returned from the hell beneath the seventh hell to the
desert, he had chased after his chariot, just managing in a
wild leap and snatch to grasp the sheaf of spears in the
right-hand scabbard strapped to the side of the car. The
spears had come loose and Odan had pitched backwards,

tumbled into the dust, tangled in his cloak. Then the sand-storm had whirled him aloft.

He stood, glaring about, head jutting. Grass covered a sloping meadow slanting down to a stand of trees. In the blue distance hills lifted and he thought he could glimpse the white gleam of houses, huddled into a tiny town in a cleft between two hills. He looked about. The Cave of Jewelled Sleep, his father had said, placing the words into his heart. Where, here near the coast of The Sweet Sea, was that cave to be found?

In those few brief moments in which he'd sent a grifting to speak through the hideous mouth of Littly he had seen clearly that Master Kidu had not received his plea kindly. Not kindly at all. He must put out of his thoughts any idea that Kidu or Asshurnax would help him. He hoped they would. He would more than welcome their aid. But he must assume they would not assist him.

The lifted sand strewn by the sandstorm, whipped up in so divine a fashion, lay like a long finger across the grass. Odan stared at it. Like a pointing finger . . .

At once he started to run across the meadow, pacing the long straggle of yellow sand.

A dark hole in a low, bush-crowned back, seemed to him the most likely spot. The last few yellow sandgrains lay scattered a half-dozen paces from the entrance to the hole. Odan approached. A smell whiffed from the opening, a smell he could only identify with rotting meat, charnel houses, the dankness of fungi-infested bat caves. With a long last breath of the clean fresh air, Odan the Khuzuk ducked into the hole. Dank earth fell about his hunched shoulders, pattered against his hair. Ahead, a long way ahead, gleamed a milky-green light.

A quick and furtive rustle, the flash of teeth and eyes, the lumbering rush of small excited bodies, caused Odan's right hand to snap up, the poised and deadly spear ready. He considered a moment. Then he rejected his idea. These small subterranean animals could not harm him and if he injected his ka into one of them and explored ahead; he felt absolutely certain the presences ahead—whoever they might be—would sense the sorcery instantly. He preferred to wait and see what sorcery might be used, reserving that until after he had hurled his spears. For a half-god that was proper procedure, although for a normal mage the result might be death.

He moved on, keeping away from contact with the crumbling walls. If Zenara was here, chained up, imprisoned, caged, he would free her. He would not consider that she might not be here.

He well-realized this might be a trap.

He didn't care if it was a trap.

For Odan the Half-god the trap in this cruel world of Khepru was wherever in this world he might be without Zenara.

The milky-green light brightened. A strange noise—a weird nose—echoed up the earthen tunnel. The sound was like the sucking slopping the spades of the ditch workers made as they cleared out the irrigations. Odan prowled on, his left hand grasping the sheaf of spears, his right poised.

He was a Half-god, the son of a god and a mortal woman. He was not immortal. He possessed no magical sword, no ensorcelled weapon. He was only half a god. But he did possess some little resistance to sorcery, a resistance that would work the instant a mage hurled a spell at him, however much the power he held might wane and attenuate as the sorcerers grew to understand his limitations and so to enwrap him in their higher thaumaturgy.

He was more of a man than a god. He trusted to his mortal weapons of bronze as a good Hekeu would do—and, in the end, trusted more to the primeval weapons with which he had been born.

And, he had come to distrust and contume the gods.

The light broadened about him, washing over him with a leprous tint, turning his face into a hideous semblance of Littly's ghastly countenance.

He stepped into an earthen cavern, and halted. He stood, rooted, repelled and disgusted, and gruesomely fascinated.

All around the walls the light glowed and rippled from interlinked strands of gems. The gems formed loops and nets of color, green and blue and indigo, milky white and vomit yellow, and he could not be sure if they were jewels or if they were merely mineral deposits secreted upon the wide-spun webs. In each net-like web, cradled, hanging, hung the body of a man or a woman. Stark naked, they were, and they were being eaten.

The worms slobbered.

Odan had met the worms conjured by the gramarye of

the Raven. But these worms were real. He sensed that with
the god half of him that would not be deceived.

The bloated forms fed. White they were, wrinkled and
moist, and the reflected colors ran in transparent rainbows
across their fat bodies. Pincers ripped and tore at the
hanging meat. Large, these worms, fat and juicy, eating,
and as Odan stood on the threshold so first one and then
another left off their slobbering sucking and turned their
black beady eyes upon him. He saw their numbers, and he
knew he did not have spears enough for them all.

At the far end of the earthen chamber an opening
matched the one in which Odan stood, poised, his spears
at the ready, feeling nausea and, also—dare he believe
this?—an eerie levity, a kind of black giggling that wished
to take over his responses. Repulsive, the worms. Evil, horrible, ghastly—and yet, as they left off feeding and with
their beady black eyes fixed on him began to wriggle
across the damp earth floor, were they not ludicrous? Pathetic? Left over abominations from an older, darker,
best-forgotten time?

The dank earth ceiling pressed in on him, the dark
crumbly mass leavened and illuminated by the scattered
blaze of embedded jewels. The walls extended around him,
loaded with their bloody freight. And the worms wriggled
and writhed toward him. Ichor dripped from their sharp
pincers. Their beady eyes leeched on him, hungrily, yearning, seeing him already as fresh juicy food for their
ravenous mouths.

Ludicrous and pathetic, they might be, cast into the
present day from the black womb of time—but they were
dangerous and deadly and would kill and devour him just
as a wolfpack would kill and devour him if he gave them
half a chance.

The heavy spear in his right hand slapped into the sheaf
in his left. His bronze sword came out with the blood-stir-
ring shirr of sharp metal. A glint of light struck the bronze
blade, glittering like a star.

Steadily, Odan the Khuzuk advanced into the undulating mass of worms. Steadily, Odan the Half-god walked
toward the far opening. As he went so his bronze blade
choked and ran thick with the grue of worms.

An aroma so fierce, so vile, so gut-wrenching, stank in
the close air of the earthen cavern so that all the Khuzuk's

wild senses arose, and he fought to keep himself from
vomiting.

This was no phantasm conjured by sorcery. These
worms were real. No sense of power, no phantasm of primordial strength powering his arm, came to reduce Odan
to smallness. He was here to take Zenara away from these
scenes of horror. This he would do, or his own bones
would moulder and rot here, forever.

The far opening reached, he turned for a final severing
slash, and the worm, hissing, fell away. These worms
feeding here must be a guard. On through the tunnel
prowled Odan, shaking drops from his sword, ready to
face what fresh dangers and terrors surely lay ahead.

The whole hill was honeycombed with passageways.
Chambers hanging with more carcases met his stony gaze.
He saw the bloated flesh of men and women and knew
that within their tortured bodies the eggs of worms grew
and ate and fattened. If he lived, if he regained the sanity
of the outer air, if he continued his life in the land between the Two Seas, he would return to this pestilential
place and destroy completely all trace of the worms who
fed upon humans and planted their eggs in the live bodies
of men and women.

He brushed through a hanging spider-worked web,
feeling the strands vibrating as spiders ran. He crushed a
half-dozen and then walked on. The passageway curved,
the damp rich earth walls glowing with gems. He felt the
familiar tingle along his limbs, and he knew they—
whoever they might be at the inner recesses of the labyrinth—had at last sensed his presence and were practicing
their black arts of thaumaturgy upon him. He must
hurry. His demigodhood conferred some immunity to sorcery. But he remembered with anger how the Raven had
halted him with a spell of paralysis. He was stronger, now,
more cunning in gramarye—but he doubted his powers
were yet sufficient to withstand all the ancient wisdom
hurled at him in an onslaught by one of the wormpeople.

A savage Zuman kept himself oriented. Odan had no
need to attempt any mechanical remembrance of each
runnel and passage; the very marrow of his bones would
tell him the way back, as the savages of the Zumer hills
tracked their paths across the mountains and valleys, as he
had followed the high runnels of the sky borne here in a
whirlwind of sand.

The impalpable feeling of evil, pressing in, encompassed him. Omnipresent forces of an ancient darkness, curtailed with the debris of time, hemmed in this place. Odan walked through caverns of horror, passageways leading on to terror, down earthy runnels where his sword-hand gripped more fixedly about the hilt of the bronze blade.

When the loose dirt beneath his feet appeared to shift and lurch and move, Odan fought the enchantment, summoning up not only his god-given innate strengths of resistance but the hard-won lore culled from the baked clay tablets in the musty library of Asshurnax's eyrie on Yellow Lotus Street. He fought. He ploughed on, shoulders hunched, head straining up, his eyes glaring with that fey murderous stare. He would not be denied. Zenara was prisoner here. Odan the Khuzuk battled on as though he strode against the very flood waters of The River itself.

The lights slanted their green and blue brilliances across the crumbling earth. Vertigo sought to claw him down. How had Zenara resisted the devil-driven witcheries of this place? They would not have used her as food or for breeding—the hard, jagged, impossible thoughts had to be faced. Odan must face them and conquer them. The goddess Tia had said men who bore him and his father no good will had taken her away, and that meant she was a political prisoner confined here and not held for meat or breeding.

It meant also that the wizards who had called forth this blasphemy were in league with the wormpeople to a degree completely unknown to ordinary mortals. As he forced his way on so Odan forced all feelings other than obsession for Zenara from his heart. Force, will-power, self-reliance—if ever he needed the cruelly learned lessons of the Hekeu in his life, he needed them now.

Chapter Nineteen

A Hekeu Fights for Zenara

Master Ubonidas bowed with great obsequiousness, ushering in the lord Gabal-ayin, dismissing the ghostly servitor, fussing. The ghostly servitor vanished with a clank and the slaves who had carried Gabal's great carven traveling-chair here ran from the sorcerous chamber with the utmost alacrity and relief. Not one of them relished this visiting of their lord and master, for the Abode of the Bats had gathered about itself a dark and sinister reputation, a notoriety of terror.

Gabal turned his shrunken face and fierce impatient eyes upon the scarlet curtain. He spoke in that rat-wheeze of his that drove shivers of apprehension up the spine of Ubonidas, for all that Master Ubonidas was a famed mage, and feared.

"And the princess is safely mewed up? The witch, Amenti—she has fulfilled her great promises?"

"Yes, indeed, lord. The princess is safe. But—"

Gabal scowled. "But?"

Ubonidas placed both his hands together, and pressed, and conjured a swift spell of the dispellment of anger and the softer protections, and said: "The prince Odan seeks to free her."

The spells must have worked, for the expected explosion did not burst like the flood along The River. Gabal lifted the thin gilt-bronze dagger, and toyed with it, and a small smile flitted across his face. "The prince Odan? The wild Khuzuk? Then the witch will have her pleasure."

"Oh, yes, lord. Amenti has the command of great powers."

"If you admit that, Ubonidas, then I believe she has."

"The princess is safely held in an inner chamber of the Cave of Jewelled Sleep. Amenti has a grifting watching—"

"Let me see the witch!"

Like some scuttling spider, Ubonidas clawed at the scarlet curtain, drawing it back to reveal the recess beyond.

Upon a bier of black pleated cloth the form of Amenti glowed like pearl. Her red hair coiled about her shoulders. Her eyes were open, a blazing blue in the lights from the tapers burning at the four corners of the bier. Her breast rose and fell evenly; but both men knew her ka was not here, in the eyrie of the Abode of the Bats.

Abruptly the witch's face contorted. For a frightful moment the face of a demoness glared through those perfect features. In the next instant Amenti sat up and once more her face showed a lily-like white purity. But she scowled ferociously, and her hand went to her full red lower lip, to pull it down fretfully.

"The mage Kidu—and the old dodderer Asshurnax! They attempt to interfere! Ubonidas—I need your help." She saw the lord Gabal and her chin went up and her hand dropped away from her mouth. "My lord! Your friends, the wizards Chaimbal and Sebek-ghal refused you their assistance. It might have gone better had they chosen to help."

Wrath flared along the wrinkled brows of Gabal.

"Do you tell me you cannot prevail? That you will fail?"

"Prevail, fail! What do they mean in the higher sorceries? My arts show me the truth, and this Odan, this wild Khuzuk, possesses powers he is not aware of. That is always the way. A big, lumbering, male-ox, and brains not fit for a sheep. Yes, lord Gabal-ayin. The Sapphire and her gramarye must needs use cold bronze to defeat this wild man from the mountains of Zumer."

"Then let bronze be used!"

With deep malicious viciousness, Amenti said: "Do not forget, lord, this Khuzuk is the son of a god."

"I do not forget." Gabal-ayin returned all the viciousness, all the spite. "He is also the son of a mortal woman, who should have been strangled long ago. He can be slain by bronze, and if your spells are not powerful enough, I will find a wizard or a witch whose spells may wreak the final damage I require."

Amenti lay back on the black bier, and the tapers threw long shadows across her white flesh. She closed her eyes.

"Odan is a mere man, only a demigod, and for all the powers he has and does not wot of, he can be slain, by sorcery or by bronze." Her breast rose and fell with a quick, spasmodic inhalation of breath. Her hands clenched at her sides. "The Sapphire—she is concerned—the powers approach—the wormpeople are ancient and proud and take heed of humans only when it suits the needs of the worms. The event may not turn out quite as you visualized, Lord Gabal-ayin . . ."

"It does seem to me, Master Kidu, that we are being altogether too lenient with young Odan. He has been ungrateful, traitorous, a very young Terror of the Souks all over again—"

"And, Asshurnax, have you then lost faith in the Khuzuk?"

Old Asshurnax humphed and grumped around, twisting in the massive carven chair. "No, old friend, I do not think I have—not quite. Anyway, even if I had, I think I would joy in this struggle against Ubonidas and the witch Amenti. I think this will be my last great fight, and then I shall be happy to be carried away, secure in the dream chariot of Kurd the Unmentionable."

The young mage sitting upright in the third chair leaned a little forward, his sharp jaw outthrust, his dark eyes hot upon old Asshurnax. He wore ceremonial robes, as did they all; but the robes of this Master Zehutinax were of an altogether more austere cut. Plain, dignified, exuding an aura of competent occult power, robes and mage added a new and vital note to the old eyrie in the Tower of Relicts of King Neb-ayin-Ke's palace in proud Eresh.

"You wound me, my master, in speaking this," said Zehutinax. "Since I was your famulus I have traveled the land of Ea—aye, and further!—and nowhere have I found a mage or a man I hold in higher esteem." Here Zehutinax shot a quick bright look at Master Kidu, who nodded, understanding. "Therefore, I beg you, do not speak in this vein. We have this Ubonidas and the witch to defeat only on behalf of Prince Odan. This, we shall do. But we have the mages of Karkaniz and the welfare of our city always before us—"

The mage in the fourth chair, Dorhutinax, coughed and

wiped his mouth on a cloth and, somewhat surly, said: "This is work of extreme fatigue and extraordinary travail, for which we are paid nothing, for we cannot charge the king fees. You are the court wizard, Master Kidu, and rightfully the task is yours." Dorhutinax, in his usual huffy way, would have gone on expounding the reasons why he should have been selected by the king as court wizard, but old Asshurnax interrupted, somewhat crossly for the old fellow.

"Oh, come now, Master Dorhutinax! Eresh is our city. The king needs our help—and Master Kidu has always treated us fairly. If the rumors of Zadan the All-Glorious are true—"

"They have extended downriver," said the young Zehutinax. "I was in Zhorzuppak. I went to their temple of Zadan, as is my custom in a foreign city, and there I heard. I returned to my own city at once—"

Kidu leaned forward. "We shall have need of your carpet very soon, Master Zehutinax. I shall make very sure the king hears and understands. Your return is most welcome."

"All young apprentices dream of traveling The River as mages," said Zehutinax. "I would not have missed it. But to return home—there is the real experience."

"Even when the city is in such a plight." Kidu stiffened and the others, catching the aura from him, fell silent and linked into a super-ka to face the next onslaught.

The four mages of Eresh, linked, immobile but vitally alive and alert, sitting like mummies in the flesh, sent their combined ka out in a powerful grifting. The wizards of Karkaniz would feel the heavy occult hand of the wizards of Eresh. And, too, Master Ubonidas and the witch Amenti would not escape the telling aura of the mages of Eresh.

The bronze sword slashed away a hanging net of spiderwebs. The clinging stuff shredded and fell away and Odan the Khuzuk stepped through into a wide, low-ceiled chamber. All around him extended the moisture-oozing black earth walls, their loamy surfaces brilliantly lit in the glare from the massed jewels. Truly, this was indeed a Cave of Jewels—and the Sleep part of the name became apparent as Odan stared at the serried ranks of piled bodies.

Not all were human. Many beasts lay there, also, piled

up in frozen death awaiting use. He looked in a way that
revealed his repugnance. Zenara, he knew—he knew!—
would not be here. She had been taken for a purpose beyond that of mere food.

Odan prowled on. A second vast cavern opened from
the first, containing more bodies. If they were truly dead
or merely slumbered, as the name of this place suggested,
Odan could not know. The smell of a charnel house clung
everywhere; but he was accustomed to it now, and ignored
it.

The third cavern revealed heaps of skeletons, man and
beast, piled up in a wild grotesquerie of scattered and
heaped bones. A mess of small worms squirmed in and
out of the hollow eye sockets of skulls, and wriggled
through gappy jaws. Stomping in squashy filth where he
must, slicing with the sword when necessary, Odan forged
on across this chamber, leaning forward even more as
though physically leaning into the steady psychic wind that
sought to hold him back from his goal.

An arch of craggy stone framed the far opening. Odan
paused. In all this labyrinth of damp earth, stone must
mean he entered a place of importance. He took a breath,
hardly aware of the stench, and pressed on, the bronze
blade ready.

Inside the stone-framed opening a cavern vaster than
those through which he had so far passed opened out, the
jewel glitter dimming in the overreaching roof from which
moisture dropped in long streaks of glitter. The floor
puddled. Odan moved on warily. He heard the scuffling
sounds, moving up from the shadows beyond a large central black pillar, long before the dwarfs burst into sight.

The worms used the kaleidoscopic refractions of color
shimmering over their bodies to conjure their magics.
They had, perforce, in their armless and handless state, to
use beasts with those appendages to perform menial tasks.
Now they launched these hairy dwarfs at him. Clad in
stained leather aprons, with large, pale, bearded faces, the
dwarfs bounded screeching from the shadows below the
gems, howling in sorcerous glee, goaded on by the malice
of their worm mistress.

Odan knew that the wormwoman was aware of him,
had been sending spells to destroy him, and had now
reacted by flinging this force of spear-armed dwarfs at
him.

He bellowed a great mocking laugh.

"Wormwoman! You admit failure! You cannot destroy me with your puny spells—now these midgets for all their hair and their spears will die—as you will die!"

Only a faint and distant hissing answered him.

Odan the Khuzuk laughed as he prepared for battle; but the laugh was a laugh that would have chilled the blood in any normal mortal. It was a laugh that a Hekeu might utter as he plunged his blade into the throat of a Dragon.

Creatures of the underworld, these dwarfs. Troglodytes, possessing two eyes, to be sure; but stunted, malign, vicious, deformed creations doomed to the runnels of eternal night, vouchsafed light only by the glitter of the gems studding their earthen mines.

Beyond the massy black pillar lofting from floor to the distant roof the troglodytes halted. Odan circled warily. He saw what the pale-faced dwarfs were up to. One stepped forward and with a powerful muscular heave sent his spear hurtling. Odan moved just enough and the spear flew past. Another followed. Odan bared his teeth.

With a crisp snap the bronze sword slapped back into the scabbard. The sheaf of spears in his left hand, held by the strap that bound them securely, would take enough dwarfs out for him to get to close quarters. And, truth to tell, the wild Khuzuk felt the relief of hurling spears. This was a sport practiced in earnest by the Hekeu, this hurling of spears at one another. The spears might be pointless and padded; but one driven into the ribs with a thump from a muscular Hekeu arm would teach a young cub to dodge the flung spear and to hurl his own in accurate reply. Now the spears darted at him with their keen bronze points ready to suck his blood. Odan braced and hurled, dodged and ducked, swirled another spear out and threw.

Two dwarfs screeched, their bodies burst through, the bloodied bronze protruding. Odan bent, and straightening with a snap, threw again. He ran forward, hurling spears one after the other. He had four left, when a change passed over the scene.

He saw the dwarfs facing him alter in appearance. One moment they were prancing and shrilling, hurling spears, filled with rage, but dwarfs still. The next—and Odan stopped. He felt the tremble along his legs and arms, the thrilling pain in his head. The dwarfs' skins grew a mass of brown warty escrescences. From the overlapping mass of warts disfiguring the skin long black hairs grew. Odan saw the hands of the dwarfs, lifted, the backs of the left hands towards him. He saw the back of each left hand as one huge wart, brown and wrinkled, festooned with black hairs. He saw—he saw a man in slaver's leathers, with a spear, hurling the spear, saw the spear piercing the undefended side of Nadjul the Quick. Odan saw—he saw the left hand of the slaver, saw the brown wart, saw and remembered.

Odan the Half-god shrieked in remembered pain.

This was an hallucination spelled on him by the wormwoman, a superior sorcery at last breaking down his barriers, tearing aside his god-given resistance. From now on he could expect little aid from the half of him that was a god.

With a great cry Odan hurled his spear. The keen bronze head smashed through the wart-covered body of the dwarf, spun him about, destroyed him. He fell, shrieking, and as he fell so the warts vanished and he was once more a vicious little troglodyte, malignant and evil, dominated by the wormwoman, but only that and not a thing of warts that dredged up the deepest experience of pain.

The wormwoman had looked into his heart and had culled the thing he feared most and so had unleashed that horror at him. His love for Nadjul the Quick, so brief a time and yet so rich and intense in his life, had been turned against him.

"By Ke and Hekeu!" panted Odan. "Nadjul the Quick will never stand between me and Zenara!"

Again the spears flew, bright glints of bronze gold in the cold glitter of the jewels.

The use of Balniodor's Invisibility would not aid him now for the wormwoman would see him through that spell. To allow his ka to leave his body would be fatal. He forged on, walking as though among snakes, and now he could hurl his last spear and burst in a smother of blood into the rib cage of a dwarf. Now he could draw his sword and with all the skill taught him by Nadjul the Quick could snick and slice, cut and hack, and so force his way on.

The dwarfs screeched and fell back, and now there were fewer of them than there had been, and now they were running and he could flick the blood drops from his blade, and stare about, his powerful face fierce and arrogant, jutting from between his stooped shoulders.

A voice hissed from the empty jewel-brightened air.

"Be very sure, Odan the Half-god, that you are a doomed man!"

"Oh, I am doomed, wormwoman! But not by you!"

And another voice, a distant and yet reverberant voice, echoing emptily in the corpse-littered chamber.

"Strike the black pillar, Odan the Khuzuk!"

"Kidu!"

"Strike as you value your life."

Odan strode for the black pillar. Dark, massy, awe-inspiring, the blackness reflected no light from polished surface, but absorbed light, taking in the substance of the gems and giving forth in return only coldness and the musky stink of fear.

Odan lifted the bronze blade and struck the pillar.

Instantly it collapsed into a spreading shower of black bats, leathery wings fluttering madly, a wild bluster of wings and jaws and bright glittering eyes.

And—on a basalt rock revealed by the whirling dispersal of the bats—Zenara!

Zenara!

Clad in a filmy white gown, her hands crossed upon her breast, she lay with her pale brown hair unbound and loose, her eyes closed. Her face struck a shock through Odan. Pale, that face, white as a white rose, pale and wan and frightening.

He bent and took her up. She weighed passing little. He turned, looking for any movement within the chamber. Only dead dwarfs and a last few panic-stricken bats fluttering madly up into the high shadows of the earthen roof met the cool methodical stare. Now, now more than ever, he must use all his professional skill as a fighting man and all the wild savagery of his primeval upbringing as a savage of Zumer. For now he held the princess Zenara cradled to his breast, and for her everything mattered and without her the world of Khepru might totter and fall and slide into the encompassing oceans.

A faint voice, shirring like a fingernail on glass, reached him over the last panicky flutter of the bats.

"Take care, Odan—we cannot see, cannot guide you—but there is a great evil here—a wrongness—we are blind and Karkaniz presses and the witch Amenti is strong—strong—"

The voice faded. Only a lingering hiss hung in the

high-vaulted chamber, one with the shadows and the bats.

Odan did not waste time trying to see from what manner of animal the grifting from Kidu was spoken—probably one of the bats—but a swift understanding of the occult power being exerted from far Eresh touched his heart. So his appeal had been answered! He felt renewed strength. With the slight limp form of Zenara in his arms he pressed back through the damp earth caverns and the labyrinth of gem-illuminated tunnels.

Of course there was a great wrongness here. These dank runnels and their loathsome freight of worms belonged back in the womb of time. Their continued existence on the earth affronted Odan, and all his instincts of revulsion and aversion were aroused by the blight in the world of Khepru. He held Zenara tenderly, and looked this way and that with the fey arrogant stare of madness, and pressed on and he resolved he would return here and cleanse this filth from the land.

No guiding lamp hung unsupported in the air before him, leading him into the outside world. But his savage sense of survival and his primitive instincts for directions led him unerringly back the way he had come to the exit. The bones crunched underfoot. Small worms squirmed away. The hanging carcases stank and rotted away. He felt sure the eggs within many of the bodies had hatched and the worms were steadily eating their way out. Ignoring the fetid evil of the subterranean labyrinth Odan made swiftly for the clean outside air.

He had to stop and put Zenara down tenderly and take his sword into a quick and brutal action only twice. The first time he slew five dwarfs before the rest, emitting high shrieking shrills of fear that overcame their worm-driven ardor, ran off, caterwauling, bloody, shattered. The other occasion he had to slice a group of worms who squirmed toward him, shooting foul liquids from their proboscises, a drenching stinking liquid that filled the lower earthen passage with a miasma, green and putrid, and which persisted as an obnoxious effluvium. He scooped Zenara up again, seeing with concern the pallor of her face. He ran for the exit, brushing through clinging spiderwebs, dodging flung spears, feeling the lingering tingling of gramarye working on him, insidiously.

The wormwoman had so far failed to entrap him with her sorceries, and her dwarfs and her worms could not

stop him. He knew he would escape, he knew he would
step out into the fresh air and the sunlight holding the still
form of Zenara in his arms. He knew it. All the worms in
the land of Ea would not stop him now.

A long faint hissing followed him down the last gem-glit-
tering runnel. Dampness stained the walls. The earth
crumbled beneath his feet. But no thaumaturgical art practiced by the wormwoman could deceive Odan the Half-
god, for he *was* a demigod and now the god half of him
came triumphantly to the fore and took him through the
chamber of feeding worms and out through the long um-
bilical tunnel to freedom.

Odan ran fleetly out onto the grass. The sun appeared
hardly to have moved. He felt Zenara in his arms, still and
unmoving, her breast barely rising and falling. Her hair
fell across her face. How white and limp she was!

A shadow dropped over him and, in the same instant,
he had ducked and dived convulsively to his left. He still
held Zenara. He hit the grass and rolled and still Zenara
was unhurt, unruffled. He looked up. Many and many a
time had a mere fleeting shadow saved a Hekeu from
destruction.

Odan saw a flying carpet sailing through the air toward
him, the gaily colored fringes rippling with the wind of its
passage, the mage sitting cross-legged in the center, peering downward. The keen eyesight of the Hekeu picked out
at the distance the uncertainty on the mage's sharp-featured young face. Odan did not know him.

He placed Zenara on the grass and stood a little way
off, drawing his sword, glaring up, balefully.

"Put away your sword, Odan, Prince Odan, Odan the
Khuzuk. I am here at the request of Master Kidu and
Master Asshurnax to carry you away from this sink of in-
iquity."

The flying carpet settled with a sigh and the mage
jumped up, moving with the alacrity of a youthful man in
full vigor anxious to be gone.

Odan glared at him. "Who are you?" He did not put up
his sword.

"I am Master Zehutinax."

There was a perceptible emphasis on the word Master.

"Yes?"

"And the sign in Yrn. Yrn. Now, Prince Odan, hurry—"

Yrn. The sign given him by Zadan, his father. He had

not used it once. He had not considered it, and yet, surely, had he used the sign Yrn within the caverns might not his whole escapade there have been easier? The remembrance of his father chained and torn at so cruelly convinced him it would not.

Odan picked up Zenara and walked across to the carpet. He sat down, cradling his princess, and Zehutinax took his seat again. With a serpentine undulation the carpet rose into the air and flew off strongly to the northwest.

The motion of the ride was pleasant, peaceful, almost soporific. The wind blew gently about his ears; yet he could see by the swift passage of the grass and then the sand dunes below the speed of their flight.

"We struggle against Karkaniz, prince. I act thus because my old master, Asshurnax, requested, and the king's wizard, Master Kidu."

"So you were famulus to Asshurnax, also? Yes, he did mention a fumble-fingered wight who was always breaking alembics and trying to cast spells that caused untold mischief."

Odan felt light-headed. He wanted to prattle, to bait this eager young wizard, so keen and smart. At the same time he wanted to thank him profusely and to heap all his worldly wealth upon him.

Zehutinax looked ahead. His sharp jaw set.

"The lord Gabal-ayin and his mage mage Ubonidas employed the witch Amenti. They it was who arranged the abduction of Zenara. They suborned a poor handmaid away— they had their way and they thought the princess safe in the Cave of Jewelled Sleep."

Zehutinax started as Odan let a curse fly.

"Gabal! And the princess was for his son, the lecherous Galad!"

"Yes, prince."

Zehutinax looked at the princess. His dark eyes hardened. He furrowed up his brow. His sharp jaw took on even more angular planes.

"What ails you, Zehutinax? Put the beauty of the princess out of your mind." Odan did not look down—not just for the moment. His heart conjured only black and evil designs against Gabal and Galad and their pack of wizards and witches.

"The princess is indeed beautiful. Never have I seen such beauty in all the land of Ea."

"She will soon recover once we have her home in Eresh. The king will spare no effort. Zenara will once more bloom, once more be the greatest princess in the world."

"I think, prince, that the princess Zenara. . . ." Zehutinax did not go on. Then: "I will send a grifting—I can insinuate my ka from here. The Cave of Jewelled Sleep holds life that may be manipulated . . ." His voice trailed off.

Odan looked down at Zenara. He had gained all he wanted. Now that the princess was safe he must look to repairing the damage he had done his cause in attempting to obey the instructions of Tia. Absolute confidence swept over him that he could convince the king. Betrayal, enchantment, yes, these were what had overtaken the prince Odan, so that he had so traitorously marched up against Eresh. But now—his thoughts worked feverishly over his plans. Ankidu and Kufu the Ox would play a part. There would be regiments to marshal, men to handle, the arrow storm must break about the damned heads of the men of Karkaniz and their vassal cities. He felt the soft cold form of Zenara in his arms and he hugged her to his breast, consumed by the desires tormenting him.

Zehutinax was still sitting cross-legged, erect; but his ka was away, behind them, ferreting about in the caverns of the worms.

Odan looked most tenderly upon Zenara. He brushed back the pale brown hair from her white forehead. How pale she was! He bent and pressed his lips gently upon her cheek. Cold! Her face was as cold as the winter hills of Zumer. Yet she breathed, she lived. Odan took up her hand and began to chafe it, and ever and anon he would press it against his lips.

He heard Zehutinax stir. A moan escaped the mage.

"You are in trouble, Zehutinax?"

The young wizard shook his head, unable to speak.

For some reason Odan no longer held Zenara's hand.

He looked down.

His heart battered like a bat trapped in a well.

His throat parched as dry as the desert below.

Even as he looked down at the slender form of Zenara across his knees she changed.

Her head with its freight of brown tresses swelled. Her white gown thinned and desiccated away into a crumble of grey dust. Her body that would intoxicate a man's senses thickened, grew moistly white, grew rounded and ridged. Her breasts slopped into her stomach which distended and joined. She became a great fat slug, a white worm, a worm, a worm, a worm.

Odan the Khuzuk sat holding a great white worm in his arms.

With a frenzied cry of revulsion Odan sprang back. He almost toppled over the fringed edge of the flying carpet. The worm lay, writhing, turning its blind head up and around, squirming up at him. The charnel house aroma whiffed at his nostrils, a thick and cloying stench, nauseating.

Zehutinax said, speaking very quickly: "She was not used for breeding, prince. She is dead. The princess is dead. This is an hallucination, a worm provided to deceive you. It is all done now, and there is no going back."

Odan drew his sword and the great white worm drifted into a fine grey dust, that sifted away on the wind, leaving no trace whatsoever. Odan was left holding his bronze blade, stupidly.

He looked at Zehutinax and he did not see the young mage.

He looked at his sword.

That, he did see.

"Gabal and Galad-ayin," he said. "And Master Uboni-das and the witch Amenti." His head hurt. It was difficult to breathe. But he was a Hekeu. He knew what ought to be done. He would do it if he could. If the gods spared him. Oh, yes, he knew.

"Gabal," he said, and his voice sounded like a sword of Zadan's metal drawn across stone. "Galad. You have wrought a terrible mischief this day, and you have destroyed yourselves."

Chapter Twenty

Odan the Khuzuk Lifts his Sword

"The abode of the Bats," said Odan the Khuzuk. "Take me straight to the Abode of the Bats."

"But, prince, the palace—the wizards, the king, they expect you—"

"Do not argue, master wizard, or you go overboard. Take me to the ebon tower. There is a matter to be settled."

"Yes, prince."

Zehutinax looked away from the face of Odan the Khuzuk, and he shivered.

"Princess Zenara is dead," said Odan. He said it again. He savored the taste of the words. "My Zenara is dead."

The words made no sense to him. They were just words. He gripped his sword. That, he could understand.

"Zehutinax! Send a grifting ahead. Spy out the tower."

"Yes, prince."

About a hundred and eighty miles northwest. That was the distance and bearing of Eresh from the Cave of Jewelled Sleep. The flying carpet would cover the distance in roughly three and a half glasses. In that time Master Zehutinax, acting with extreme caution, made a careful reconnaissance of the Abode of the Bats. He reported to Odan that the sealings were powerful; but that by using a spell he had worked on during his time south of The Sweet Sea, they might be broken—for a short period.

"I shall need only the time necessary," said Odan, gripping his sword.

Speaking was an effort, words an affront. He sat hunched, his head hanging, fondling the sword, his heart overflowing with remembrances of Zenara.

He had nothing of Zenara left, apart from his memories. He could not even cradle her dead body in his arms. Only a black remorseless rage filled him, a savage and berserk fury for revenge, driving him on, making him disregard any and every thing else save this one thing he craved. After that—he was in no case to think about anything beyond what immediately obsessed him.

They flew into sight of The River and the glittering mass of proud Eresh. They swooped over the city. The countryside bordering The River and the irrigations had been swept bare of people. An army was being formed to meet and challenge and destroy the hosts of Karkaniz. No thought of his place with that army, no thought of the consequences of his action, nothing remotely resembling rational thought possessed Odan. The carpet slanted down over the crowded huddle of houses toward the unkempt gardens and the squat ebon tower, the Abode of the Bats.

"I can protect you from Ubonidas, prince," said Zehutinax, with a slight motion of his hand indicating what he thought of Ubonidas. "But the witch Amenti is another matter."

Odan did not reply. He stared hungrily down at the squat and evil shape of the ebon tower rising to meet them. Zehutinax would not necessarily know of Odan the Half-god's powers. The witch Amenti would have to be dealt with as he intended to deal with Master Ubonidas, the Lord Gabal-ayin and his son Prince Galad.

Zehutinax drew himself into that particular huddling crouch that at the same time conveyed a sense of vast expansion of the physical body. Odan knew the mage's occult powers were being extended to the full. His sharp-featured face drew down in intense lines of utter concentration. Words dropped from his tightly drawn lips like grave-clods from the diggers' spades.

"I can open the sealings. The window. But, after, you must—"

"I will."

The flying carpet swooped down like a great eagle of the mountains about to carry off a lamb. The lighted window rushed up toward Odan. He braced himself, relaxing, breathing lightly, feeling his blood thumping, judging the distances. The wind bustled past, flaring his hair wildly.

The carpet hovered for only a moment and in that moment Odan sprang.

He hit the thick window ledge on his knees and rolled forward over the sill as the carpet span away high into the air. Bat droppings crusted away from his legs. He felt the ethereal strands of the broken sealing pulling at him, still feebly attempting to deny him entrance, proof that Zehutinax had worked against powerful forces and had done his work well. Odan rolled over, going forward and downwards off the sill, sprang to his feet within the blasphemous eyrie of the Abode of the Bats.

Ubonidas surged up from his chair, his face unbelieving, his eyes bulging, his mouth opening to shriek the incomprehensible words of a spell. Odan saw the wizard. Beyond him Gabal's ornate carrying chair crouched on the floor and the thin haunted face of the noble peered past the hanging curtain of embroidered cloth. A scarlet movement in the corner of his eye brought Odan's vicious stare to center upon the witch Amenti.

She swirled her scarlet gown before her face, concealing that chalk-white face and those blazing blue eyes. Her red hair vanished under the settling cape. Odan felt a tremble in his legs, a tremble throughout his body, a tremble akin to that onset of paralysis that had seized him when the wormwoman, the Raven, had ensorcelled him beneath the ground in his own hallucination. He was not fully aware of his own thoughts and actions. The scarlet of the cape merged with the crimson flicker surrounding every object he could see, a blood-red miasma of fury emanating from his own heart. Odan lifted his sword and hurled himself forward at the sorcerer.

The master mage, Ubonidas, died with a foot of hard bronze through his heart.

Odan withdrew, careful to withdraw cleanly so the blade would not catch on bone. Ubonidas stared with an appalled horror upon his chamber. He fell. He fell and twitched for a little space. Odan would not have been surprised had he changed into a frog or a lizard, if he had desiccated to a handful of crumbling dust, or dissipated in a puff of smoke. But the mage's body lay upon the rich carpets, and his blood crept out to stain the fabric a more deadly color.

The lord Gabal-ayin threw up a hand before his face.

Urt, the seeming-spider, shuddered in his web, scuttled back and rolled himself up into the tightest ball he could contrive.

From the adjoining chamber a clank sounded; but the partitioning door did not open.

Gabal regained control of himself. He drew his sword.

"Odan!" he said. "Prince Odan—come to slay a poor wizard and a crippled lord—great deeds for a mighty hero!"

Odan the Khuzuk made no reply.

The light struck across Gabal's sword and the slender leaf-shaped bronze blade glittered. He held the sword in the cunning practiced grip of the professional sword fighter; but he was chained to his chair, unable to stand up, a doughty fighting man crippled and easy prey for the chopping.

"Why were you ever born, Odan—why did the savages of Zumer not strangle you on sight—why did you come back to plague me?"

The glittering blade flashed its reflections about the somber room. A brilliant shaft of golden light struck across Odan's face as he advanced.

At last the wild Khuzuk spoke. "Save your clever stratagems, Gabal. You are to die. That is an end to it."

"If my son, the prince Galad, were here! He is the most renowned swordsman of The River! You would not so easily contume an old and crippled man then, you bastard—"

Before Odan could make a reply the long black curtains at the left-hand door swayed and parted. Prince Galadayin stepped through. He had already drawn. His sword flamed as his father's had flamed. And on his left arm he bore a great oval shield emblazoned with the device of the sun and the sword, sacred to Zadan and to Eresh.

Galad looked confident, powerful, resourceful. But above all, he looked arrogant.

Odan the Khuzuk had seen that look of prideful arrogance, that overweening sense of superiority before among the nobles of the land of Ea, and he felt—for the tiniest fraction of time—a breeze sweeping in from the icy flanks of the mountains of Zumer. The rage that possessed and sustained him, the reaction of frightful horror and despair that had nearly destroyed him, the awful sense of loss and loneliness engulfing, all impelled him to fling himself murderously upon this bright and glittering noble.

But Odan paused. He switched a quick methodical look about the chamber, ignoring the eerie evidences of the necromancer's art. There was no sign of the witch Amenti. Her griftings no longer sought to drag him down to paralysis and deaden his muscles and sinews. She had gone.

"Yes." The hoarse whispering of Gabal's voice echoed from the chair. "The witch has betrayed us." And now the voice thickened into a choked gloating triumph. "But my gallant son will soon finish you, *Prince* Odan. For Galad is known along The River among swordsmen."

This was true. Odan knew it. But, also, he knew that Nadjul the Quick had been noted as a swordsman. He knew, and with a deeper and darker sense of desolation, that he, himself, Odan the Khuzuk, was not yet as fine a swordsman as Nadjul had been, that he needed a couple of years more of practice and experience yet.

But he set himself and faced the sword and shield man, and the bright anger burning in his heart set a face of bronze across the dark and somber chamber.

"Kill him, my son—strike off his damned head."

"Gently, my father. I do not think the dog deserves to die so quickly as that."

"Ah!" Gabal's throaty voice choked on spittle, and his bony hand clutched his own sword in vicious mockery of the powerful bronzed fist that gripped the sword in his son's grasp.

So violent were the emotions of hatred and detestation and desolate grief gripping Odan that no idea of hurling a spell at Galad occurred to him. He just wanted to bash and strike and cut with his sword, to beat down the bastard to his knees, to see him broken beneath his blows, his blood spouting in a votive offering to the shade of Zenara.

The flashing leap and the wild stroke brought only a smooth slanting of the shield, the clang of the blow and, after a quick return slice that barely missed, only a low contemptuous snort of amusement from Galad.

His amusement infuriated Odan. This Galad carried the refinements of civilization into his fighting, so that he could mock the brutal savagery of Odan, taunting him with superiority that was the noble's inalienable right.

Again Odan rushed and again his savage blow was deflected. He circled, and with his sword pointing, sought once more to fling himself upon Galad.

This time the slanted shield was not quite quick enough. In a wild scurry of blade meeting blade Odan felt the strength in Galad's sword arm. And, too, held off as he was by the shield, he saw that this maniacal assault would do him little good.

But the thought of Zenara burned him like branding irons. This Galad had lusted after her and had planned and now Zenara was dead. Odan let out a shriek of sheer savagery that shocked Galad back. With his hair flying wildly, his eyes blazing, Odan rushed upon the noble and beat and hacked and cut as though driven by the manic frenzy of a madman.

The artfully slanted shield withstood his blows.

He felt no pain, no fatigue, he felt only fury.

Galad stepped aside, neatly—aye, neatly!—and Odan felt the thin kiss of bronze across his thigh. Stepping back he looked down stupidly. Bright blood welled up from the long sharp cut across his thigh. He shook his head, clearing the hair from his face. Now Galad laughed, jeeringly.

"You are finished, Odan Crookback! The wild man from the land of primitives, uncouth, stupid, dull, brutish! Go back to your ancestors and pray their forgiveness—"

And, as he taunted, so Galad moved in with quick deceptive cunning. His brand scorched toward Odan.

Almost, almost, Odan the Khuzuk was deceived. But he had fought the hekeu. He had taken wolves with his bare hands. He was a Hekeu. His reflexes powered him into a superbly sudden convulsion. His sword glittered once as it struck and then dulled with blood as he withdrew.

Galad let out a screech and staggered back. His left ear hung down in tatters and streams of blood ran down his cheek.

"You bastard! I'll chop you slow for that!"

Odan did not reply. He circled. Nadjul would have dealt with this puppy—shield or no damned shield. Nadjul the Quick had spent long hours aboard the crawler drifting down The River showing and explaining to Odan the tricks and stratagems of the swordsman against the sword and shield man.

Again Odan leaped. This time he checked his rush, got

his left-hand fingers hooked around the bottom of the shield. He feinted with his sword to take Galad's eyes and weapon and then heaved up on the shield. The top rim crunched into Galad's nostrils.

His nose opened like a flower. Blood flowed down. Galad screamed.

"Kill him, my son! Kill him—and kill him now, quickly."

Hatred from the lord Gabal made Odan turn and spit out words he hoped would frizzle the crippled old bastard's soul.

"When he is dead it will be your time, Gabal-ayin!"

Thus speaking and spewing out the hatred and venom roiling in him, Odan saw in a stunned flash the swift decisive blow of Galad's sword slicing down for his head. No time to curse himself for a babbling fool, time only to dive full length and roll over and so come up, snarling, and fling himself once more upon his enemy.

Almost, Galad had split his head, then. Now Odan set himself to the task. As his old training told him, as Nadjul had drummed into him, as he knew—he knew! he must drive all anger from his heart and allow his superb muscles and body and skill to drive his sword arm. But Galad was almost finished. He knew as Odan knew that he could not master the wild Khuzuk. Now Odan slashed at an exposed thigh and drew bright crimson. Now he cut overhand over the shield and drew spouting blood from a shoulder. The shield drooped. Odan methodically butchered Galad, trying to finish him in the knowledge that, still, Galad might pull a trick that would also finish Odan the Half-god.

This fight had been all on a mortal scale. No sorcery had aided either combatant. Because Odan was the son of a god he had no expectations that Zadan would aid him. He had fought as a mere mortal. As a man he could be slain, spitted or chopped. Galad, notorious along The River as a swordsman, and Odan Crookback had fought as equals within the sorcerous and divine spheres.

At last Odan, spattered with Galad's blood, stepped back from the reeking wreck.

Some of his own blood ran to mingle with that of his enemy's.

Odan gulped huge draughts of air. He turned to Gabal. The lord's hollow face looked green. He held his sword and the blade snouted. Odan felt nothing for Gabal-ayin, the king's uncle, save contempt riding the hard bile of hatred.

Gabal's eyes flicked sideways.

Without turning his head Odan leaped to the side.

The cast spear passed through the air where his heart had been a moment before. Odan swung about like a cornered leopard.

He saw a hand grasping the edge of the door, a hand hauling the door shut. It was a left hand. On the back of that left hand a large and hairy wart disfigured the skin with black and brown. A low guttural snarl burst in on Odan and he leaped for the closing door. The door slammed and a bar slotted into place outside. Odan lifted his sword to hammer on the door—and then lowered the blade and turned and walked quietly toward Gabal.

The spear had not slain the lord. It had added to his injuries, for it had smashed through his right shoulder. His sword lay abandoned on the rich rugs of the floor.

Odan the Khuzuk said: "I should refrain from slaying you, Gabal, so that you might live out the rest of your life in pain and misery. But I find I cannot do that—"

"What do you want, Khuzuk? I can offer—"

"You cannot offer me my sister. She is dead. She is dead because you commanded it. I cannot let you live and foul the land of Ea between the Two Seas. I cannot let you live and sully the air of The River."

"The king will be wroth if you slay his uncle—"

"I think the king will be more wroth if I let you live."

And then, at the last, Gabal's nerve broke.

He was in pain from his smashed shoulder. He saw the death in this savage's eyes, the primeval force of the wild Khuzuk that no sane reasoning could alter, and he felt his soul shrivel.

Gabal-ayin began a fearsome babbling, a shrill lament of pleas and cries for mercy—Odan kissed the lord's neck with the edge of his bronze sword.

"Just say, as you die, you bastard, that I am putting you out of your misery."

King Neb-ayin-Ke looked across at the walls of Dilpur. The sun shone down on the irrigations alongside The River. The host of the army waited to welcome their king to the victory. Standing in a light chariot adorned with much gilt and many feathers, Prince Odan-ayin approached his father.

"So you have won me back Dilpur, Odan."

"It was not difficult. Once the army of Dilpur returned their allegiance to Eresh, and we attacked, the men of Karkaniz were thankful to retire along The River."

"Yet it is a great victory and must be celebrated as such."

"We have yet to clear the rest of the dogs who serve Tia from The River. Until we stand under the walls of Karkaniz itself I shall not be satisfied."

Neb-ayin-Ke did not smile; but a corner of his mouth lifted in a tiny painful pucker. "Will you ever be satisfied, Odan my son?"

"No man can answer that question."

"I have only conditionally pardoned you. What you have done has brought great mischief to Eresh, and has ruined trade along The River. But you serve me well, and you fight for Eresh and Zadan. And, too, I have listened to your mother Momi—and there is no man in all Ea who can do that and not obey."

"I will say ahmeen to that, with all my heart. But we must press on. Dilpur is only a beginning—"

"No, my wild Khuzuk. We have regained what is ours. King Norgash will return to his city and the alliance will continue and Karkaniz must retrench. This is ordained of the gods." The pain that crossed Neb-ayin-Ke's face was now open and plain and very real. "Since we fight without a god—or so the priests say although no word has passed to the people or the army—we must rely on ourselves until Zadan returns to us."

Odan had said nothing about his interview with his father.

Now he nodded, abruptly. "Your wish is my command, king. But we must check Karkaniz and we must destroy Endal. These two strategies dominate our lives."

"True. But we must take them as the opportunity offers."

"Whilst Master Kidu lives Eresh will remain strong against her sorcerous foes. And Master Zehutinax, also."

The king looked past Odan. The white plumes of his chariot horses nodded. The army waited to greet its king. Neb-ayin-Ke shook his feathered staff, the gold blazing in the sunshine, for this was the war staff, brandished for battle and victory.

"Kidu tells me my uncle Gabal was the villain many have known for long and long. Zenara—the words are painful to me. I think the death of Zenara and Momi's pleas worked to save you from my wrath. And you have proved yourself loyal. But the time must come, and soon, when repayment must be made."

Odan was not quite sure what the king meant. At the signal the chariots rolled on. Soon the king's chariot was engulfed between the lines of cheering men as the regiments of the army welcomed their king to the city they had conquered. Odan let his chariot roll on after the king's. He pondered. Much had happened since he had taken a just revenge upon Ubonidas, Gabal and Galad for the death of Zenara. Justice had been done, as the Law proscribed. Although a Hearing might be held in the cities of The River, in the land of Zumer a death must be repayed with a death, so that the spirits could be satisfied, so that pride and honor might not vanish from the land. What Odan had done had been done within the letter of the Law, inscribed on baked clay tablets and there for all to see. Justice was of importance in a civilization, Odan the Khuzuk could see that, but Odan the Half-god saw also that the justice meted out in the harsh mountains of Zumer counted also in the land of Khepru.

The chariots rolled and the banners flew and the standards glittered brightly in the sun. The united yells of the soldiers brought a tingle to the blood. Odan saw Kufu the Ox and Ankidu and others of his comrades, and he felt the silly, prejudiced pride of the fighting man in the prowess of his army.

So Odan Crookback, hunched, awesome, feral, followed his king into captured Dilpur. And he pondered long on the meaning behind the king's words.

The remote stars shone cold and hard upon the desert sands and the irritable flicker of his sand scarf about his neck made Odan haul the thing off and hurl it viciously into the bed of the chariot. He had taken to driving for long periods across the desert at night. Remoteness, aloneness, isolation—these seemed to Odan the only fit companions for him. This day they had welcomed the king into Dilpur and what would happen on the morrow might

shake the land of Ea or might evoke nothing more than a
yawn. Odan did not care. He drove across the harsh sands
of the desert and he tried to banish all rational thought
from his heart.

But this he could not do. He had avoided Ankidu. Kufu
the Ox had withdrawn with a hurt and puzzled frown after a burst of bitter invective from Odan. But, for Ankidu,
the young noble who had loved Zenara and would have
killed or died for her, for him, Odan had no words.

The star glitter and the tiny night wind and the vast
silence of the desert encompassed Odan Crookback. He
drove with his habitual stoop-shouldered stance, feet
braced diagonally, one hand flicking the whip, the other
ready to grasp chariot rail or spear or sword as the occasion demanded.

He had hungered to be a god. He still felt the desire in
him, like a live ember, red and hot beneath ashes. His father, Zadan of the Sword, had denied him. What was there
in life now to draw Odan on to godhood? Zenara was
dead. Zenara, whom he had loved past reason, Zenara was
denied him by grisly barriers far stronger than those of
blood-kinship. Why did he bother to live, save for the
strictures of the shamans of the Hekeu, who would not allow a man to give up this life, even when he was dying?
What was there of life left to him, now?

The sky in brightening with a glow that did not come
from Zamaz merely heralded a fresh experience with the
gods. Odan stared up as the light grew, limp, empty, indif-
ferent.

The dream chariot glowed with light. It burned. It cast
greenish rays of light upon the sand and sent scuttling
shadows hurrying away.

"Odan-ayin, prince of Eresh! You are summoned before
the gods! Attend lest worse befall you."

The godvoice boomed, as a godvoice should. Odan dismounted from the chariot. He waited. Presently he felt
himself lifted up. For a space, a mere heartbeat, he
thought he dreamed. He rose high and higher, merging
with the radiance. He felt cold metal beneath his feet. The
upward pressure forced his knees to bend and drove his
stomach down with a wrenching jolt.

A band of cold greyness covered his eyes. The coldness
was of a strange quality, associated with no comparable
experience he had ever undergone. When he opened his

eyes he stood in a small railed enclosure of a thin blue-grey metal, and a bright light shone in his eyes, so that he blinked, and beyond the brightness he could see vague and awesome figures, shadowy, half-seen, immense.

"You have been brought here, Odan, so that you may speak in your defense."

He blinked. The voice rumbled like an avalanche of Zumer.

"I do not see who speaks—"

"I am Hoveuz. It is not necessary that you see me."

"Of what am I accused."

"You know that in your heart."

Odan found he did not much care for anything, now.

"If that is so, then, of whatever you choose to accuse me, I am innocent."

A sharp indrawn breath from a silhouetted figure at the side brought Odan's attention there. The light cleared. He saw Tia Nin-Apsish seated on a rug-strewn golden throne, surrounded by her handmaids and her beasts, bending forward to frown upon him.

"You are forsworn, mortal! You betrayed me—"

"In that, Tia, you lie."

The gasp of surprise and horror—and of a dry relish, also—ran around the seated gods. They were here to sit in judgment upon him. He was past caring for them. He was a man, even if he was half god.

"The lady Tia cannot be spoken to thus," said Kanikan, the god of Kheru, in fee to Karkaniz. He sounded flushed and annoyed.

"Your city bows and scrapes to Karkaniz," said Odan. "Your words have no weight."

The next voice to speak brought Odan's out-thrust head around sharply. The voice spat, thick and ugly, filled with a vicious power.

"Slay the dog now, and have done! He is forsworn to me, also."

Odan made his craggy face sneer. He spoke so that his words fell like the icicles falling from a Zumerian cave.

"You, Nirghal En-Theus, are the devil incarnate. You sought to trap me, betrayed me, abandoned me. Do the assembled gods know what you plan, through your son Nirghi? Do they know you seek to throw them down and place your foot upon their necks and usurp the paramount power?"

If Odan had expected a shocked reaction from this as-
semblage of gods, he was disappointed. As the light
cleared he recognized from the statues he had seen and
from their attributes, many of these powerful young gods.
There were Redul and Anki, Sakhmet and Farbutu. Mut
of Zemlya did not appear among the gathering; no doubt
she occupied some dolorous place after her defeat by Tia.
He looked about, more carefully, searching for one god;
but he did not see him. The gods' reaction was one of
amusement, one or two laughs, a snort, a polite titter. If
they were prepared thus to regard Nirghal and his ambitions so lightly, then Odan, for one, thought them fools.

"You show no fear, Odan-ayin." Hoveuz lowered from
his high throne. "Yet have you found much displeasure in
the eyes of the gods. The land of Ea is in turmoil—"

Odan interrupted violently.

"Blame Tia, the so-called goddess of love, for that! She
betrayed me, suborned me, set me against my own—she is
the blameworthy one." He fairly spat the words. "And the
devil Nirghal is no better. I seek nothing for myself—"

"In that, Odan Crookback, you lie also! You seek godhood."

"I did, once. But I see no virtue in gods, now."

"We would not allow you to join us in godhood. We
will not speak of it further. Your origins are wiped—"

Odan turned his head and saw, as through a slowly
opening doorway, the molten fires, and the cavern, and the
dripping gold. He saw the vulture and the eagle preening,
ready once again to begin their obscene assault upon his
father. Odan knew Zadan was not with this company of
gods, for Zadan was fast chained in the eighth hell; but his
face and voice could be seen and heard here. These were
the small miracles of the gods.

"This Odan-ayin, prince of Eresh," said Zadan. "He is
my son, and he has no claim on godhood, and I have no
claim on him for any prophecy." The dark, prideful look
of power that crossed Zadan's face echoed the black look
of anger on Odan's. "For now. But for the future, I will
not say. The boy has been tricked and maltreated and his
sister is dead. You chain me here, my fellow immortals.
There is no need to punish my son."

Wily Anki of Shanadul said: "Zadan of the Sword
speaks words that cannot be gainsaid. I counsel moder-
ation."

"Let the bastard be put down," growled Nirghal.

"Yes! Let him be sent to lie and rot in chains with his father!" said Tia, in a waspish voice most shrewlike.

But Odan looked at the brilliance that was Hoveuz, and he was comforted.

"Odan-ayin shall live and return to his place in the land of Ea," said Hoveuz, in a voice that brooked no argument. "What may happen thereafter must be weighed—" Odan did not understand the rest of the words.

Odan had derided these gods. He had cursed them as meddlers in mankind's fate. Because they had given mankind the opportunity to defeat the wormpeople the gods now battened on men's fears and superstitions. They used men as men used beasts.

"But I will not bow the neck to you. You may kill me—you may send me to join my father—that is all one to me. My place is with men. From now on I will eschew gods."

"That is wise," said Hoveuz.

"Odan," said the apparition of Zadan his father. "Odan—may good go with you, always."

As the light faded and the gods vanished, Odan cried with a loud voice: "And with you, Zadan of the Sword, Zadan the All-Glorious—Zadan my father."

Odan the Khuzuk would have no more truck with gods.

From them he had reecived only wounds, fatal scars that he could never obliterate. His father, Zadan, might have stood in better stead had he agreed to make Odan a god, and then, why, then, perhaps, between them they might have made such a stir in the heavens that Zadan would never have been banished to his torture in the hell beneath the seventh hell. From his father Odan had received little after the first impetus to life. Or so Odan considered.

The madness that had not left Odan for far too long, a madness compounded and made hideous by the death of Zenara, prodded him to great schemes, violent designs, insane ambitions. But he said, and he spoke aloud as he turned the chariot back to Dilpur, shouting at the heavens: "I am done with the gods! From now on I take my place beside men."

There were certain things he must do, certain designs he must accomplish, before he could at last sink down into dull anonymity with the ruck of mankind. He would not forget he was a demigod; but the knowledge would only appear to him dim and unimportant. So Odan the Khuzuk reasoned as he drove furiously back to Dilpur. The king's messengers welcomed him, saying the king, whose name be praised, wished to see him urgently. Odan went up to the private rooms apportioned for the use of Neb-ayin-Ke and he shouldered in, lowering, shoulders hunched, hair hanging, feeling little affection for man or god.

Neb-ayin-Ke received him in private, waving away his servitors and slaves. He did not offer Odan wine. He sat slouched in a carved ivory chair overstuffed with ornate cushions, one hand propping his chin, his robes trailing from his still vigorous frame. He looked like a man who has come to a difficult decision, and now faces the more difficult implementation of that decision.

"King?"

"I call you my son. Kidu tells me Odan En-Ke was not your father. Zadan of the Sword—yes, it all makes sense. Would not Zadan the All-Glorious bring you to his own city? And yet, and yet I wish I had known, for I would have acted differently."

"What is done is done. Have you news of my mother?"

"The Queen Momi, who shines fairer than any star in the sky, is well. She wishes to see you before you leave."

Odan waited a moment, and then said: "Leave?"

"Of course. You have caused much grief and agony. Any normal king would have hung you by the heels from the battlements. But I am no ordinary king and you are the son of a god."

"I have finished with gods."

"That is as it may be. But you will leave Eresh, after you have said goodbye to your mother."

"You exile me?"

"If you wish to call it that. Perhaps, one day, I shall send for you, for you are indeed a mighty warrior and have won great renown along The River in the land of Ea."

"Then I shall travel beyond Ea—the world is wide, there are the two seas, and all the length of The River—I may return to Zumer. I do not think, king, you punish me in this."

"That is good. I think my days are numbered. I have lately been troubled by pains that worried me in my youth. Master Kidu works wonders, and the doctors are helpless. It may be, my wild Khuzuk, I shall never see you again."

Odan, in the midst of his madness and grief, felt the pang of that. "I pray Zadan that be not so."

Neb-ayin-Ke looked up under his brows at Odan. "Yes. Yes, I think, perhaps, you do. But Zadan is gone—well. The priests must do what they can. The people do not know and must not know."

Odan did not tell the king where Zadan waited out his torture.

"I have called you my son and treated you like a son. You have created a great storm along The River. The pieces have been broken and scattered and much labor will be needed to restore them. I have another son. The future is dark and the mages and the priests can see nothing certain. I live from day to day. When you are gone about your travels in Khepru—you may think of Eresh. But I am the king! My word is law. Only death can reward those who seek to gainsay my word."

Odan nodded, understanding. It was a fair warning.

"But I, king, am not a civilized man of The River. I am a Hekeu, a wild Khuzuk from Zumer. And my sister Zenara is dead. And I do not much care what happens in Ea, now."

"Then I pray Zadan goes with you."

Neb-ayin-Ke lifted his hand and the audience was at an end.

Going out of the luxurious apartments and finding his chariot and cursing at the slaves, Odan found he was dissatisfied with the way the interview had gone. He would see his mother in Eresh and other people, also, in pursuance of the object whose end now obsessed him. But the king had not looked as a king should look. The thought of prince Numutef-ayin passed away like a vapor. That ninny could be crushed by a puff of wind. But Neb-ayin-Ke— what would befall Eresh when the king died?

Mounting up and with a skirling yell and a slash of the whip sending his chariot flying out of the city, Odan the Khuzuk went hurtling along the pathway beside the irrigations. He headed east for Eresh. After that . . .

Despite the madness burning like a fever in his blood he acted and spoke with a surface rationality inherited from his cruel Hekeu training. Self-sufficiency and survival en-

sured that he did not place himself in that kind of unnec-
essary jeopardy. But as the years of his exile went on he
would tip over the brink of madness, that he knew with a
darkness of his soul that almost welcomed the ebon wings
of oblivion. Life was to be lived, despite that Death beck-
oned.

Zenara . . . Zenara . . .

He would try—he must try—a last gamble. He must
fling one last defiance in the face of gods and sorcerers.
For was he not a Hekeu?

So Odan the Khuzuk drove his chariot like a maniac
toward proud Eresh and the beginning of his banishment
from the land of Ea between the Two Seas.

Appendix

The Story of Abak

When the Young Gods of Power flew down to the world of Khepru in their Dream Chariots and beheld what the Old Gods had wrought in the Land of Ea between the Two Seas they were well-pleased and saw that the land was rich and would bring forth milk and honey.

And they settled in the land and brought their shining Dream Chariots to glitter at the side of The River. But the Great Grey Old Ones were not pleased and they called, one to the other, saying: "How may we drive these new gods away?"

And the sun god, Ke, who had created all things, sent forth all the powers of the sun, which is called in some cities of The River Atun and in some cities of The River Zamaz, and the sun's rays smote upon the Young Gods sorely.

And Adad blew with all his strength and the burning wind of the desert parched the lips of the Young Gods.

Then were the Great Grey Old Ones pleased. But the new gods were not pleased and they took counsel one with another, saying: "How may we shield ourselves from the sun and the wind?"

In that time the new gods took the dust of the earth and the water from The River and they mixed them and fashioned the clay into the form of a man. And him they called Abak. And Abak was the first of all men.

To Abak, the first mortal man of the land of Ea between the Two Seas, they said: "Take clay and make bricks and dry them in the sun and build of them a wall."

All this Abak did. Then said the new gods unto him: "Dig the soil and open the banks of The River and plant trees and fair bushes and sweetly perfumed flowers and all things to make a garden comely in our sight." All these things Abak did. And Abak built the garden in the sight of the gods and the gods walked refreshed in the sweet-scented shade.

The new gods walked in the garden Abak had built and were well pleased, for the heat of the sun and the violence of the wind did not touch them.

When Abak had finished his labors he said: "What other thing may I do for their pleasure in the sight of the gods?"

They took counsel, one with the other, and they were well pleased with Abak, first of men, and they spake unto him, saying: "Come walk with us in the garden, Abak, first of men, and enter into our shining Dream Chariots with us."

So Abak walked in the garden and was clothed as the gods are clothed and rode in the chariot of fire and, lo, Abak was a god like unto the other gods.

GREAT NOVELS OF HEROIC ADVENTURE ON EXOTIC WORLDS